CRAVING TRIX

The Aces' Sons

By Nicole Jacquelyn

Craving Trix
Copyright © 2015 by Nicole Jacquelyn
Print Edition
All Rights Reserved

No part of this book may be reproduced or transmitted in any form or by any means, electronic or mechanical, including photocopying, recording, or by any information storage and retrieval system without the written permission of the author, except for the use of brief quotations in a book review.

This is a work of fiction. Names, characters, businesses, places, events, and incidents are either the products of the author's imagination or used in a fictitious manner. Any resemblance to actual persons, living or dead, or actual events is purely coincidental. The author acknowledges the trademarked status and trademark owners of various products referenced in this work of fiction, which have been used without permission. The publication/use of these trademarks is not authorized, associated with, or sponsored by the trademark owners.

Dedication

Every book I write is for the readers, but this book more than most.

This is for every message and comment and tweet you sent me, asking for Cam and Trix's love story.

If it wasn't for you, it would still be unwritten.

And what a shame that would've been.

Prologue

TRIX

I KNEW HER. I *knew* her. *Goddammit.*

I ground my teeth together as I watched her move above him, giggling and flipping her hair around. She was a senior at my high school—obviously eighteen, or they would have never let her into the clubhouse—but she went to my fucking *school*.

My stomach clenched in self-pity. I'd gotten my driver's license today, and I'd been feeling like pretty hot shit as I drove my little brother, Leo, around town before dropping him off at our house. He'd thought I was pretty hot shit, too—probably because he knew I'd drive him to his friends' houses whenever he wanted just so I could take my new Honda out on the road.

I'd practically strut my way through the forecourt, grinning back at the guys who'd smiled indulgently at me for driving my car over when I could see the garage from my front porch.

God, I was such an idiot.

A few of the guys had tried to pull me into conversation as I'd walked toward the front door, but I hadn't let them distract me from my goal.

I was at the clubhouse I'd practically grown up in for one reason.

Cameron Harrison.

And he was currently getting what looked like a lap dance from a senior in my high school.

Motherfucker.

I stood frozen as she ground all over him, a part of me unable to comprehend what I was seeing. She was wearing a short, flowery skirt that swished with every movement of her hips and a grey tank top that barely covered her small breasts.

I sighed. At least my boobs were bigger. I had that going for me.

After a few moments spent standing dumbly in the doorway, I was knocked out of my daze by the sounds of men's voices arguing cheerfully at my back. They were coming in behind me, and I knew without a shadow of a doubt that if I didn't move from the door, I'd be greeted with long, pitying looks the minute they saw me.

I took one step forward, and then another, until I was moving swiftly through the room. It didn't take me long to reach the couch I'd sat on a hundred times before, but never would again.

"Are you kidding me right now?" I asked thickly, making the girl's head spin in my direction. Her name was Abbie. Fucking Abbie.

"Excuse me?" Abbie asked with a snicker.

I swallowed hard as my eyes automatically met his, then felt seething fury and overwhelming hurt build inside my chest. His face was completely void of emotion.

"We're busy." Abbie made a shooing motion with one hand that I ignored.

"Is this how it's going to be?" I asked him, tucking my thumbs into my palms to stop myself from fidgeting as I heard conversations around the room go quiet. *She goes to my fucking high school, Cameron.*

He raised his eyebrows, the expression so condescending I could barely breathe. It was as if I was boring him, as if he didn't give two shits about me.

As if he didn't know why I was *bothering* him.

My heart began to pump loudly in my ears as my pop, gramps and uncles came walking into the room, their voices cutting off abruptly when they saw me.

Berating a member in the clubhouse. Berating a member like I was his nagging old lady and not a seventeen-year-old girl with absolutely no rights to him whatsoever.

The feeling in my chest grew and grew until I could barely breathe past it.

In that moment, the tramp did something incredibly stupid.

Turning her face back to Cam, she asked loudly, "Why the hell is she still standing there?"

I don't think I could have stopped myself if I'd tried.

I took one step forward, grabbed a handful of her mousy brown hair and ripped her ass off his lap and onto the floor.

I heard a loud, "Oh, fuck!" from across the room, but I ignored it.

I also ignored Cameron as he stood, quickly buttoning his pants and buckling his belt. *Oh, God. His pants had been undone.*

Instead, I watched as the mousy haired senior got to her feet and rushed toward me. She shouldn't have done that. Things would have been so much simpler if she'd just fucking left it alone.

As she reached for me, I felt tears of humiliation blur my eyes. Then I leaned away as she tried to hit me, using her momentum to grab hold of the back of her head and slam her face into the edge of the pool table on my right.

The room was completely silent for a full thirty seconds as she slumped to the floor.

"Little Warrior!" I heard my pop yell, his voice growing louder as he ran toward me.

"Bea," I heard softly spoken. "What the fuck?"

I met his eyes as the first tears fell down my cheeks. My humiliation was complete.

"Fuck you, Cam," I rasped. "Don't ever come near me again."

"The fuck are you doin' here?" he hissed, reaching for me. I stumbled back, tripping over Abbie's legs before righting myself.

I watched Cam's eyes dart over my shoulder as booted feet made their way toward us, but before I could turn to face my pop, Cameron was moving toward me—his shoulder meeting my belly so hard that it knocked the wind out of me as he slung me over his shoulder.

"Give me a minute?" he asked my pop angrily as I gasped and pounded on his back. What an asshole! I could smell her, I could fucking *smell* her on his clothes.

"She's fuckin' seventeen years old," my pop ground out, obviously furious.

"Seventeen or not, you see that shit?"

"Saw it."

"I need a fuckin' minute," Cam ground out between his teeth.

There was a tense silence that gave me hope, but then my pop murmured, "A minute," and my entire body deflated.

I was so fucking embarrassed I wanted to crawl into a hole, so I wasn't going to make it worse by fighting Cam as he carried me to the back hallway and through the door to his room.

This wasn't going to end well.

I'd finally gotten my breath back when the door to Cam's room was slammed behind us and I was tossed onto the bed.

"You asshole," I yelled, pushing my hair from my face as I scrambled onto my knees.

"You wanna tell me what that was about?" Cam asked, crossing his arms.

"Fuck you," I mumbled back, shaking my head. I was an idiot.

I'd let my emotions take control and I'd made myself look like a complete moron in front of every single man sitting in the clubhouse. There was no excuse, no way I could explain it away. Frankly, I knew better.

I may not agree with the rules, but I knew them.

I crawled to the edge of the bed, clenching my jaw to keep from spewing my hurt feelings all over the place. I needed to get the fuck out of there.

A hand planted in the center of my chest had me falling back into the bed.

"Explain!" Cam yelled, finally losing patience.

"Fuck you! I don't have to explain *shit* to you!" I yelled back, climbing to my feet again.

"You jealous? That what this is about?"

I scoffed, turning my head away from him.

"You knocked that girl out, Bea!"

"She fucking deserved it," I mumbled back, refusing to look at him.

"She didn't do fuck all to you!"

"She's a bitch."

"She's hot as fuck and down for anything. Don't fuckin' care if she's Miss Congeniality," he shot back.

My body jolted as if he'd slapped me.

"You're right," I told him around the lump in my throat, making eye contact and smiling ruefully as stupid tears began to leak out of my eyes again. "You can fuck anyone you want to."

"Bea," he murmured softly as his shoulders slumped forward.

"I'm sorry for bothering you," I told him, jerking away from his hand when he reached for me. "My problem with Abbie has nothing to do with you."

"Baby girl—"

"Don't," I cut him off, shaking my head as I got to my feet once more. "I'm going to go."

The moment I tried to step past him, he grabbed me, pulling me into his huge chest. He was big, one of the biggest guys I'd ever been around, and usually his thick arms and broad shoulders comforted me when nothing else could.

But they didn't comfort me then.

"Let go," I ordered, pushing away from him and slapping his hands as he tried to pull me back.

"Bea, come on—"

"I'm done," I whispered, backing toward the door. "Whatever we are—it's done."

"Don't be so fuckin' dramatic," he said in exasperation, reaching for me again.

I think we were both surprised by the sound of my hand meeting his cheek.

"I got my license today," I said with a humorless laugh as I backed away and grabbed hold of the doorknob. "I came by to see if you wanted to go for a ride with me. Didn't realize you were already getting one."

He lurched toward me, but I got the door open and was running toward the main room before he could catch me.

I heard his door splinter as he roared, "Goddammit!" but I didn't slow. I raced past my pop as he paused in a conversation with Cam's dad, Casper, and didn't stop until I'd reached the door to my new car.

I needed to get the fuck out of there.

Cam had been my best friend for as long as I could remember. He'd taught me how to ride my bike without training wheels and how to change both a flat tire and the oil in a car. He'd been to every birthday party I'd ever had, and even though he was almost six years older than me, he'd let me tag along with him whenever I was having a bad day or just needed some attention.

Like an idiot, I'd even waited to get my license because I liked it that he drove me around when I needed it.

I was completely in love with him.

Unfortunately, he wasn't even a little bit in love with me.

★ ★ ★

CAMERON

Six months later…

"Got the parts in today, wasn't sure if you wanted to—*ow, man!* What the fuck?" I yelled as Dragon shoved me face-first into the cement wall of the garage. I'd been talking to Casper and minding my own business, when the guy hit me like a fucking linebacker.

"You got somethin' you wanna say to me?" Dragon growled as I shrugged him off my back and spun around. He looked like he wanted to rip my head off, and I had no clue why.

Dragon and I had no problems, as far as I knew. We weren't tight—I was closer with my adopted uncle, Grease—but we were cool.

"Nope," I replied, watching him warily.

He was practically shaking, he was so livid.

"You sure about that, kid?"

"Not a kid, and I've got no fuckin' clue why you're in my face." My shoulders bunched as he glared at me. I wasn't taking his shit. I'd gone through the same probation period he had and I was a full fucking member of the club. I didn't answer to him—not until he had the gavel, at least.

Dragon crossed his arms over his chest, but I kept mine loose at my sides. I was bigger than him—no question. But the guy was twice my age with twice the experience. He'd kill me.

"You been keepin' those hands to yourself?" he asked darkly, searching my face for some sort of guilt.

Hands to myself? What?

Oh, shit.

"She's seventeen!" I replied incredulously. "*Yeah*, I've been keepin' my hands to my fuckin' self. What the fuck?"

"So, you know nothin' about my girl askin' her mama for birth control, huh?"

It took longer than it should've for his words to register. I was fucking blindsided. I stepped back, bumping back into the wall as the implication behind his statement became clear.

She was *not* having sex. No fucking way.

"You fuckin' joking?" I rasped, the back of my neck growing warm.

"I look like I'm jokin'?"

"Did you let her get it?" I roared, completely forgetting that the man could kill me with one well-placed blow.

"I look like I wanna be a grandpa?"

"Jesus Christ!" I knew my eyes were wide and I knew that my chest was heaving and the veins in my neck were visibly throbbing, but I couldn't seem to curb my reaction.

My Bea had asked for birth control?

No. Fucking. Way.

"Didn't touch her," I finally ground out, glancing over at Casper as he glared at Dragon. "We done here?"

"Yeah, boy. We're done," my adopted dad replied. "Come over to the house tonight—family dinner, no excuses."

"Will do," I agreed, already moving away from them to strip off my coveralls and grab my shit off the huge tool box in the corner.

I hadn't talked to Trix in months, not since she'd gone fucking nuts in the clubhouse—but that shit stopped today. What the hell was she thinking? Birth control? Not. Fucking. Happening.

She didn't need birth control, because she wouldn't be having sex with any needle dicked high school kid.

I pulled my cut over my shoulders and stuffed my wallet into my pants as I headed outside, catching a bit of Casper and Dragon's conversation as I passed them.

"You know my boy better than that," Casper said angrily.

"Yeah, I do. Girl doesn't fuckin' listen to me, though," Dragon said with a sound of disgust and a nod in my direction. "He'll put her on a fuckin' leash."

"Don't listen to a word ye say?" Poet asked laughingly as he passed me with an absent slap to my shoulder. "Wonder where she got that?"

I didn't hear Dragon's reply as I climbed on my bike and slid my helmet on, re-checking to make sure Trix's helmet was still strapped to the back of my bike.

I pulled up in front of the high school fifteen minutes later and parked in the fire lane. I wouldn't be there long enough for them to give me shit about it.

It only took minutes before the secretary was calling Bellatrix White over the intercom, but I was too fucking keyed up to wait in the office, so I stepped outside. I knew she'd come looking for me.

The office knew me—I'd picked up Trix quite a bit in the past few years. My showing up at two o'clock on a sunny afternoon wasn't anything noteworthy.

But apparently Trix didn't get that memo, because as soon as she saw me, she threw the front doors open with an angry slam as she stormed toward me.

"What are you doing here?" she snapped as she came closer, her black hair flying all over the damn place.

"Let's go," I ordered. Shit, I could barely speak, I was so pissed.

Trix growled. *She* was angry? Really? What the fuck could she be pissed about?

"I have class," she argued, stopping abruptly.

"Never stopped you before."

"Yeah, when I actually *wanted* to leave."

"Get on the fuckin' bike, Bea."

"No," she replied stubbornly.

"Got your friends lookin' out the window," I said, glancing over her shoulder. "You want them to see me makin' you get on, or you wanna climb on without the dramatics?"

She glanced back toward the school, then started toward me with a scowl. "You're such an asshole."

I ignored her as I climbed on my bike and handed her helmet over, waiting a few minutes while she got it situated and swung her leg over behind me. We'd done this dance a thousand times, and she wrapped her arms tight around my middle as I fired up the bike and pulled away from the curb.

It had taken years for her dad to let her ride on the back of my bike, but she'd worn him down eventually. Thank fuck. I hated driving the piece of shit truck Casper had given me when I got my license at sixteen, but I'd driven it often back then—for her.

Fifteen minutes later, I rode slowly down a gravel driveway and stopped at a large gate so Trix could unlock the pad lock and let me pull the bike through. As soon as I'd gotten a few feet inside, I was off the bike and turning toward her as she locked the gate behind us.

No one except us ever used the gate at the back of the club's property. It was secluded and there was nothing much back there but trees and blackberry bushes. The road stopped a hundred yards from the gate, probably because at some point, they'd wanted to carve a path all the way to the clubhouse, but had lost interest.

"What are we doing here?" she asked, stomping toward me.

She was either completely oblivious to how pissed I was or was itching for a fight, because she didn't stop until she was a foot from me and glaring up into my face.

"You need birth control?" I barked, the words torn from my throat.

I wanted her to tell me no. As she opened and closed her mouth twice, I waited for her to tell me that she had just been curious or some shit.

So, when she spoke, I had a hard time not reaching out and shaking her.

"Don't really wanna be a teenage mother," she snapped, throwing up her hands. "Is nothing freaking sacred around here?"

"Are you shitting me?" I growled.

"How did you even *know*?" she asked, tucking her thumbs into her fists and leaning up on her toes in a pathetic attempt to get in my face. She was almost a foot shorter than I was—she'd need a fucking step stool.

"You gonna have sex? That's what you're tellin' me?" I sneered, leaning down until our faces were inches apart. "Got a little boyfriend?"

"I've *already* had sex with him," she spat back.

I'd never looked at Trix in a sexual way. Never. She was my little Bea. My other half. When we were kids, she'd been best buds with my little brother, Curtis, and after he died in the fire that killed my family, she'd somehow switched her affections to me. I didn't know if it was because she missed Curt or she'd just had no one to play with, but she'd followed me around and I hadn't had the heart to make her leave me alone. She'd been so sweet, with her long dark hair and big brown eyes—I hadn't stood a chance.

She was mine.

She'd always been mine.

And suddenly, the thought of her being someone else's made me livid.

She'd fucked someone else?

She'd let someone else see her body?

I couldn't even feel my hands when I reached out and fisted her hair between the fingers of one and gripped her jaw with the other. It felt like a fucking out-of-body experience as I watched her eyes go wide and her body freeze.

"You've been fuckin' someone else?" I hissed as her hands came up to grip my forearms, her nails biting into my skin. "You belong to *me*!"

"Fuck you!" she yelled back, pulling at my arms.

It was like waving a flag in front of a bull—and later, I'd wonder if she knew exactly what she was doing—but in that moment, all I saw was red.

I pulled her mouth to mine and kissed her hard as she went completely still. Her fingers went lax on my arms and she stopped pulling away, but she didn't move her mouth, either. That pissed me off even more.

I spun us around and pushed her up against a tree, the wet bark and moss soaking the back of her shirt and hair within seconds.

"You wanna be fucked, *I* fuck you," I ordered into her mouth.

"Yeah, right!" she screeched back, reaching up to grab my head. My hair was too short for her to latch onto, but her fingers wrapped around the back of my head hard, neither pushing me away or pulling me forward.

As if she wasn't sure what to do.

"You let a boy touch you, I'll break his fuckin' legs," I growled, stepping in closer until my knee was wedged between her thighs.

With a moan, she finally relaxed against me, and my heart started pounding in my ears when she opened her mouth for my tongue.

God, she tasted good. Like cinnamon gum.

I inhaled deeply as I ran my tongue over her lips, letting go of her jaw so I could wrap my hand around one of her thighs and pull it up high on my hip.

I loved Trix's thighs. I'd never thought of her as a conquest—that wasn't how we worked, but I was a man. Hard to ignore it when a girl was shaped like she was. She was far from fat, but her thighs and ass were *thick*. Round. When she wore a bathing suit, no matter what type, bottoms rarely covered her ass—to the point that I'd forced her to start wearing shorts when I took her to the river during the summer, so I didn't have to kill anyone. It was the type of cushion men dreamed about. The kind of thighs that you fucking *knew* would squeeze you to hell when they were wrapped around your waist.

I hated that I was still too tall in the position we were in, so I dropped my other hand, using both to hike her up my chest until I could notch my dick right between those gorgeous thighs.

Shit, that felt incredible.

I wasn't prepared for her to bite my lip, and I jerked my head back in surprise to find her glaring at me.

"Does that go for you, too?" she asked breathlessly, moving her hand to press against my throat as I tried to catch her lips again.

"What?" I asked dumbly. Did she expect me to talk to her when I could feel the heat between her legs pressed against me?

"I don't sleep with anyone else, you don't sleep with anyone else," she ordered, immediately pissing me off.

"What?" I asked again, lower.

"If I'm fucking you, you aren't fucking anyone else," she said, finally letting go of my throat so she could kiss me.

Oh, fuck no.

"I'm not gonna *fuck* you," I snapped back, shaking my head.

What the fuck was I doing? All of a sudden, I was thinking clearly again, and I couldn't believe what the hell I'd just done.

This was Trix.

My little Bea.

Jesus Christ.

I stepped back quickly and dropped her legs, making her stumble as she tried to catch her balance. "This isn't happen—"

My words were cut off as she punched me in the face.

"I hate you!" she yelled, her chest heaving. *"What the fuck is wrong with you?"*

I watched her, dumbfounded, as she stomped toward the small break in the trees, moving so quickly she was almost running.

Reaching up to wipe a drop of blood off the side of my mouth, I grimaced. "You're seventeen years old!" I yelled at her back.

She stopped, spinning around to glare at me. "I'm eighteen in three weeks, dick!"

"I'm still way too fuckin' old for you! Where are you going?" I took a step forward, then stopped. She was on club property and half a mile from her house—I wasn't following her ass through the forest.

"Fuck off!" she yelled, flipping me the bird as she stomped away until she disappeared in the trees.

"Eighteen," I grumbled, slapping myself on the side of the head as I turned and headed toward my bike. "You fuckin' asshole."

Chapter 1

CAMERON

Four years later

"GOT A PROBLEM," Slider said to the open room, glancing around to the brothers gathered. There were at least twenty of us, young and old, new and seasoned. Some of us had dealt with "problems" before, some looked like they were going to shit their pants, some looked bored.

I felt… ready. I knew I could handle it, whatever it was. I'd gone through too much for anything to surprise me.

"Got some assholes down from Salem, makin' noise," Dragon cut in, leaning against the bar top. "Tryin' to take over territory that's belonged to us for over thirty years."

"We can handle it—" Poet said confidently.

"Can handle it, but we need to be keepin' an eye out," Slider finished.

"Are we lockin' down?" one of the younger brothers asked. His name was Mack and I knew he had a girl and a brand new baby at home. He was sweating.

Christ.

"Not lockin' down," Slider said with a small shake of his head. "No reason to think we need to—not yet. Been quiet so far."

"So, what do we do?" another guy called out.

God, they sounded like a bunch of pussies. I rubbed the back of my neck in annoyance.

"You tell your women to stay alert." Grease finally spoke up. His jaw was locked as he glared. "You keep your kids home."

Grease's woman, Callie, had gone through some shit when they were young, dealing with a gang out of Southern California. It was clear by the way he stood that he didn't like whatever we were dealing with, but he was calm. Far more calm than my adopted dad, Casper.

Casper looked like he was ready to explode.

"Go on home and keep an eye on things. Quickest way for shit to go south is fuckin' loose women, so from here on out, no bitches inside the gates except old ladies," Dragon ordered, making the crowd groan and grumble.

"And no callin' some gash yer old lady to get her in here. I'll toss her out on her arse," Poet warned, pissed at the complaining going on.

As people filtered out of the club, I moved to a stool and took a seat. I didn't have an old lady, and at the moment, I didn't even have a house. I slept at the clubhouse most nights, or at my parents' house. The shit hole I'd been renting got fucking condemned and they'd booted my ass out.

"Hey, boy," Casper said quietly, thumping me on the back as he sidled up to the bar.

"You okay?"

"Yeah. Hate when shit like this happens, but it happens. Just have to deal." He reached over the bar top and grabbed two glasses and a bottle of Jack, pouring us each a couple of fingers.

"You already talk to Ma?"

"Yep. Her and Rose got things covered, keepin' an eye on the girls and a hand on their guns. Farrah's a crazy bitch when she's protectin' her own, not worried about that."

"Yeah, no shit," I joked, remembering back to a time when Farrah had stepped between me and armed policemen, screaming about how she'd have their jobs.

Grease and Dragon moved in behind us, so I turned to face them, leaning back against the bar. Poet and Slider had moved to some chairs across the room and were talking quietly, their faces and bodies tense.

"Got a bad feelin' about this," Grease said softly, running his hand down his beard.

"Callie and the kids?"

"Sent Will home to his mama. Pissed him off, kid wanted to stay here, but I feel better if he's there." Grease shook his head and looked down at the floor. "Pissed that I'm thinkin' about the panic room I built in the house."

"You think we should be callin' everyone in?" Casper asked, tilting his head to the side.

"I'm thinkin' we don't know enough. Makin' the hair on my neck stand up."

"I'm not feelin' good about shit, either," Dragon finally admitted, reaching up to tear the rubber-band out of his hair before scraping it back up into a knot. "Got Leo and Brenna inside the gates, but Trix is still at school."

My stomach rolled.

Shit between Trix and I was so complicated, it was a joke.

After she'd caught that chick giving me a lap dance when she was a teenager, things had never been the same between us. At first I'd been pissed, but eventually, it had just become our new normal.

She didn't want to be around me, and as long as I knew she was okay, I let her do her thing.

I still didn't understand why she'd cut me off like she had. We'd gone from talking a few times a week to complete radio silence in the matter of a few hours. It was bullshit. But fuck, I wasn't going to beg her.

"You gonna bring her home?" I asked, trying to act as if I wasn't crawling out of my skin.

I couldn't imagine anything happening to Trix. I didn't want to imagine it.

"She's got graduation comin' up. Can ask her to stay nights at our place, but since we're not goin' on lockdown, she's gonna bitch."

"So, let her bitch," I said darkly.

"Unless I fuckin' kidnap my own kid, not a lot I can do if she says she ain't comin' home," Dragon shot back. "I throw my weight around, she's gonna do the opposite of whatever I tell her."

"I'll take care of it," I blurted without thinking.

"What's that?" Grease asked in amusement.

I glanced at Casper to find his lips twitching. "Fuck off," I growled, making him laugh.

"You don't have a place—" Dragon mumbled.

"I'll stay at hers."

"Want your throat slit in your sleep?" Dragon asked incredulously.

"Fuck, she wouldn't wait 'til he was sleepin'," Grease chimed in.

"Yeah, it's real funny," I growled, pulling a pack of cigarettes out of my pocket so I could flip one over my fingers.

"We're not laughin' at you—" Casper said, trying to stem his chuckles.

"Nah, man. We are," Grease cut him off, nodding his head.

"I hate every single one of ya," I said, accidentally snapping my cigarette between my fingers.

"If ya think ya can handle her, have at it," Dragon mumbled through his smile. "Been a while since that happened."

"I get to do it my way," I warned, meeting his eyes.

Years ago, when she was younger, I'd been careful. Out of respect for Dragon and Brenna, I'd played by the rules and kept my hands off what had belonged to me since we were kids. But Trix was no longer a child. Our age difference no longer mattered.

And if I was taking responsibility for her, I'd be doing that across the board. Dragon would have to hand over the fucking reins—because she wasn't going to be crying to her papa when shit went sideways, which I knew would happen at some point.

I was surprised by the fist that slammed into my face.

What was it about that family that made them fucking punch me without warning?

"The fuck?" I asked, turning my face back toward Dragon.

"Had to get at least one in," Dragon said calmly, watching to see if I'd hit him back.

"It *is* tradition," Grease agreed.

"Nobody hit me when I got with Far—" Casper started to argue before taking a shot to the face.

"Yeah, 'cause Slider didn't wanna piss her off," Grease said, shaking out his hand before pointing at Casper. "You had that comin'."

Casper punched Grease back, splitting his lip, then followed it with a hard blow to his stomach. "You fucked my sister—think you had it comin,' too."

I stepped down from my stool as Grease tried to catch his breath. While I knew they had each other's backs, Grease was a fuck of a lot bigger than my dad, and any fight between the two would not go well.

"Jesus Christ," Slider called out, walking toward us with a scowl on his face. "Knock it off, you idiots. We got enough on our plates."

"You get a hold of Eastwood?" Poet asked as he made his way to the bar. Mark Eastwood, or Woody, was the son of one of the original members. Doc hadn't had a medical degree, but he'd patched up Aces until the day he died of old age. Most of us hadn't even known Woody existed until after Doc died and the boys had stepped in to support him. He'd grown up in Salem with his mother, and he'd rarely been around the club until he was already half grown—but he'd sure as hell fit in.

We were hoping that he'd heard something around his hometown, but the little fucker wasn't answering his phone.

"Nah. Hasn't called back yet," Grease said, wiping the blood off his lips with a dirty rag from his pocket. "I'll call Sherry in a couple hours—see if she's seen him."

"Make sure he's not been an asshole to his mum," Poet ordered. "Last time I checked, boy was in trouble again at school."

"Leo's doin' the same shit," Dragon said, shaking his head.

"Not the same. Leo's got a pop and a gramps to knock sense into him. Sherry's got no man to keep the kid in line," Poet reminded him.

"I gotta run for some parts," I finally said, bored with the conversation.

I didn't give a shit what Woody was doing. The kid was cool, but he was still young and he acted like it. Eventually, he'd get his shit together or he wouldn't. I didn't give a fuck either way, though I knew that Poet and Slider felt a responsibility to their old friend's kid.

"I'll head to Trix's place," Dragon told me with a chin lift. "Give her a bit of warnin' before ya show up."

"Tell her I'll be there around—nah, just let her know I'll be by."

"Will do."

I smacked Casper on the shoulder and nodded to the boys before spinning toward the door.

"Good luck!" Grease sang out.

I flipped him off, but didn't pause. I had shit to do.

"HELL, NO," TRIX snapped, glancing down at the duffle in my hand.

I'd finally stopped working on an older Ford Taurus when it started getting dark, packed my shit, and headed straight for her apartment. She'd moved into the sweet two bedroom place the year before. It was in the same complex my adoptive parents had lived in when I'd met them, but in the past five years, the owner had given the place a hell of a facelift. New windows, wood floors, appliances that weren't purchased during the Reagan administration, and countertops that weren't scratched to shit meant that the place always looked clean and inviting.

Like a home.

Not that I'd been there enough to get a good look at it. When Trix's stepdad died before Brenna had divorced him, all his money had gone to her. It wasn't something anyone talked about, but I knew that Dragon hadn't wanted to touch it—so they hadn't. Instead, they'd put it into a college fund for Trix, so she wouldn't have to work during the school year. Trix didn't seem to have any problems with using the dead fucker's money. I guess she figured they deserved it after what he'd put her mom through. I'd helped when she'd moved in and I'd only been let in twice since then. Once when she bought a new couch, and the second time when she'd bought a new bed.

I'd been having dreams about that bed for the better part of a year.

"Gonna let me in?" I asked, taking a step forward.

"Nope."

"Wasn't really a question, Sweetbea."

"Don't call me that."

I ignored her scowl and kept moving forward until she had no choice but to step out of my way or be pressed up against my chest.

"Is this really necessary?" she asked, shutting the door as I walked farther into her living room.

"Yeah."

"I don't want you here."

"That's pretty clear," I replied, walking down her hallway. I knew she had an extra bedroom that she kept for when her brother spent the night, and I found it easily. I remembered which door held her bedroom—it wasn't something I'd ever forget, but I figured I'd get a lot less fight out of her if I didn't put my shit in her room.

"If there's an issue, why aren't we on lockdown?" she asked, trailing behind me. "I mean, that I could understand. I don't know why you have to—*oomph*." She rocked back as I tossed my bag on the bed and turned into her. My hands came up to grasp her hips to keep her steady, but within seconds, she was taking a huge step back.

"Jumpy?" I asked, a small smile pulling at my lips.

"No."

"Alright." I nodded and stepped around her. "What's for dinner?"

She sputtered and stomped after me as I made my way to the fridge. Even though I'd barely ever been to her house, when I opened the door, I found a six pack of my favorite beer in her fridge. Interesting.

"These old?" I asked, lifting one up before setting the neck against the edge of her countertop.

"Don't!" she yelled, startling me. "Those counters are new, you idiot."

I watched her silently as she searched for a bottle opener, finally finding it in the bottom of one of her kitchen drawers. She obviously hadn't used it in a long time.

"No, they're not old," she mumbled, reaching to grab the beer out of my hand and opening it with a flick of her wrist before handing it back. I took a long pull as she tossed the top into the garbage.

"You get 'em for me?" I persisted as she pulled a package of raw pork out of the fridge.

"Obviously."

"Thank you."

"Don't mention it."

I took a seat at her kitchen table as she moved around the kitchen, cutting vegetables and stir-frying them with pork in a big wok while she grumbled.

"You live with Rose, so you'll have to cut me some slack," she told me over her shoulder. "Her food is insane."

"Christ, I can't eat there much or I'd be as fat as I was in high school."

"You weren't fat!" she argued, spinning around to glare at me.

"Oh, yeah, I was." I chuckled. I'd been so glad when I'd been able to burn off the extra weight once I got a little older.

"No, you were the perfect size."

"Perfect, huh?"

"Shut up. You know what I mean."

She spun back around just in time to keep the food from burning and put another pot on the stove so she could steam some rice.

We were quiet as she brought me a second beer and finished cooking, and a little while later, she was setting a plate full of steaming food in front of me.

"So, how's this going to work?" she asked as she poured herself a glass of water and sat down across from me. "You're staying here? For how long?"

"Holy shit, that's hot!" I moaned, covering my mouth so I could open it to cool off the pork burning my tongue.

"No shit, Sherlock. I just took it off the stove," she replied, rolling her eyes.

I scowled back, finally swallowing the food in my mouth. Damn, even hot enough to burn, it was some good shit. "You're not going to fight me?" I asked, scooping some more food onto my fork.

"I know how this works," she said ruefully. "I stay with my parents or you stay here. You're the lesser of two evils."

"Those the options your pop gave you?"

"Yep."

I nodded. Good man. "What's your schedule like?"

"I have classes Monday, Wednesday and Friday. Tuesdays I visit my mom, Thursdays I usually try to study most of the day. Weekends are free."

"You workin'? Got a boyfriend?"

"Not working at the moment. I'll start waitressing again for the catering company once summer break starts. The boyfriend status is none of your business." She stood from the table and grabbed both our plates, taking them to the sink.

"My business if I need to invest in some earplugs," I said, following her to the sink and stepping in behind her.

"What?" she asked, spinning to face me. "Why would you—" Her understanding dawned and her jaw dropped.

"Not gonna listen to you fuckin' someone else."

"You're disgusting!"

"Just sayin'."

"I wouldn't have sex with someone if you were here."

"Well, you're not stayin' anywhere else while we've got this shit goin' on."

"I don't even have a fucking boyfriend!"

A smile spread across my face as I watched her get more and more riled up. "Good," I said softly, reaching up to touch her cheek, then letting my hand fall as she dodged under my arm and walked toward the living room.

"This how it's gonna be the whole time I'm here?" I asked reasonably as I dropped down on the couch with her a couple minutes later. "You jumpin' around like a rabbit every time I try to touch you?"

"Stop trying to touch me," she said flatly, turning some home improvement show on the TV.

"You know that ain't gonna happen."

"What is your deal tonight?"

"No deal."

"Just because you're staying at my apartment doesn't mean you get some sort of perks," she huffed, refusing to look at me. "If anyone gets benefits, it should be me. I'm the one paying the fucking rent for you to live here."

I waited for her to realize what she'd just said, but she didn't.

"Take all the perks you want, Sweetbea," I told her with a slow smile.

She stood abruptly and glared at me, tossing the remote at my head with a small squeak of frustration before stomping off to her room.

I couldn't help but laugh as I heard her bedroom door slam.

As if a flimsy door would stop me.

Chapter 2

TRIX

"Wake up, Sweetbea," Cam called softly, making me groan. "I'll take ya to your parents."

"You go," I mumbled, pushing my face into my pillow. "I'll drive in later."

God, it was early. Why the hell was he awake already? It had been almost a week since Cam moved in, and living together had been surprisingly painless until he decided to wake me up at the butt crack of dawn.

He wasn't messy. When I was studying or reading, he pulled out his laptop and plugged in his earbuds, checking the news and watching TV shows without bothering me. He even showered at night, so I had the bathroom to myself in the morning.

If it wasn't for the fact that he insisted on touching me constantly, little brushes of his hands and body, he'd be the perfect roommate.

"Come on," he said softly as I felt him sit down next to my hip, his hand brushing down my bare arm. "Want you on the back of my bike."

"Sleep time, no bike."

"You got twenty minutes to get ready, or I'm takin' ya the way you are."

"Can't. No pants." I pulled my arm away from him and flung it over my face.

He inhaled sharply, and before I could stop him, he ripped my comforter down to my knees.

"Cold!" I gasped, pulling my knees to my chest. "Give the blankets back, ass!"

"Jesus," he mumbled, his gravelly voice jolting me completely awake.

I turned my head to look at him just as he pulled his t-shirt over his head.

"What are you doing?" I asked in alarm as he dropped his jeans to the floor. "Get the fuck out of here."

"Warmin' you up," he replied, crawling in behind me as he pulled the comforter up around us.

He wrapped a muscular arm around my waist and jerked me into the curve of his body as his lips met my neck. "Nice and cozy."

"You're out of your damn mind," I said, completely motionless. "What the hell?"

"Been waitin' on you to come to me—that ain't happenin.' Looks like I gotta go to you."

His hand that had been wrapped securely around my waist pulled up slowly, running up my belly and then back down over my bare thigh until he'd reached my knee, jerking it up so he could press one of his legs forward into the gap.

"This is a bad idea," I warned, my body softening.

"Best idea I've ever had."

"No, really. My pop will kill you."

"Already talked to your dad, Sweetbea. He won't say shit."

"What? You *what*?"

"You wax your legs? So fuckin' soft, damn."

"Cameron!" I hissed, slamming my elbow into his gut. "You talked to my pop?"

"Jesus, watch the elbows. Yeah, I talked to him. Laid it all out. It's all good," he replied against my shoulder, before opening his mouth wide and running it up my neck.

Shit, that felt good.

"Laid what out?" I asked stubbornly, ignoring the way my heart raced.

"Us."

"There is no *us*."

"Oh, really?" He gripped my hip and rocked against me softly. "You sure?"

"Just because you crawled into my bed uninvited doesn't mean there's—" My words cut off as his hand slid forward, pressing beneath my belly button as he rocked harder against me.

"Tell me no," he whispered into my ear as he slid the arm he'd been braced on under my head. His hand moved slowly, tracing my collarbone before sliding down to cup one of my breasts. "You want me to stop?"

I made some weird noise in the back of my throat, but words seemed to be beyond me. How many years had I fantasized about Cam's hands on me? I couldn't even remember. I'd wanted him for so long that it seemed to be soldered into my personality. Sarcastic, smart, a little weird, outgoing, fun, wants Cameron.

My mind went blank and I closed my eyes. I didn't think about what the aftermath would entail, or that I hadn't even brushed my teeth. Shit, I didn't even think about the fact that I didn't keep condoms in my room.

All I could think about was Cam's large body behind mine and his massive hands on my torso.

"No," I gasped as his hand slid off my breast.

"No?"

"Keep going." I grabbed his hand and pressed it back against my breast as he chuckled against my neck.

"I can do that," he whispered into my ear. "I'll make it even better."

I was nodding my head before he'd even finished speaking. Damn, I knew I was going to regret it, but I was far more worried that I'd never have the chance again than any regrets I'd have afterward.

We were adults. I'd deal.

"You wet?" he asked, sliding his fingers into the front of my underwear as I shook my head. "I better do somethin' about that."

My entire body jolted as his fingertips met my pussy, barely skimming over the skin as I tried to widen my legs.

"Stay still," he warned, tightening the hand on my breast. "I'll do the work this time, yeah? You just—goddamn, you're sexy—you just lay right here."

"This is stupid," I argued hoarsely, reaching behind me so I could grip his hip. "I won't come like—"

"You won't come at all unless you stop movin'," he warned, pinching my nipple before moving his hand to my other breast. "I know what I'm doin'," he whispered into my ear as his fingers between my legs pressed harder against me.

"I love this," he said, running his fingers over the short hair. "Trimmed short, so when I go down on you, it'll be out of my way."

"You're welcome," I panted, trying really hard not to work my hips against him.

He laughed. "I can't wait to see what you look like. Bet you're dark—" His fingers spread my outer lips apart, then slid down between them. "Yeah, you're dark here, to go along with all that gorgeous tan skin."

My back arched, and his fingers clamped down against my nipple.

"Look how wet you are now," he teased, kissing my neck. "Soakin.' I bet if I pressed—"

"Shit!" My entire body jolted as the heel of his hand pressed down on my clit and two fingers slid inside me.

His palm ran in small circles as he slowly pumped his fingers in and out, and I was so close to the edge, I could have cried.

I took care of business myself on a pretty regular basis, but this impending orgasm was way bigger than anything I could have accomplished on my own. Holy shit.

I turned my face toward his, my dazed eyes meeting his warm ones as he smiled. "I bet your little clit turns bright red when I suck on it," he said seriously.

That was it.

My orgasm hit hard, and my entire body locked as Cam murmured praise to me, his hand still moving against me as I rode it out.

By the time my body had calmed again, I was turned and pulled halfway on top of Cam's wide chest.

"Let's go back to sleep," I said, sighing.

"Glad you're all worn out," he replied dryly, kissing the top of my head. "But we need to hit the road."

"You want a blow job?"

"Are you offering me head so you don't have to get out of bed?"

"You're a poet, and… yes."

"Yeah, I'm sure that would be fun. Much as I'd like your lips wrapped around me, you'd probably fall asleep on my dick."

"Would not, and if I did, that'd probably say more about you than me, anyway."

"Come on, babe," he said with a laugh, slapping my ass. "Up."

He pulled me from the bed and slapped my ass again to get me moving.

"You owe me!" he called as I stumbled into the bathroom.

"Yeah, a hand job—maybe," I called back, swinging the door shut behind me.

I focused on showering and brushing my teeth, refusing to think about the can of worms I'd allowed to be opened. I'd think about it later.

★ ★ ★

"You woke me up early to go to my parents'?" I asked incredulously, climbing off the back of Cam's bike.

"Gotta work, I'll pick ya up when I'm done," he replied, making no move to follow me.

"Are you kidding? I'll be stranded here all day without my car."

"You'll be fine. No use drivin' when I can drop you off."

"Maybe I had shit to do today!"

"Ya said Tuesday was your day with your ma, right?"

"Not all day!" I argued, getting annoyed. A part of me had hoped that we were just going for a ride, that he'd been planning to spend the day with me. I was irritatingly disappointed that he was just dropping me off.

"I'll come get you for lunch, then," he said calmly.

"I don't want to have lunch with you," I snapped back as I finally ripped my helmet off my head.

"Yeah, ya do."

"I really don't."

"Bullshit."

"Ugh! Go away." I spun to walk away when his words stopped me.

"Come kiss me goodbye."

"Not happening," I said flatly, moving toward the front of my parents' little house.

He was off his bike and stalking toward me before I'd reached the front porch.

"Quit," I ordered, pointing at his face. "I'm not kissing you."

"Come here," he replied calmly, moving closer.

"No! Knock it off." I threw my hands out in front of me as I backed toward the house, starting to laugh nervously. "Go to work."

His mouth curved up into a small grin as he watched me scrambling away, then his hand shot out and grabbed one of my wrists, jerking me toward him.

"Kiss me goodbye," he demanded again, his smile never wavering as he wrapped the other arm tight around my back.

"I'm not kissing you!" I stated stubbornly. At that point, I actually *did* want to kiss the asshole… but it was the principle of the thing. I wasn't backing down, dammit.

"I need to warm you up first?" he asked, his hand sliding down to grip my ass.

Oh, shit.

"Stop it!" I hissed, glancing over my shoulder toward my house. "My pop's still home."

"And?"

"Quit it," I ground out between my teeth.

"Kiss me goodbye," he repeated with a squeeze of my ass.

"Fine!" I went up on my toes, but I wasn't anywhere near his lips until he bent down to meet me halfway. "You're so annoying," I mumbled against his lips.

"You love me."

I jerked back at his words, the sentiment hitting too close to the past I'd put behind me, but he didn't allow me to go far before his mouth was covering my lips and forcing me to open.

He pulled my arm over his shoulder as he sucked at my bottom lip, then gripped my ass hard as he jerked me up his chest so I could wrap my legs around him.

It was the first time we'd kissed in years, and it was more than I'd remembered. Kissing Cam was like falling into cool water on a hot day. Shocking at first, then it felt so good I didn't want to come up for air.

One of my arms was wrapped around his neck and the other was cupping the side of his head when I heard my mom laughing behind me.

"Shit," I gasped, yanking my face away from Cam's.

"Come back," he murmured, smiling.

"Unless you wanna leave without your balls, you'll put my daughter down," my pop said quietly, making me jump.

"Put me down. Put me down," I ordered frantically, pushing at Cam's arms.

God, I'd set out to not kiss him and I'd ended up eating his face in front of my parents. How the hell did that happen?

"Relax, Sweetbea. Your dad's not gonna cut off my balls." He chuckled, letting me slide down until I was on my feet.

"Don't bet on it, Hulk," my pop warned, making me take a giant step backward.

"Seriously, man?" Cam asked in irritation, glancing at my parents, who were standing on the porch. "We gonna do this every time you see us together?"

"We're not together," I cut in eagerly.

Both men ignored me.

"You can call me, 'sir'."

"Fuck off."

My pop started laughing, the chuckles coming out deep and raspy, and I couldn't help but smile along with him. My dad was a good-looking guy, but he didn't smile very often—so when he did, it was staggering.

"I'll follow you over," Pop said with a nod once he'd caught his breath.

"I'll be here to pick you up at one for lunch, Bea."

"I'm having lunch with my mom—"

"No, you're not," my mom argued.

"See ya in a few hours, little liar."

I stood with my hands clenched as Cam strapped his helmet on his head and fired up his bike.

"Seriously?" I griped at my pop as I brushed past him. "What the hell was that?"

"Watch your mouth," he warned, following me into the kitchen.

"You pretty much just gave me to Cam, but I still can't swear in front of you? You do realize, he doesn't want to play charades at night, right?"

"Watch it, Little Warrior," Pop said softly, reaching past me to get a cup of coffee before kissing the side of my head. "Knowin' you're an adult is one thing. You rubbin' that shit in my face is really fuckin' different."

"Sorry," I replied glumly.

"What the heck, Trix?" my mom asked in surprise as she finally followed us into the kitchen. "You've been after that kid for years, and now that you have him, you don't want him?"

"I had a crush on him when I was young—that's it."

"Not five years ago you broke a girl's cheek for sitting on his lap," my pop reminded me with a smile.

"She was a bitch."

"Of course she was."

I rolled my eyes at him and pushed him roughly out of the way so I could get my own coffee.

"You're acting weird," I accused, staring at my dad as he relaxed back against a kitchen chair.

"I'm taking a shower," my mom announced, walking over to give me a kiss. "You guys need a couple minutes."

"Nothin' weird about it," Pop said, watching me closely after my mom was gone.

"So, you're okay with Cam living with me? Since when?"

He sighed and scratched the side of his head.

"Don't like it, no."

"Then what was all that?" I bitched, flinging my arm toward the front porch.

"Ya gonna give me time to speak before you fly off the handle?"

My mouth snapped shut, and I crossed my arms over my chest.

"You realize your ma is the only woman I've ever let speak to me like that—right?"

I nodded.

"Still stands."

Point taken.

"You and Cameron—" he sighed again. Good grief, get to the point already. "I've never liked it."

I tilted my head to the side, waiting for him to finish. I wasn't going to get yelled at for interrupting.

"Fuckin' weird the way he let you follow him around. I hated that shit. But hell, after the shit you and your mama went through—I couldn't force you away from him. He wasn't doin' nothin' wrong, and neither were you. He helped ya with your shyness, made ya more outgoing. And as he got older, he made sure there was enough distance between ya that no one ever got the wrong idea."

I remembered that. Around the time Cam started high school, he stopped hanging out with me as much. It had hurt my feelings, until my mom sat me down and explained that Cam was working at the club more, so I had to stop whining about it. I hadn't realized that he'd stayed away for a different reason altogether. Made sense, though.

"Sit," my pop ordered as I shifted from one foot to the other.

As soon as I was seated, he leaned forward in his chair and braced his forearms on the table. "Do I like ya with him? Fuck, no. I don't want ya with anyone, but that ain't reasonable or normal. You're a full grown woman."

He reached out and pulled at my messy hair.

"If somethin' happened to me—"

"Don't say that," I blurted. I never wanted to have that conversation. Ever.

He glared at me, shutting me up. "Somethin' happened to me—that boy would protect you until the day he died. Doesn't matter if you were with him or married to someone else. His loyalty to you is unquestionable—"

"He fucks anything that moves!" I argued, scowling.

"That ain't the same and you know it. He could fuck half the country and it'd still be you he came home to."

"You don't care that he'd cheat on me?"

"Course I'd care—don't want you hurt—but that ain't my business."

I scoffed in disbelief and leaned away. What a shitty thing to say.

"Stop poutin' and fuckin' listen for a minute. Jesus Christ, between you and your ma…"

"Fine."

"Look at me, Little Warrior." He waited until I met his eyes, then continued speaking. "Hulk is loyal to you. As much as I hate the thought of you with anyone, he would die for you. I might hate it that you've got a man, but I've gotta be thankful for that shit, too."

"Oh good, you're thankful," I said derisively, ignoring the scowl that grew darker and darker on my pop's face. "It's fine with you that he'll fuck around, just as long as he keeps me safe from some invisible boogeyman. Makes perfect fucking sense."

"Goddammit, Bellatrix!" he yelled, slamming his hand down on the table. "You need to *listen* to what I'm sayin'."

"Enough," my mom ordered, coming into the kitchen with her hair still wrapped in a towel. "You need to get to the garage."

"Talk to your daughter," Pop snapped back, standing up. "She doesn't listen to a fuckin' word I say."

"Oh, I heard plenty," I mumbled, rolling my eyes.

"Are you fuckin'—"

"Out!" Mom ordered again, pushing at my pop until he moved toward the front door. "I'll see you later. Love you."

"Love you, too, baby," my pop said, his eyes growing soft as he shrugged his cut on over a plain t-shirt.

They walked out to the porch and after a few minutes, my mom came back in alone. It was almost funny how little I looked like her. She was petite, pale and freckled with wild red hair that she kept long because my pop loved it. I was tan year-round, with thick black hair that had lost its curl as I got older and enough junk in my trunk for us to share.

"What was all that about?" she asked softly when she got a good look at my unhappy face.

"Cameron."

"Ah."

"Pop was acting weird this morning."

"Yeah, well, lots of stuff happening at the club, I think," she said, grabbing her mug from the counter so she could sit in Pop's vacated chair.

"What's going on? No one tells me shit—but Cameron's living in my apartment all of a sudden. It's annoying."

"They don't tell me much, either," my mom said ruefully, pulling the towel out of her hair. "But your pop's not sleeping, and things are tense."

"Maybe I should just move back in here."

"You want to move back in?"

"Not really."

"Do you want to stay with Cam?"

"Hell, I don't know." I dropped my forehead and proceeded to bang it against the tabletop as my mom laughed.

"Shit, don't do that. You're going to leave a bruise," she worried.

"Not everyone bruises like you, Princess Peach," I replied, turning my head to the side so I could look at her.

"You'll figure it out—we all do."

"He's a manwhore."

"He's a guy."

"Did Pop ever cheat on you?" I asked, making her jolt in surprise.

"No way. I'm your dad's be-all-end-all. I don't think he's ever even been tempted."

"It's not like that with Cam."

"I'm pretty sure it's *exactly* like that," she commented dryly.

"He's a whore. He's slept with freaking everyone. I can't even walk into the club without tripping over a chick he's had sex with."

"Yeah, I dealt with that, too."

"You did?"

"When we got here, your pop was with someone."

"I don't remember that."

"Yeah, well, she wasn't around for long. She glared at you one day and I knocked her ass out."

"Go, Mom!" I sighed in surprise. My mom was not the type to get into it with another woman. I couldn't even imagine it.

"Not my finest moment."

"Sounds pretty great to me."

"For what it's worth, I don't think Cam would cheat on you, and neither does your pop."

"Yeah, he already said it wasn't his business."

"Trix, babe, you've always been able to read between the lines with your father. So why the hell are you missing the point today?"

"I got his point," I argued.

"Your dad is in an awkward position, alright? He loves you more than anyone on this earth—maybe even me. But he has to work with Cam, he has to trust him, and one day, he's gonna get the gavel and he'll have to lead him. If he thought Cam would hurt you—

emotionally or physically—he would've never let him near you. But he can't step in later if Cam's being an asshole—not if you're Cam's old lady. Okay?"

"Yeah, I get it," I mumbled back, letting her words roll around in my brain. "You don't think he'd cheat?"

"Let's put it this way—are you a virgin?"

"No."

"Have you ever slept with Cam?"

"No."

"So, you've slept with other men?"

"Obviously."

"You love Cam?"

"Yeah, but we weren't—*ahh*, I see what you did there."

She stared at me silently.

"Fine," I grumbled, standing to stretch. "I should probably go smooth things over with Pop."

"That would probably be a good idea, baby. He's wound pretty tight already, doesn't need to be fighting with you, too."

"You wanna walk over with me?"

"Nah, I'm going to mop the floors."

"Have fun."

I left the house and walked slowly toward the clubhouse in the distance, swishing my feet through the long grass. Apparently, when I was little, my mom had dropped me out her window and I'd had to run across this same field to get my pop when her psycho estranged husband showed up. I didn't remember any of it—which was probably a good thing—but I'd heard the story a dozen times. I think whatever happened that day had been the reason my parents never moved off the club's property. Her first husband was dead, but my pop was still crazy protective of us, which made what I'd insinuated that morning even shittier.

Cameron made me crazy. He always had. After our little make-out session when I was seventeen, I'd lost my ability to be rational about him. While my mom had made a valid point about my sexual history and the hypocrisy of judging Cam because he'd fucked other women, I still couldn't get over the *number* of women he'd been with. I'd slept with two other guys—both boyfriends. Cam, however, was indiscriminate in his bed partners.

I couldn't decide which of us was worse—me, who'd been in actual relationships with other men, or Cam, who'd never cared about any of the women he slept with.

Chapter 3

CAMERON

"THAT GIRL'S GONNA give you trouble," Grease informed me, pointing at Trix as she crossed the field, coming toward us. "Glad I'm done with all that."

I took a drag off my cigarette and nodded. I knew she was. "Got any advice?" I asked, glancing at him before looking back at Trix, who looked pretty deep in thought.

"*Yes, dear,*" he said in a completely subdued voice before slapping my shoulder and putting out his cigarette. "Only two words you need to know."

"You're so full of shit," I scoffed.

"You'll figure it out, we all do." With a slight nod, he walked away as Trix reached me.

"What're you doin' here?" I asked, dropping the butt of my cigarette so I could wrap my arms around her.

"Need to talk to my pop, you know where he is?" she asked, gripping my biceps hard.

"Everything okay?" I asked, going in for a kiss that she surprisingly gave me without a fight.

"Just need to apologize," she replied with a huff as I pulled away.

"Ouch."

"Yeah, not my favorite thing to do."

"He's in the second bay, I think. Want me to come with you?" I didn't like that she was apologizing. That meant she'd done something to piss her old man off.

"I think I know my way," she teased with a small smile, stepping back.

"Find me when you're done?"

"Sure."

She spun and walked toward the garage bay her dad was working in, and I couldn't help but stare at her ass. She was wearing a pair of jeans that were snug in all the right places. Damn.

"You gonna help me finish this or what?" my little cousin, Will, griped, sticking his head out of the garage. The kid was twenty, but I swear to God he was still growing. His dad, Grease, was a big guy, so everyone had expected him to be big, too, but not this late in the game.

"You juicin'?" I asked, stalking back into the garage. "You're pretty damn pissy lately."

"I'm not usin' steroids, asshole."

"Gettin' bigger," I murmured, watching him closely.

I didn't give a fuck what the other guys did. I wasn't their daddy. As long as they did their jobs and had my back—we were cool. But my little cousin was a completely different story, and he still wasn't as big as I was. I'd kick his ass.

"Steroids don't make you taller, idiot."

"Fillin' out, too."

"Yeah, because I've been working out and eating a shit ton of food," he snapped, leaning under the hood of the Chevy we were working on.

"Just lookin' out," I said calmly, still watching him.

"I don't need you to look out for me!" he roared, making my head jerk back in surprise as he came out from under the rusted hood. "I'm a grown ass man—"

"Yeah, little tantrum you're throwin' sounds real manly," I shot back. Where the fuck was his attitude coming from?

He took a step toward me and I braced my feet. I didn't think he'd be stupid enough to take me on, but I wasn't letting him knock me off balance if he tried to take a—*yep.*

I guess he was feeling stupid.

"This will not end well for you," I growled, dodging his fist.

"Pussy," he sneered, swinging again, this time making contact with my lower ribs. Fuck, that didn't feel great.

"Will!" Slider yelled, making Will freeze. "Take that shit away from the cars!"

I nodded and turned toward the open doors, catching a glimpse of Trix's worried face as I moved outside. I didn't make it two feet before Will took a cheap shot. My head snapped forward and I stumbled onto the gravel.

I was suddenly just as pissed as he was.

"You fuckin' kiddin' me?" I yelled, spinning to face him and slamming my hands into his chest.

No way the kid wasn't on steroids. No fucking way.

He spit on the ground between us.

My hand swung out without conscious thought, and I watched with satisfaction as I connected with his jaw, knocking him back a pace. All around us, the boys had come to watch, keeping their distance and staying mostly quiet.

"Takin' cheap shots at family? The fuck is a matter with ya?" I asked as he swung again, his fist glancing off my jaw as I dodged him.

"Not my family," he spit back.

I hit him again. And again. And again. I hit him four or five times before he fell, and I ignored the throbbing points where he'd gotten me back as I watched him land hard on the gravel.

"The fuck was that?" I asked quietly, breathing heavily as I met our VP Poet's eyes.

"Get him up, boys," Poet ordered. "Find one of the girls to patch him up. Christ, we need a fuckin' doc."

"You start that?" Grease asked as I finally made eye contact with Trix. She looked completely freaked out as her pop held her tight against his side.

"Hell, no."

"Alright," he said with a small nod, following the guys carrying Will inside.

I prodded the inside of my cheek with my tongue and found two cuts from my teeth. I spit the blood out of my mouth with a grimace, finally feeling the full extent of Will's fury. I was going to be sore as hell tomorrow.

"Take the rest of the day," Slider said calmly before walking away.

"Christ," I mumbled, shaking my head. Then Trix was there.

"What the hell happened?" she hissed. "I'd barely walked away and all of a sudden, you're having a schoolyard fight with Will."

"Hell if I know," I answered, bracing my hands on my hips. "Damn, that boy's got some mitts on him."

"Yeah, you look like shit."

"Don't feel real great, either."

She sighed, reaching up to wipe gently at some of the blood smeared across my cheek. "Wanna go home?"

"You get shit straightened up with your dad?" I asked quietly, ignoring my throbbing head as I leaned down close.

"Yeah, we're good," she whispered back before pulling away.

"We're gonna go, Pop," she called to Dragon, who was standing a few feet away talking to Casper.

"How you feeling?" Casper asked as we made our way toward them.

"Not as bad as he is."

"No doubt." He chuckled. "He's lucky you kept your shit together. Got any idea what set him off?"

"No, and I wasn't gonna go crazy on the kid. He's family."

"Gonna have to watch him," Dragon said darkly. "Don't have time for this shit."

"Think he might be juicin'," I mentioned, feeling like an asshole for saying anything about it.

"Done right, that shit won't fuck you up," Dragon said with a shake of his head. "Has to be somethin' else."

"Might be doing it wrong," Casper pointed out. "He's what—twenty? Who's he getting it from?"

"No idea—not even sure he's doin' it," I mumbled, reaching out to pull Trix against my side.

"Nah, you're right. He's doin' it," Dragon said. "Boy's gotten huge."

"We done?" I asked tiredly, scratching at the blood that was drying on my face.

"Yeah, get outta here," Casper said with a sympathetic smile.

"Love you, Papa," Trix said softly, stepping away from me to give Dragon a hug.

"You, too," he mumbled back, kissing the top of her head as he glared at me.

I shook my head and turned as Trix moved back to my side and we started walking toward my bike. Goddamn, I was sore.

"WHAT DO YOU want for lunch?" Trix called out as I situated the ice on my face. My jaw had some mottled bruising that I would have ignored, but my girl was all about babying me and I wasn't going to stop her.

I wondered if I should moan a little so she'd come check on me.

"Don't have to make me lunch, Bea," I called back, leaning farther into the couch with a sigh.

Will had gotten some good hits in, but he'd been too sloppy. I knew he'd been taught better, so he had to have been completely out of his mind when he went after me. It drove me nuts, because I couldn't figure out what had set him off.

He'd been a moody little bitch lately, but I figured it was just his age. We'd all gone thorough that stage—the one where we wanted to be the big man on campus, but were surrounded by much bigger men on a daily basis. You had to just grow out of that shit, eventually find your place in the pecking order and work your way up.

"I can make you soup," Trix said sweetly as she came back into the living room.

"Baby, I don't need soup."

"Applesauce?"

"You're joking, right?"

"You should have something soft—"

"Steak," I cut in. "I want steak and mashed potatoes."

"Your mouth, though—"

I reached out and grabbed a hold of her hips, letting the bag of ice fall onto the couch as I pulled her onto my lap.

"You're sweet, you know that?"

"Your face looks like it hurts," she replied, reaching up to run her fingers through the short hair on top of my head.

"It's fine, Sweetbea," I reassured her, sliding my hand up her side. "Looks a lot worse than it feels."

"You still shouldn't have steak. Your cheeks are cut—"

"Mouth feels fine, too."

"It was bleeding."

"Not bleedin' now."

"I didn't like watching that," she confessed softly. "I know I should find it hot or something, but I didn't. I knew you would win, but I still hated it."

"Shouldn't have had to watch it. Wish your dad had kept you inside."

"There was no way he could have kept me inside."

"Doesn't make a lot of sense," I teased quietly.

"I didn't want to see it, but I had to know what was happening."

"Shit like that doesn't happen very often," I said, sliding my hand up her back until I could run my fingers through the ends of her hair. "But you're gonna have to get used to not knowin' what's happenin'."

"I don't think I'll ever get used to that."

"You can handle it. Hell, you were born to handle it."

"Doesn't mean I like it," she replied with a frown.

"Kiss me," I murmured, ready to change the subject. I reached up to grip the back of her neck.

"But, your mouth—"

"You don't kiss me right now, I'm gonna be usin' my mouth for other things in about three seconds."

"Is that supposed to be a deterrent?" she asked laughingly, leaning forward to press her lips gently against mine.

"Such a badass," I said into her mouth, licking her bottom lip. "I get in a fight and you don't get pissed or hysterical, you just wait until it's over and then baby me."

"Was I supposed to be hysterical?" she asked, smiling.

"Well, I wouldn't have objected to a few tears," I murmured back jokingly.

"Sorry I couldn't be the swooning maiden to your conquering hero." She sighed and rolled her eyes, leaning back. "What are we doing here, Cam?"

"Well, I was tryin' to kiss ya. Not sure what you're doin'."

"Do you want—are we together? Is this a thing?"

"A thing?" I asked incredulously, trying to figure out what she was getting at. We weren't a thing—we were us.

"I just want to know where we stand—alright? Stop getting pissy."

"Not getting pissy, just wonderin' where this is comin' from."

"I want to know what you're doing! I want to know if this is—do you just want to have sex? Is that what this is about? I know about the ban on sluts at the club."

"You're kiddin,' right?"

"No."

I laughed humorlessly and pushed her off my lap so I could stand up. I was fucking insulted. After all the shit I'd done for her when we were kids, after all the shit we'd been through and the fact that she'd ignored me for almost five years because I wouldn't fuck her—and she thought I just wanted sex?

And then what? We'd just go back to being strangers? I didn't even know how that would be possible.

"Yeah, Trix. I was thinkin' we'd just fuck while I was stayin' here. Convenient, ya know?" I shook my head and grabbed my cut off the back of the couch as I headed toward the front door.

"Where are you going?" she asked, jumping to her feet.

"Be back later," I called over my shoulder, not stopping as she tried to follow me.

I slammed the door behind me as I got outside, then stomped toward my bike. I froze just as I was about to climb on. I was taking off like a fucking pussy just because she'd hurt my feelings.

I'd almost just left her, when keeping her safe—not getting my dick wet—was the whole reason I was there. Sure, she was probably safe inside her apartment in broad fucking daylight, but that didn't mean I should run away like a bitch.

I ran my hands restlessly over my head, then turned back toward the apartment building.

Trix was standing on the landing, barefoot, with her arms wrapped around her chest. Watching me.

"Get back inside," I said, walking toward the stairs. When I reached the top of them, she was still standing in the same spot. "I said to get back inside," I ordered, pushing her gently toward her apartment.

"Where were you going? Were you going to fuck someone else?" she asked quietly as I opened her door.

"Jesus. You've got a real high opinion of me."

"You fuck anything that moves." She wrinkled her nose.

"Not quite—I like pussy, not dick," I said with a smile. I could hear the words coming out of my mouth, but I couldn't seem to stop them, even though I could feel her pulling away from me. What did she expect? She was acting like I was disgusting—did she think I'd just lie down and take it?

She thought I was dirty? Fine. No skin off my back.

"I just wanted to know if we were exclusive, and you freaked—"

"No," I cut her off, locking the door before turning to face her. "You wanted to know if I was gonna fuck around on you."

"Well, I just—"

"When have I ever done anythin' to hurt you, Bellatrix? Huh? Yeah, you were pissed when you were younger because I wouldn't put my hands on ya—but that was for your benefit, not mine. I've done nothin' but take care of ya our entire lives. So, why the hell would I fuck someone else knowing that shit would bother ya?"

"You've been fucking club skanks for years! You think that didn't hurt to watch?"

"You shittin' me right now? You were a kid, Bellatrix! You sayin' I shoulda been a fuckin' monk? We were *friends*. You were sleepin' with scrawny high school kids. Jesus, what planet are you livin' on?"

"You kissed me! You kissed me and then went right back to them!" She pointed toward the front door like there was a line of women out there waiting on me.

"We seriously discussin' somethin' that happened four years ago?" I ran my hands over my head. God, she was so fucking irritating.

"Yes."

"You were too young, Bea. Still in fuckin' high school."

"I wasn't too young." She crossed her arms over her chest stubbornly. "And *Abbie* was in high school!"

"Who the fuck is Abbie?" I asked in confusion.

She growled, and I waited for her to stomp her foot like a fucking two year old.

"You *were* too young. You think I didn't want you then? 'Course I did. But you wanted to go to fuckin' college. Shit, you were seventeen years old! Poet and Dragon would've hung me up by my balls. Kissin' you was a lapse in judgment—" My words cut off when she rocked back like she'd been hit. I softened my voice. "That whole scene was a lapse in judgment, Sweetbea, because if I woulda waited just a bit longer, we coulda been together. But I was fuckin' crazy jealous thinkin' about you with some kid. I fuckin' snapped. Then you got pissed and stopped talkin' to me, and it's taken me four fuckin' years to find a way back in."

"You just gave up! You walked away and started fucking other people again, and I wasn't going to be the stupid girl that waited around and watched you do it. I'd already been that girl, remember?" Trix's eyes filled with frustrated tears.

"You wouldn't even be in the same room with me, Trix," I mumbled back tiredly. "After bein' friends for all those years—you cut me off at the fuckin' knees."

"I'm sorry," she said, dropping her arms to her sides.

I didn't want her "sorry." I kicked off my boots, then moved past her toward the hallway. "I'm takin' a nap. This has been a shitty fuckin' day and it ain't even noon."

She sniffled as I walked away, but didn't say another word as I left the room.

I didn't like it that she was crying, but I was done trying to explain myself. I'd never done anything to hurt her—*she'd* been the bitch. *She'd* been the one to completely cut me out of her life. *She'd* been the one to act like I was some kind of whore for fucking other women. What had she expected me to do?

I'd never make comments about the men she'd been with. I hated that she'd had sex with anyone else, and I didn't want to hear about it or think about it—but I'd never make her feel badly about it, either. I'd known after she left me in the clearing when she was seventeen years old that I'd gone about shit the wrong way—but even when I'd been livid about her having sex, I'd never made her feel bad about it.

Was I pissed back then? Yes. Did I think there was anything wrong with her for wanting to have sex? Hell, no. I just wanted to be the man in her bed.

I peeled off my clothes and climbed gingerly into the guest bed, lying flat on my back as my ribs protested the movement.

I needed to get some sleep so when I saw her again, I didn't want to pack her ass up and leave her with her parents just to get the fuck away from her.

Chapter 4

TRIX

I MESSED UP.

Well, to be honest, I wasn't sure if I'd messed up or if I'd done myself a huge favor by pissing Cam off. He was right—completely right. I was the one who'd ended our friendship. I just hadn't been able to watch him with other women, and by the time I was old enough—mature enough—to be with him, I was doing everything I could to avoid him. I'd expected him to be celibate, even though we'd had no relationship whatsoever at that point. Not exactly fair… or realistic.

If I was thinking clearly, I knew he wouldn't do anything to deliberately hurt me. But when I was with Cam, I wasn't thinking clearly. I was all twisted up, eager to hold on to the chance of having him, but at the same time, completely afraid of what that would mean.

What if it didn't work out? How would I be able to handle seeing his parade of club skanks at every birthday party and barbeque? Even worse, he might find someone he wanted to be with for good—and that would kill me.

If things did work out—if we did end up staying together, did that mean I would have to become my mother? She had a degree from the same university I was almost graduated from, but she'd never used it. She'd been a housewife when she was married to my stepdad and had continued staying home once she and my pop got back together. It seemed like all of the women I was close to except my nan stayed home to take care of the kids—and while I didn't think that was a bad thing, it also wasn't what I wanted.

I'd worked my ass off for my business degree, and I wanted to use it. I didn't want to own my own business, but I *really* wanted to run someone else's. It didn't matter what kind of business I ended up in—a tattoo parlor or an advertising firm—I just wanted to put my new skills to good use. I wanted to strategize and implement new ideas, make money and feel the thrill of a job well done. I thrived on that shit.

A part of me loved the idea of settling down with Cam and having a house full of babies, but the other part of me wanted to make my own way, stand on my own two feet. If I got with Cam, I knew that he would take control. Our dynamic from the very beginning had been of a leader and a follower. Because of the age difference, I'd always been the follower, and I'd never questioned it.

But a lot had happened in the last four years. He was no longer the adult—we both were, and I couldn't be content with following him anymore. I wanted us to be equals.

I paced around the quiet living room, fidgeting and worrying as I tried to figure out what to do. I hated that Cam was pissed at me. I'd never liked fighting with him, not even when we were kids. Frankly, I didn't like anything that made him unhappy. I'd been able to ignore the gnawing in my stomach every time we'd crossed paths the past four years and I wouldn't look at him, but that had been pure self-preservation. Even then, it had hurt me to hurt him.

I let Cam sleep for almost an hour before I couldn't stand it anymore and finally made my decision.

"WHAT'RE YOU DOIN'?" Cam asked groggily as I slipped into bed beside him.

The sheets were cool against my skin and I shivered, immediately moving toward his body when he reached out an arm to pull me close.

"I'm sorry," I whispered against his chest.

"Me, too." He sighed, turning his head to kiss my hair.

My whole body seemed to relax at his words. This was my Cam. He didn't hold a grudge, and I knew if I never brought up our fight again, he wouldn't, either.

"I know you wouldn't hurt me," I mumbled past the lump in my throat.

"I'm with you, I'm not with anyone else, Bea. Alright? I know a lot of men are cool with that and their women look the other way, but I knew from the moment you busted that chick's face—that would never be us."

"I'm jealous."

"Good."

"I don't know how to *not* be jealous. I just—this feels like it came out of nowhere, and I'm—"

"Mighta came outta nowhere for you—but it feels like I've been waitin' forever."

"You didn't act like you were waiting," I said quietly, before snapping my mouth closed.

"Bea," he scolded softly. "What was I supposed to do, baby? First you were pissed I was fuckin' around, but at that time, you were seein' me in a way that I wasn't seein' you. Knew you wanted me—didn't feel the same. So I tried to keep that shit quiet, didn't want to hurt your feelings. But you kept pullin' away, no matter what I did, and after that shit went down at the back of the property when I realized—holy fuck, I've got a serious hard on for my best friend and I don't want her with anyone but me—you wanted nothin' to do with me."

"That was never true," I argued softly.

"Sure as hell felt true. I went from talkin' to you every day to nothin'."

"I cried myself to sleep for weeks," I said, making his entire body stiffen. "Though that probably had a lot to do with the birth control pills I'd started taking. It made me crazy."

Cam pressed his fingers under my chin, making me raise my face to his. "Why didn't you come to me?"

"I was embarrassed that you turned me down. Angry. And then I started seeing you with women, and I couldn't watch that."

"One word from you, Bea," he said hoarsely, "One word is all it woulda took. Thought you didn't give a fuck."

"I wanted you to figure it out on your own," I said, laying my head back on his chest.

"Jesus, I'm not a mind reader."

"I wanted you to not want anyone but me."

Cam groaned as he lifted and dropped the back of his head against the pillow a couple times. "I'm gonna tell you somethin' about men, Sweetbea."

"Oh, this should be good," I grumbled.

"If a man has a thing for a woman and she wants nothin' to do with him? He's gonna get his dick wet someplace else."

"Charming."

"Truth. A man may love a woman, but if she ain't feelin' that, if there's no chance of him gettin' her? He's gonna get laid someplace else."

"So, if I'm not putting out—"

"Don't even go there, Trix," he growled softly. "Told you I wouldn't fuck anyone else and I won't."

"I know," I sighed. "I'm sorry I hurt your feelings earlier."

"You didn't hurt my feelings," he replied gruffly. "You pissed me off. You think I'd fuck you and bail? Really?"

I shook my head and Cam kissed my hair.

We went silent for a little while as I listened to Cam's heart beat beneath my ear.

Cam's hand traced the tattoo covering my shoulder, then suddenly pressed forward to my collarbone. "You're naked," he said, sounding both confused and excited.

"I was hoping if you didn't forgive me right away, bare skin would sway you in that direction."

"Damn, I shoulda held out," he said with a laugh. "Well? Kiss me."

I leaned up, braced myself on his chest and had to stop and stare at his wide smile. He was so handsome. His light brown hair was kept short and he rarely wore a beard because he hated the way it itched as it grew in, and he was too impatient to wait it out. Blue eyes, long lashes, a nose that had been broken twice, full lips, a strong jawline, and a little mole on his right cheek that I used to stare at when I was ten because I wanted to kiss it. Every single part of him was perfect to me.

I pressed a kiss to the mole that my ten-year-old self had been so fascinated with.

"Was hoping for some tongue," he joked, running his hand through my hair.

I licked his cheek.

"Aw, come on now," he whined, dragging me until I was lying on top of him. "You want something to lick, I've got better parts for it."

"We should probably talk first."

"You're naked, pressed up against me, and you want to talk?"

"How is this going to work?" I asked nervously.

"I'm going to push these boxers down and fuck you for the next two hours. That's how it's gonna work."

I rolled my eyes at his disgruntled expression. "Are we announcing this? What is this? We're together—"

"Yeah, we're together. Didn't we just discuss this?"

"You're my boyfriend, then."

"I'm not a boy. I'm your man and eventually, I'll be your husband."

"Getting a little ahead of ourselves aren't we?" I asked with raised brows.

"Sweetbea, what do ya think we're doin' here?"

"Dating."

"I don't date," he scoffed.

"Yeah, I'm well aware," I said ruefully.

"Didn't ever want to be with anyone long-term but you—wasn't with you, wasn't doin' long term."

"Just to be clear, long-term to you is more than a couple hours."

"Jesus Christ," he murmured, sitting up and taking me with him so I was straddling his thighs. "You didn't used to bust my balls."

"Yeah, well, we never got naked together, either." My words seemed to remind him that I was sitting there bare assed, because his eyes immediately dropped from my eyes to stare at my breasts.

"You can bust my balls as much as you want," he said reverently as his long fingers cupped my breasts, making me laugh.

His eyes rose to meet mine again with a soft look. "I know I should say somethin' good—somethin' that you can remember later. But, fuck, Bea. I'm just so happy right now, can't think of nothin' to say."

"That sounded good enough to me," I replied quietly.

"Kiss me."

I leaned forward and brushed my lips against his, my fingers roaming over his shoulders and neck. This wasn't some frantic sex on a couch or against the wall. We had all the time in the world and I wanted to savor it.

He must have felt the same way, because his hands left my breasts in a smooth glide, and he wrapped his arms around my back, pulling me into a tight hug as our lips continued to play.

After a few moments, though, what little control I'd had over the situation was completely demolished as Cam's hand ran up my back to tangle in my hair. His tongue tickled my top lip, then slid inside my mouth, curving to run over my front teeth.

I pulled away laughing.

"What's funny?" he asked, smiling huge.

"That tickled."

"Your teeth?"

"No, the roof of my mouth." I dodged his mouth when it came for me again and stuffed my face into his neck, still giggling.

I yelped in surprise when he turned and threw his legs over the side of the bed. I tightened my arms around his neck as he wrapped my legs around his waist.

"What are you doing?" I breathed against his neck, making him shudder.

"Goin' to your bed."

"Why?"

"Cause that's where we'll be sleepin' when we're done."

He walked to my room, his hands braced under my ass to keep me steady. Sometimes I didn't notice how big Cam was—he was so familiar that I didn't really think about it. However, looking over his shoulder as he carried me easily across the hall reminded me just how tall and strong he actually was.

"I love your bed," he said seriously, as he pulled at my legs and dropped me on top of the comforter. "Have a lot of good ideas for this bed."

"Oh, yeah?" I asked as he pulled his boxers off. I couldn't look. For the first time in our lives, we were completely naked and on display, and I was having a hard enough time not jumping up and locking myself in the bathroom. Instead, I focused on the small "B" he had tattooed on his chest. It wasn't his first tattoo, or even the most recent, but it was the one that meant the most to me. B for Bellatrix. He'd gotten it during my freshman year in high school, something to cheer me up when I'd been dealing with mean girls. I don't think that it had meant much to him at the time, he'd already been covered with tattoos, but for me, it had meant everything. It was my brand on his skin, and even through the years I'd avoided him, he'd never had it covered with something else.

"Yeah," Cam breathed, looking me over. "But we're gonna have to get a new one."

I looked at him in confusion for a moment, then smiled. "You won't fit."

"I can fuck ya in it, not sure I can sleep in it without my feet hangin' off the end."

"But I like this bed," I argued as he came down over me, bracing himself on his forearms.

"I'll buy you a better one."

He leaned in and kissed me deep, sliding his tongue along mine in a smooth motion before pulling away and sucking my bottom lip into his mouth. My hands went to his hair as his mouth moved down my chin, and I arched my neck as he slid further down, running his lips against the skin of my throat.

"I love your skin," he murmured as he reached my collarbone. "Love the way you smell."

His eyes met mine for just a second before he tucked his chin and licked around my left nipple, teasing and teasing it before finally pulling it into his mouth. My hips arched off the bed at the jolt of sensation, and one of his hands slid down my side so he could anchor my hips to the bed.

"So pretty," he said, moving to the opposite nipple to give it the same attention. The hand on my hip went on the move again as I pulled my knees up to grip his waist, and within a moment, he'd burrowed his hand underneath my thigh and was sliding his fingers over my wetness.

My entire body curled inward in response, and my mouth met the warm skin of his shoulder just as his fingers reached my clit. I think I made some weird sound in the back of my throat, but I wasn't sure, because all of my focus was torn between the teeth gently biting my nipple and the fingers playing between my legs.

"Like that?" he asked happily, pushing his face between my breasts as his breathing grew heavy. "I wanted this to last all fuckin' day, but that's not happenin'."

His head lifted, and his pupils were so dilated that only a small amount of blue shown at the edges.

My breathing grew choppy as two fingers slid down, notching at my opening before sliding in with one smooth thrust. No hesitation.

I pulled my legs higher on his sides.

I'd had sex before—even good sex. I liked sex, but nothing in my experience had ever come close to the way I felt with Cameron. It was as if everything was magnified because I loved him so much, and because I could read every emotion on his face, I didn't have a moment of self-consciousness. He liked every movement of my hips against his hand, and every shuddering moan that came out of my mouth—and it showed.

Cam moved up my body, his fingers still sliding in and out, until his face was right above mine. As his hips settled between my thighs, he pulled his fingers out slowly, completely cupping me for a moment before bringing his hand to his mouth.

Then he slid his fingers between his lips and moaned as he sucked them clean.

My heart beat fast in my chest as his hand gripped my jaw, but I jerked my hips away as I felt the end of his cock at my opening.

"Condom!" I blurted out, my eyes wide.

"I'm clean," he assured me, pressing forward.

"Stop!"

My frantic urging must have finally sunk in, because he completely froze above me.

"I'm not on birth control."

"What?" His face was a mask of confusion. "Why the fuck not?"

"Because none of it works right," I explained, my face growing red. I really didn't want to discuss it with him. "I tried everything."

"You got pregnant?" he asked through clenched teeth.

"No! Jesus." His nostrils flared as he waited for me to explain myself.

"I bleed all the time, okay? It doesn't matter what type I try to use, it screws up my hormones and I just have my period constantly. Plus, the hormones make me batshit crazy—I cried constantly, about *nothing*."

"Is that normal?" he asked, his voice softening.

"It's not abnormal—it's just a thing. It happens to some women."

His body seemed to deflate at my words and his forehead dropped to rest on mine. "Shit."

"It's not a big deal, we just have to use condoms."

"Didn't want anything between us," he grumbled, leaning down farther to kiss me gently.

"No glove, no love."

"Can we just—"

"No."

"I'll pull out."

"You won't get in," I replied seriously.

I was not prepared to be a mother.

"Okay." He sighed loudly, and I chuckled as he pulled back and reached for his jeans lying on the floor.

Within a minute, he was kneeling back above me, rolling a condom on.

"Thank you."

"You're not welcome," he replied with a half-smile, his eyes shining.

"Someday, okay?"

"No worries, Sweetbea."

He lifted my legs, hooking my knees at his elbows as he leaned forward to kiss me.

Then he pressed inside.

My eyes slammed shut and my entire body tightened in response.

"Shit, Bea. Relax," he choked out.

"I'm trying!" My voice was all wobbly.

"Hey," he crooned, rubbing his lips over my cheeks and eyes. "What's wrong?"

"It's been a while."

He let out a long exhale, then was suddenly no longer on top of me, but gripping the backs of my thighs and pressing his mouth against my pussy.

"Shit!" I yelped, frantically reaching for his head.

He wasn't messing around.

His tongue came out and he began licking from top to bottom, over and over again, deliberately stopping right below my clit. It was incredible. I could feel myself growing wetter and wetter as he ate at me, tilting my hips at every upward pass, trying to force his tongue where I wanted it.

"So pretty and dark," he murmured against my skin. "Knew it."

Then he was above me again, my thighs at each side of his hips as he pressed hard against me.

He slid halfway inside.

"There you go," he panted, wiping his palm over his mouth. "God, that's it."

"Holy shit," I groaned as he pulled back and pressed forward a little more.

"You feel so good," he mumbled, his eyes half closed as he watched me.

He pulled back and pressed in.

Then he did it again.

On the third thrust, his balls slapped against my ass and we both groaned.

"Knew you could take me," he gasped, kissing me hard as his hips moved faster, pulling out slowly and then snapping forward, again and again.

Sweat slicked our skin as I ran my hands over the flexing muscles of his back. God, it was as if he was completely surrounding me. I could see nothing but him.

The friction of his pelvis against my clit grew more pronounced as he ground against me with every thrust, and soon I was moaning each time he slid forward. The noises coming from my mouth were completely involuntary and were soon joined by Cam's grunts and groans.

Our mouths were just centimeters apart as I got closer and closer to the edge, and just when I raised my head to kiss him, every muscle in my body went rigid as I came.

"Fuck, fuck, fuck," he panted, slamming inside of me before shuddering.

My arms flopped back down on the bed as Cam struggled to keep his weight from crushing me.

"Pretty," he said finally, grinning as he kissed my lips softly. "I ever tell you how much I like this?" he asked, tracing down the full sleeve on my left arm.

"Yeah?"

"Suits you," he said simply, giving me a sweet kiss. "Put on a suit and you look like a business woman, change into a tank top and you look like *my* woman."

He reached down to snag the condom as he pulled out, and my legs snapped together as soon as he pulled away. Shit, I was going to be sore.

"Be right back, baby," he said gently, pushing my sweaty hair away from my face.

He'd just crawled off the bed when someone started banging on my front door.

Cam's head snapped to the side. "What the fuck?"

Chapter 5

CAMERON

"Hey, Hulk. Pop asked me to come get ya, since you and Trix aren't answerin' your phones," Leo said with a grimace when I answered the front door in nothing but my jeans. "Can you get dressed?"

"My tits makin' ya uncomfortable?" I asked, reaching up to run my fingers around my nipple.

"Jesus Chri—"

"Knock it off, Cam!" Trix called out, laughing. "You're gonna scar my brother for life."

"Make him put some clothes on, sissy," Leo begged, watching me with a snarky smile as Trix pushed past me to hug him. "Whoa! Damn, dude. Those bruises look painful."

I glanced down at my chest and noticed the fist-sized bruises on my lower ribs. Huh. They'd grown darker in the past few hours.

"Holy crap," Trix said softly, lifting apologetic eyes to mine. For a split second, I vividly remembered her thighs pressing hard against the purple splotches on my skin.

"No worries, Bea," I assured her with a smile, biting my tongue so I wouldn't tell her that I hadn't even felt them as I'd fucked her. Leo didn't need to hear that shit, he'd probably have a heart attack.

My woman's hair was a mess, tangled and knotted, and her face was still flushed. Leo knew what we'd been up to without me saying a damn word.

"What are you doing here?" Trix asked happily, turning back toward Leo.

"Just came to get Hulk. Pop needs him at the club."

"Why didn't he call—" Her eyes widened and shot to me as her mouth snapped shut. She knew why we hadn't gotten any phone calls. "And he sent *you?*"

I gripped my ribs and laughed hard.

"Okay, this has been fun as a fuckin' turn-your-head-and-cough physical. I'm gonna head back—you followin' me?" Leo asked, not looking at either of us as he stepped back out the door.

"Yeah, I'll be right behind ya."

I swung the door shut as he turned to walk away, and immediately pulled Trix against my chest. "Gotta head in," I said softly.

"Yeah."

"Not exactly how I wanted to end our first time together."

"It is what it is." She sighed and leaned her chin on my sternum. "I guess I'll have to get used to it."

"I'll try to be home for dinner—not sure if I'll make it, though," I told her with a grimace. Shit.

"I know the drill, Cam."

She tried to pull away, so I tightened my arms. "You mad?"

"No. Frustrated."

"Well, we'll pick up where we left off when I get back."

Trix rolled her eyes and pulled away. "I'm not sexually frustrated," she called over her shoulder as she walked toward the kitchen.

"Better not be after the way you came not twenty minutes ago!"

"Oh, shut it," she grumbled, making me smile.

I went back to the spare room to grab my shit and get dressed, and by the time I made it back to her, she was standing with her hands full by the front door.

"What's all this?" I asked in surprise.

"Ham sandwich, chips, thermos of iced tea," she replied, pushing a small pink cooler into my hands.

"Uh—"

"You didn't have lunch."

"Sweetbea—"

"I know you don't wanna bring that pail into the clubhouse, but I didn't want your sandwich heating up in your saddlebags since I put mayo on it. So, I don't know, just pull it all out before you go in or somethi—"

I cut off her words with my mouth.

Jesus.

I had to bail on her right after we'd had sex for the first time and she was sending me off with lunch? Who was this woman?

"You're the perfect old lady," I mumbled against her lips, making her jerk back.

"That's just what every woman wants to hear," she scoffed, scowling.

"Hell, yeah, it is," I said, pulling her back to me.

"You've obviously been with the wrong women," she commented before sucking on my bottom lip.

"With the right one, now."

I slid my tongue into her mouth and my hand into her hair as she groaned. God, she made me hard. I was seriously contemplating saying fuck it and carrying her back to bed when she finally pushed away and took a couple steps back.

"Go. The sooner you leave, the sooner you'll be done."

I nodded, trying to clear the Trix fog from my head. "Don't go anywhere."

"I'll call you if I do."

As I opened my mouth to reply, she raised her eyebrows, so I snapped it shut again. I didn't want to fight with her—especially when I was leaving. With my luck and Trix's temper, she'd probably take off just to prove a point if I pushed her.

"Be back soon," I said with a nod.

I strode out the door and closed it, then moved away as I heard her engage the deadbolt. I only got a few feet from the door before I had to turn around, though.

Pulling my keys from my pocket, I unlocked the door again, then peeked inside to yell, "See you soon" so she didn't think I was nuts, right before shutting it. Then I locked the door myself, making sure the deadbolt held when I tried to open it.

★ ★ ★

"Things have gone quiet," Slider said loudly over the noise of the room, making men shut their mouths mid-sentence. "I don't know what the fuck is goin' on. The two informants that gave me information got nothin.' No news from Salem, no news about Eugene, no fuckin' news, period."

"What the fuck?" Samson, an older guy with hair down to his ass in a long, thin braid called out. He'd been a member for fuckin' ever, and I'd known him since I was a kid.

"We got no fuckin' clue what's goin' on."

"Maybe they changed their minds," Mack said seriously, making me chuckle. God, that guy was green.

"Doubtful," Dragon mumbled next to me with a shake of his head.

"Keep yer eyes open," Poet called out harshly from behind the bar. I didn't know what the fuck he was doing back there—it's not like the man would be serving drinks. We had prospects for that shit. God, I was glad I never had to go back to that.

I was a second generation Ace. My biological father was an Ace before he went fucking psycho and kidnapped Farrah, and Casper was, too. So, from the beginning, I'd had an in.

That didn't save me from the bullshit, though. Our president, Slider, and his VP, Poet, were under the impression that getting the shit beat out of you and taking on the most menial jobs in the club built character. I didn't know about that. What I *did* know was that by the time I'd been patched in, I'd had dirt on almost every single one of the men in the club, from where they stashed their personal drugs to where they dipped their dicks. When you're cleaning up after a person, you figure out things about them that they never wanted other people to know. Like Carl, who stuffed his blow up his ass when he went on a run.

Fucking nasty.

The probation period worked, though, especially for guys like me. I'd known most of the men in the club since I was a kid, and I'd seen them as uncles. But once I was a member, they weren't uncles. They were brothers. They were my equals and my greatest allies. Instead of living under the protection of the club, I'd become a part of the protection. And as I'd found my place among them, their view of me had changed, too—from the kid they'd watched play in the mud to a man they knew would have their backs.

That thought brought me back into the present and I glanced around the room, not seeing Will anywhere.

"Where's Will?" I asked Casper quietly as someone peppered Slider and Poet with questions.

"Haven't seen him. Think he went back to his place after he got patched up earlier," he replied.

"You find anything out?"

"Nope. Thought Grease was gonna fucking kill him when the kid wouldn't stop mouthing off. Didn't learn anything new, though."

I nodded and sat back in my chair. I had to track down Will and get things straightened out before shit started happening. I needed him at my back—without a fucking knife.

"Just keep doin' what you've been doin'," Slider finally called out with a tired wave of his hand. "We'll keep our ears to the ground, let ya know if we have any news."

"This mean we still can't have girls on the grounds?" some idiot called from the back of the room.

Slider glanced at Poet, then back at the room. "Gates are open again."

A cheer went up from the guys and the crowd dispersed, heading to call their sidepieces and go back to work.

The garage we ran was a legitimate business that kept the police mostly off our backs, but running the business meant actually fixing cars. So that's what we did—and we did it well. Most of the men that patched in with the Aces had started out as gear heads, their love of bikes bringing them to the club.

Our other businesses weren't quite as aboveboard, and there were only a few of us who handled those. Poet and Slider, Grease, Dragon, Casper, Samson, an old-timer named Smokey that couldn't do much anymore, me and pretty soon, Will, ran the not-so-legal side of the operation. A few others were muscle, stepping in whenever asked, but they knew very little. We kept our shit tight and our mouths shut, bringing in the other brothers if we needed them, but leaving them out when we didn't. They all knew the score, they'd all been on runs when shit went down, but they rarely had to deal with the shadier side of the Aces.

They didn't mind not getting their hands dirty, though they'd all been dirty at some point. It was a win-win. Those who wanted to be a part of shit usually were, and the others wouldn't go looking for trouble, but were more than happy to step in if the need arose. The way it was organized meant there were very few that knew the intricacies of what we were doing, which left little room for error.

"Church," Slider called as the room cleared out.

"I'm gonna head home," I told Casper as we climbed to our feet.

"Home, huh?"

"That woman—" I couldn't help but laugh uncomfortably and shake my head. Casper and I had talked about a lot of shit in the years since he'd taken me in, but I couldn't talk to him about Trix. Shit with her seemed almost sacred, too important to tell anyone about it.

"Glad you're happy, boy." He gripped my shoulder tight, then turned and walked through the doors to the meeting room.

I wasn't invited in there.

I may have been one of the few that knew exactly what was going on, but that didn't mean I got into the inner sanctum.

I'd only been gone for a couple of hours, waiting for the rest of the men to show up before Slider made his announcements—and for the first time, I was anxious to get the fuck out of there.

★ ★ ★

"TRIX?" I SWUNG the front door open and stepped inside the apartment, surprised at the low murmur of voices coming from the kitchen.

"In here!" she called back cheerfully as I locked the door behind me.

When I got to the kitchen, I stopped abruptly, my neck heating as I took in the scene. Trix was at the table with some guy, leaning over a couple of textbooks. They weren't touching—that's the only reason the guy was still breathing.

"Hey," Trix said cheerfully, standing up to greet me. "You're back a lot earlier than I thought."

"Clearly," I said flatly, ignoring the way she'd wrapped her arms around my middle and leaned up for a kiss. "Who's this?"

Trix's neck snapped back in surprise, then turned toward the kid sitting at the table.

He was clean cut. T-shirt and jeans. Plain black converse. Short hair. Black framed hipster glasses. Five-nine on a good day. Not built, but not scrawny, either.

"Hey, man. I'm Steve," he said, standing to shake my hand.

"Hulk," I introduced myself, keeping my arms at my sides.

"Is that your real—" his eyes drifted down my chest and he grinned. "Biker name, huh? I get it."

"Probably not," I replied flatly.

"Cameron," Trix warned lowly, stepping away from me.

"Since your boyfriend's home, you wanna work on this tomorrow?" Little Steve asked, his eyes moving to Trix. He smiled and shrugged like he felt bad for her, and I wanted to knock his head off his narrow shoulders.

"That's okay, we can—"

"What's for dinner?" I asked, cutting her off as I stared at Steve.

I swear to Christ, her head whipped toward me so fast she was lucky she didn't get whiplash.

"Make your own fucking dinner," she hissed, her face growing red.

The kid looked between us a few times before reaching down to gather his shit. "We can just work on this tomorrow."

"Seriously, it's fine—" Trix tried again.

"I've got plans, anyway," Steve said, shaking his head. "I'll text you later."

He left the apartment slowly, taking his sweet ass time packing up his stuff, and the longer he was there, the closer I came to putting my boot in his ass to get him moving. As soon as he was gone, I flipped the deadbolt and stomped back to the kitchen to get a beer.

"What the fuck was that?" Trix yelled as soon as she saw me, stuffing her books into a bag.

"You tell me," I replied, grabbing a beer and using the countertop to take off the cap—just to piss her off.

"I was studying, you know the thing you do when you want to pass your classes?" She sneered, "Oh, wait, you wouldn't know about that."

I ignored her jab. I'd never done well in school—it just wasn't my thing. But I could piece together any car or bike from scratch. If she was trying to get under my skin with that shit, it wasn't going to work.

"You always have men over when you look like that?" I asked calmly, even though I was feeling anything but calm.

"In shorts and a t-shirt? Yeah, pretty much," she huffed.

"You even wearin' a bra?"

"You are frigging unbelievable!"

Trix stormed out of the kitchen, which was probably a good thing—I felt ready to snap. Little Steve had obviously been there to study, but something about it rubbed me the wrong way and I couldn't put my finger on it.

I'd always been possessive of Bellatrix, but this was something else. Something beyond the need to keep her to myself.

The kid was too clean cut. Too fucking personable. Too easy to forget.

And the thing that made the hair on my neck stand up more than anything else? He hadn't been afraid of me.

Chapter 6

TRIX

I WAS SO pissed I could have screamed as I dropped my backpack on the foot of my bed.

Fucking Cameron.

I'd known he was possessive. I'd always known that he considered me his, even before the afternoon when he'd practically beat his chest and growled "mine!" my senior year of high school. Possessiveness didn't bother me. In our world, it was a sign of love, no matter how outsiders chose to perceive it.

My dad had always been super growly and handsy with my mom when there were other men around, it was just his way. She didn't have friends that were men. Her relationship with Casper was completely transparent, but I'm not sure that she'd ever spent time with him without my dad—and that guy had taken a bullet for her. But on the flip side of that same coin, my dad had no women friends, either. He didn't spend time with other women at all—not without their husbands present—and single women? My mom would have gutted him. It was a sign of respect, of loyalty.

So it wasn't Cameron's possessiveness that had me slamming things around my room. I understood that.

It was the way he'd embarrassed me in front of my classmate.

When Steve had called to ask if we could work on our group project for our marketing class, I'd jumped at the chance. It was hard as hell to get the group together with everyone's busy schedules, and as it was, our third member had been at work and unable to come over. I hadn't thought twice about it, I'd just been happy that we could get part of our project done.

I should have thought it through, but to be fair, Cam and I were brand new. Did I think about him constantly? Yes. It's not as if I'd forget him when I'd seen him naked for the first time only an hour before. But I hadn't yet wrapped my mind around the little things I'd have to do to make it work with him.

Like not having a man over to the house when he wasn't there.

I knew that he trusted me, that wasn't the issue. Not really.

But that didn't appease my anger. Not even a little bit.

"You gonna stay in here all night?" Cam asked from the doorway, just as I'd begun scooping laundry off my floor and tossing it into the hamper.

"I'm pissed at you, go away." I grabbed a pair of dirty jeans from underneath my bed and tossed them across the room. How the hell did jeans get that far under my bed?

"*You're* pissed?" He laughed nastily. "Right."

"Seriously, Cam? You were a total dick."

"Yeah, well, you knew that before you decided to fuck me."

"Yeah, well," I sneered back mockingly, "that won't be happening again any time in the near future."

"That right?" he asked softly, stepping into the room as he pulled his cut off his shoulders.

"Quit," I snapped, rolling my eyes. God, he was such a pain in the ass.

My eyes widened as he stepped in farther and gripped the back of his t-shirt, pulling it over his head and dropping it on the floor. Oh, God. His boots went next, then his socks. And then suddenly, he was a foot away in nothing but his jeans.

"Strip," he ordered softly.

"Not happening," I replied with a nervous laugh. My eyes met his for only a moment before they were drifting down his torso. God, he was big. Big and defined and tattooed. My mouth watered.

"You need some help?"

My eyes shot back to his and I swallowed hard. "No, I don't need help."

"Then get movin'."

"Maybe I'm not in the *fucking* mood."

"Your eyes are fuckin' black and your nipples are hard as a fuckin' rock. Don't give me that shit."

"I'm mad at you!" I huffed, crossing my arms over my chest.

"Best time for sex, baby. Get all that shit out."

"I'd rather punch you in the throat."

"I'd rather you scratched the hell outta my back."

My heart began to race as he took another small step forward, and without thinking it through, I pulled my t-shirt over my head.

"Good girl."

"I'm not a dog."

"You're also not naked yet," he growled.

I huffed, but still unbuttoned my shorts and pushed them and my underwear down my thighs in one movement. Before I was fully upright again, Cam was in my space, unhooking my bra and pulling the straps down my arms.

"You still pissed?" he asked teasingly, his hands sliding up the front of my torso.

"Yes," I spit back, pushing on his chest sharply with both hands so he stumbled back a bit.

His head tilted a little as he studied me, then his nostrils flared as his eyes darkened. "That's how you wanna play?"

His fingers reached my nipples and pinched, making me inhale a desperate breath.

"Okay, Sweetbea," he said gently. "Let's play."

Then his hands were in my armpits and I was being tossed onto the bed.

"You embarrassed me," I hissed, sitting up quickly to find him dropping his jeans to the floor.

"You pissed me off." He moved forward and braced his fists beside my hips, his face inches from mine.

"That doesn't mean you can treat me like crap."

"When exactly did I treat you bad, baby?"

"Don't call me *baby* in that tone. We're fighting." I scowled.

"When did I treat you bad?" he asked again.

"You—you—"

"I wanted him out and I got him out."

"You made me look bad!"

"No, I didn't."

"Yes, you did. Did you see the way he looked at me?"

Cam leaned closer until we were nose to nose, and I had to close my eyes as I felt his breath fan my face. I was still so angry, but hell, he smelled so damn good.

"Yeah, I saw the way he was lookin' at you. Didn't like it. Boy's lucky he didn't leave on a stretcher."

I leaned away and opened my eyes. "What?"

He didn't answer. Instead, he leaned forward and pressed his lips to mine, nipping at my bottom lip before sliding his tongue into my mouth.

I moaned. Hell, my entire body lit up like a firework.

Then I bit him.

"Jesus Christ!" he pulled away quickly and scowled at me, then jerked my hips, making me lose my balance and fall flat on the bed.

His hands moved to my thighs as I tried to sit back up, but before I could get any leverage, he was ripping my legs apart and his tongue was sliding over my clit.

I fell back with a gasp.

He mumbled something about a man in "his" house, as his mouth opened up wide and covered my pussy, sucking.

"Holy shit," I groaned as he closed his mouth again, his bottom teeth scraping against my flesh.

"You wanna bite, Sweetbea?" he asked darkly.

"No. No." I shook my head and leaned up on my elbows, meeting his eyes for a brief moment before I felt his teeth against my clit. "No, Cam!"

I started to panic.

"Bea?" he asked in confusion, lifting his head.

"Don't bite me." My voice wobbled.

"I wasn't gonna hurt ya. Shit."

I was panting as he leaned back down, kissing my skin lightly before lifting his head again. "I'd never hurt ya, Sweetbea. You know that."

I nodded. I did. I did know that, and I didn't know why I'd panicked. This was my Cam. Where the hell had that come from?

His tongue came out and ran delicately over my clit again, and my thighs relaxed. I didn't lie back, though. For some reason, I was still anxious and I needed to be able to see him.

He moved his mouth this way and that, running his tongue over me, then giving suckling kisses all over my flesh until my hips were undulating beneath him. I began to sweat and my arms started to shake beneath me as he finally slid one, then two fingers inside. When he finally concentrated on that little bundle of nerves at the top of my pussy, I came hard and fell backward.

I came and came until I was a boneless heap on the bed.

"I really wanted an angry fuck," he said jokingly as he leaned up to kiss my lips. When he pulled away, his face lost its humor. "But I never wanna scare ya."

"You don't." I reached up and ran my fingers through his hair, watching him close his eyes as he relaxed into the movement.

Then his eyes opened again, and any tenderness was hidden under the heat in his gaze.

"Good," he said decisively, leaning back on his knees to grasp my hips and flip me over. "On your hands and knees."

My arms still felt a little like limp noodles as I tried to get into position, but I made it work. My ass bumped into him as I slid my legs under me and rose up, but he didn't move away, his fingers sliding over my back as I braced my hands against the quilt.

I inhaled a deep breath when he went up on his knees and leaned over my back, his lips meeting my neck softly as he pushed my hair to one side. Then his hands slid gently down my shaking arms.

"On your elbows, baby. Should help." He braced me as I leaned down toward the mattress and rested my head on my arms.

Then my soft-spoken Cam was gone.

His hands slid back up my arms, over my shoulders and down my back until he was gripping my hips. I closed my eyes as one of his hands moved inward, and couldn't stop the jerk of my hips as his fingers slid between my legs, pumping inside me once.

Then there was no contact between us except a single hand on my hip.

He slid inside with no warning. He was being careful not to hurt me, but pressed hard, not pulling back or easing me with short thrusts. In one single, steady push, he slid all the way inside, while I whimpered and tilted my hips toward him.

"Fuck," he groaned as his balls came to rest against my clit.

He was motionless except for the way his dick flexed inside me, giving me time to grow used to him.

"Go," I ordered, my breath shallow. "Go, Cam. Move."

He pulled away in silence, but a deep grunt burst out of his mouth as he shoved forward again, then again.

After a few moments, I was cringing into the blanket beneath me, then throwing back my head. "Not so deep, I'm sore," I ordered through clenched teeth. "Fuck!"

"Shit." Cam pulled out most of the way and leaned back over me, turning my head to kiss me sloppily. "Sorry, Bea."

He slid inside me again, slower and shallower that time, before pulling back and doing it again.

"You have to relax, baby," he whispered, rocking his hips as I willed my body to stop tensing up every time he moved.

This guy was my friggin' soul mate. We weren't supposed to have unsuccessful sex. It was supposed to be incredible and mind-blowing from the first time. I needed to get my shit together.

"I'm sorry," I rasped, letting the top half of my body sink further into the bed.

"Shut up," he replied, kissing my shoulder and then nibbling a path to my neck. "You can take me, Bea. You just gotta relax, baby. That's all."

"It hurts," I argued, taking a deep breath.

"Does it?" he pushed in a little harder. "You sure?"

I pressed my lips between my teeth as I tried to relax the way he'd instructed, and after a moment, my breath caught in my throat.

Holy shit.

"There you go," he growled against the back of my neck. "I'm in. Fuck. Shit. Goddamn, that feels good."

He pulled out and pushed back in slower than he had before, but I no longer felt any pain as he bottomed out inside me. Instead, I seemed to be growing hazy, my entire body throbbing, sensitive to the slightest brush against my skin.

Cam's arms slid around me, his chest and belly molded to my back as he laced his fingers through mine. "You're gonna come again," he said against my ear. "You're so fuckin' wet, you're soakin' the bed."

I think I mumbled something back in response, but I wasn't sure.

His hips sped up a little as his harsh breathing rasped against my ear.

Then I was coming again, just like he'd predicted, this orgasm so different from any I'd had previously that I didn't even recognize what it was until I was literally throbbing around Cam's cock.

"Fuck. Yes," he moaned as his hips began to thrust wildly, finally coming to a complete stop.

He pulled out after a moment and my knees slid down the bed until I was flat on my stomach.

I felt so raw... so bare. It was the oddest thing. I didn't even realize I was crying until Cam flipped me to my back and his hands went directly to my face.

"You okay?" he asked, his face looking slightly panicked.

"Yeah," I sniffled, chuckling a little. "I don't know what the fuck this is."

He laughed before laying down beside me and pulling me into his arms. "I just rocked your world."

"Yeah, well, I'm still pissed at you."

I buried my head against his chest and hid my smile as his loud laugh rang through the apartment.

★ ★ ★

"YOU ASLEEP?" I asked later that night, curled up in bed with Cam, the apartment quiet around us.

I knew he wasn't sleeping. Cam freaking snored. Loudly. At some point, I was going to have to buy him some nose strips or something, but for the past week, the sound had been comforting as it filtered through the walls. I liked knowing that he was there.

I liked knowing that he was comfortable enough in my apartment to sleep deep enough to snore.

"What's up?" He asked gruffly, pulling my back tighter against his chest.

I wasn't a small girl, but I felt that way when he spooned me like he was right then.

"Please don't embarrass me again."

"Wasn't tryin' to embarrass ya."

"I have a life outside the club—"

"I know that."

"I have to get along with these people. I'm almost finished with school, and then I'll be working somewhere. You can't act like that, Cam. No one will respect me if you do."

"You gonna have co-workers in our house?"

"*Our* house?"

"You gonna have men over? Ones that stare at your tits?"

"No."

"Then I'm not sure what you're worried about."

"I swear to God, talking to you is like talking to a brick wall."

"Baby, it's eleven o'clock at night and it's been a long fuckin' day. You're lucky I'm not answerin' you in snores."

I sighed and he kissed the back of my neck.

"We'll figure this shit out, yeah? Just not tonight," he said sweetly, kissing my neck again.

"Yeah."

I closed my eyes briefly then popped them open again. "You ever figure out what was going on with Will?"

"Nah, didn't see him."

I relaxed into Cam's arms and closed my eyes again, but I couldn't fall asleep. So many things had happened in the last twenty-four hours.

Between Cam and I finally getting together, the drama with my dad that morning, knowing I'd have to face Steve in class the next day, and my little freak out when Cam had gone down on me, I had a hard time quieting my thoughts.

I still couldn't believe Cam was sleeping beside me, his breath wafting across the back of my head. It seemed like I'd wanted to be exactly in that spot for as long as I could remember, and now that I had him, I wasn't sure what to do with myself. What if becoming a couple was nothing like I'd imagined? I didn't have a whole lot of experience in any type of long-term relationship, and I knew instinctively that when Cam said this was *it*, he meant it.

Cam's arm tightened around my waist as he shifted closer, and suddenly, I was completely calm.

He was right—it had been a long day and I had school bright and early in the morning. I needed to get some rest.

Chapter 7

CAMERON

"Shit," Trix moaned as I slid into her slowly from behind. She was on her side, with one knee pulled to her chest, and even though I could barely get any fucking traction when I was on my side behind her, it was still my favorite way to wake her up in the mornings. Trix wasn't a morning person. She didn't get out of bed until her alarm had gone off at least three times, so she set them about twenty minutes apart. This meant that her goddamn alarm had been waking me up an hour before she actually needed to be awake since I'd started sleeping with her three weeks ago.

I used that to my advantage.

After the first few times I'd rolled out of bed, expecting her to follow and then not hearing the shower turn on for at least an hour, I started staying in bed.

Turns out, Trix was in a much better mood if she woke up to an orgasm, and it put me in a damn good frame of mind, too.

My hand slid up her stomach and between her breasts to hold her still and I dug my bare toes into the sheets as I thrust harder, making her whimper and groan like she always did before she came.

"Cam," she murmured, making my entire body stiffen as she got so wet I had a hard time keeping the right angle. Her body bowed forward and she started throbbing around my cock as I came with her.

I slumped into the mattress as I tried to catch my breath.

"Did you turn off my alarm?" she asked groggily as she tried to curl deeper into the blankets.

"Oh, hell, no," I warned, trying hard not to laugh as she scowled at me over her shoulder. "You're gettin' up."

"I don't have class for two more hours," she whined as I climbed off the bed and took care of the condom. I fucking hated wearing them with her, but I had to. She wasn't ready for kids yet, and I wasn't going to take that decision away. We had time to figure all that shit out.

"Come shower with me," I said, throwing back the covers and pulling her out of bed.

"I don't want to shower with you."

Okay, maybe orgasms didn't necessarily improve Trix's morning mood, but they did wake her ass up.

Even though she complained the entire walk to the bathroom, she still stripped and stepped into the shower with me. She liked it when I washed her hair.

By the time we climbed back out, I had a stiffy that I knew wasn't going to get the attention it wanted and Trix was finally wide-awake.

"Remember, we have the kids tonight," she mumbled around her toothbrush, glancing at me in the mirror as I put toothpaste on my own brush.

"What?"

"I told you yesterday—it's movie night. Leo, the Hawthorne kids and your sisters are coming over around dinner time and staying the night."

"Fuck," I grumbled, drawing out the word before stuffing my toothbrush in my mouth. "How the hell do they all fit in the apartment?"

She watched me in amusement, spitting into the sink. Damn. Her breasts swayed at the movement and my mouth started to water, making white foam drip down my chin.

"They bring sleeping bags. CeeCee usually doesn't come, but the rest of them fit fine. Boys in the living room, girls in the spare room."

I cleaned my teeth quickly, then spit while I rinsed my brush. "Why doesn't CeeCee come?"

"Too cool, I guess. Remember me at seventeen?" she laughed and I scowled.

Yes, I remembered her at seventeen. That didn't make me feel real good about what my sister might be up to.

"Alright." I sighed. "Want me to get some pizzas?"

"That's okay." She shook her head as she led our way out of the bathroom. "I'll grab some you-bake ones when I stop at the store after class. We need goodies and soda, anyway."

A little while later, I sat on the bed pulling my boots on as I watched her get ready for school.

"Why do you have all of 'em over?" I asked. "Lotta work."

"I like it," she replied, her voice muffled by the hoodie she was pulling over her head. "I didn't really have anyone but you growing up. Everyone was younger, ya know?"

I nodded. Yeah, and by the time she'd been my littlest sister's age, I'd pretty much abandoned her. I'd been sixteen—and as much as I'd loved little Trix, I'd had other things on my mind then—like the high school chicks that wanted to take a little walk on the wild side.

"They like coming over—no parents, they can eat whatever they want, talk about whatever they want, stay up as late as they want. Plus, I like knowing what's going on with them, and if I didn't make the time for movie nights, I'd barely see any of them."

"You're cute," I told her with a smile, pushing to my feet.

"Think so?" She tilted her head to the side as I stepped toward her and I couldn't help but lean down and kiss the exposed skin on her neck.

"Yeah, I think so."

Her arms wrapped around my waist and slid up the back of my shirt, tracing the bottom of the tattoo that covered my back.

"What time you get out today?" I asked, reaching up to grip her jaw lightly with my hands.

"Same as always."

"Don't you have finals comin' up? Cut out early."

She giggled, shaking her head lightly at me. "Finals means I have to work *harder* right now."

"Bullshit," I argued, making her full-on laugh.

I loved it when she laughed, and she did it a lot. After that first day when we'd fought like cats and dogs, shit had been smooth between us. We'd had dinner with my parents and hers, taken a few rides when we didn't have shit to do, fucked on every surface in the apartment, and spent time just hanging out.

I hadn't taken her to the club for any parties, but that was because we hadn't fucking had any, not because I thought it would be a problem for her.

We'd still been scratching our heads and walking around with our dicks in our hands when it came to figuring out who was fucking with us. One of our informants fucking disappeared, just poof and the guy was gone. The other said he didn't know anything, hadn't heard anything, and tried to convince us that the info he'd given us before must have been wrong.

"Will you be here when I get home?" she asked, the dimple in her cheek deepening as she grinned.

"Meet ya at the store. Text me when you're headed that way."

"Okay," she mumbled as I pressed my mouth to hers, slipping my tongue between her lips for a small taste.

I walked her to her car when she was ready to go and gave her another quick kiss as soon as she'd climbed in. "Be good," I ordered as I slammed her car door shut.

She was barely out of the parking lot before my mind was on the meeting I had to get to at the club.

★ ★ ★

"Hulk—in here with us, boyo," Poet called as I grabbed a bottle of water from the stacks Vera was making the prospects pull out of her car.

"Costco run?" I asked, as she smiled at me. "Glad I'm done with that shit."

"Get back here and help, you're like a damn packhorse!" Vera called back, her hands on her hips.

"Can't! Busy!" I laughed as she flipped me off and stepped inside the darkened main room. I made my way past the bar to the room beyond, pausing at the doorway.

"Gonna have to stand," Grease called out. "No spot at the table for you yet."

"Fuck off," I shot back, stepping inside the room and letting the door close behind me.

"We all here? Good." Slider said tiredly. "Spent the night with Mack's old lady at the hospital. Someone ran him off the fuckin' road last night on his way home."

I clenched my jaw against the need to ask why no one had called me. That was bullshit. Everyone should have been up there with them. That's what we did. We fucking rallied. I glanced around the room and noticed my dad was furious, too.

"Before you go pissin' and moanin,' I didn't call ya because his woman's fuckin' skittish and she was a mess last night. Last thing she needed was a bunch of bikers crowdin' up the waiting room."

"Could've at least given us a head's up," Dragon said quietly, leaning forward in his chair to brace his elbows on the table.

"Decision was made and now it's over," Slider replied steadily.

"Don't know who it was," Poet said, running his hand down his beard. It was finally getting long like he'd had it when I was a little guy, before he'd gotten back together with his wife and shaved it all off. "Young, though. Preppy. Mack remembered that much."

Young?

"How bad?" Casper finally asked.

"Broke both his legs, one hip. Had to do surgery this mornin'," Slider answered.

"Fuck," Grease sighed.

Slider's eyes met mine. "You hear anything new about the Wunderlich twins?"

I frowned in confusion. "No."

"Only clean cut boys I can think of," Slider said, still watching me.

The Wunderlichs were smalltime. The father and sons lived down south and had a pretty good thing going, selling designer drugs to college kids. We'd had a couple run-ins with them a few years before, when they'd tried to get a foothold at the University of Oregon, but since then, they'd kept their distance.

"Nah, saw Dan a few months ago when me and Samson went to Ashland. Nothin' had changed."

"Fuck," Poet said sharply. "You got any ideas?"

"Me?" I asked, like an idiot.

"No, the fuckin' ghost behind ya."

The men around the table chuckled.

"No," I said, swallowing hard. "Haven't heard or seen anything. Don't know many younger guys that would have the balls."

"So, we're back where we started," Grease said, tapping on the table.

"Maybe it was just some drunk college kids—" I tried to say.

"No coincidences in this world," Poet cut me off, his face grave. "This is all connected."

I nodded in agreement, wishing I hadn't said anything.

"Has anyone talked to Woody?" I asked, trying to redeem myself a little bit.

"He called his mum," Poet answered with a sigh. "Wouldn't say where he's stayin,' though. Still not answerin' my calls."

"Shit. I'll try again, too."

"We callin' everyone in?" Dragon interrupted, looking around the table.

"Over a fuckin' wreck? No," Slider said.

"Jesus," Casper murmured, running a hand down his face.

"You got something to say?" Slider asked darkly, staring at my dad.

"Nope. Nothing to say," he replied flatly.

Slider used the table to push to his feet and walked out without another word, leaving the now completely silent room.

"Fuckin' bullshit," Grease mumbled as he got up and left.

The rest of us followed, stuck in our thoughts.

I hated knowing Trix was at school unprotected for the next few hours. It felt wrong, but we had to keep living our lives. There were still classes to attend and cars to fix, even though whoever had been fucking with our informants seemed to be stepping up their game.

I walked out the front door and over to the bay I was working in that day, seeing Will inside. He'd been back a few days after our scuffle in the forecourt, but I hadn't brought that shit up and he hadn't, either. His dad could straighten him out—wasn't my business. It couldn't be my business—I had bigger shit to deal with. I didn't have time for whatever was going on with him.

I had a woman who spent her days right out in the open and there wasn't shit I could do about it without something concrete to give to her.

Meanwhile, someone had essentially declared war, and we were the stupid fucks who had no idea who was targeting us.

★ ★ ★

"CAM!" A LITTLE voice squealed as I rolled out from underneath the Honda I was working on a couple hours later.

"Hey, baby girl," I replied to my eleven-year-old sister, Lily, as she came to an abrupt stop less than a foot from my legs. "Why aren't you in school?"

"Teacher in-service day."

"Lucky."

"I know. I'm ready for summer," she said, looking around the garage. "Hi, Will!"

"Hey, sweetheart," he called back quietly, messing with something in his toolbox.

"Where's Ma?" I asked, getting to my feet as I tried to wipe the grease off my hands. If I didn't love working on shit so much, I'd hate my job. I was too big to comfortably slide under cars, my fingernails were constantly black, and in the summer, the garage got hot as fuck because the doors stayed open and there was no air conditioning.

"She's in talking to Dad and CeeCee. She's dropping us off with you so she can go do some stuff with Great Gram."

"Gram's here?"

"Yeah, she's in the car."

Lily raced out in front of me as I walked toward the large door. "Wait, you're comin' home with me? I'm on the bike."

"CeeCee drove!"

Shit. I checked my phone again as I made my way to Farrah's car, where I could see Gram's head through the front windshield. Trix still hadn't called, but it was only a little after eleven. I'd been hoping to get her home and fucked before we had company, but it looked like that wasn't happening.

"Hey, gorgeous," I called through the open passenger window, making Gram turn toward me and smile.

"Cameron," she called cheerfully. "You've been too busy for your old Gram."

"Never," I promised, helping her open the door so she could get out and hug me. "I just saw you at dinner."

"That was two weeks ago," she scoffed, pinching my side.

"Looks like I've got the girls tonight, but I'll see what Trix and I are doin' tomorrow. Maybe come and take you to breakfast."

She made a noise of disgust in her throat. "I'll make you breakfast. What do you want?"

"I want you to *not* make breakfast so you can relax."

She didn't say anything, but gave me a look over her glasses.

"Fine, I'll come for breakfast," I said in defeat.

"Good boy."

"Help! There's a giant trying to abscond with my grandmother," Farrah called out behind me as I set Gram back in her seat. "Oh, wait. I think I know him."

"Ha, ha," I replied, grabbing her as soon as she came close enough so I could spin her around in a circle. "Hey, Ma."

"Feels like we haven't seen you forever," she said, giving me a squeeze before pushing away so I'd drop her to the ground.

I opened my mouth to defend myself, but she cut me off with a shake of her head.

"I get it, kiddo. How are things with Trix?"

"Good." I felt a goofy smile take over my face. I could keep any and all expression off my face when I wanted and I kept my emotions to myself around the brothers, but I'd never been able to hide from Farrah.

"Rad," she said softly, reaching up to rub my bicep for a moment. "Seems like just yesterday, I was wiping your ass…"

I choked on my own spit. "You never wiped my ass."

"Oh, right. That was Cecilia. Should've remembered—different parts and all."

"Speaking of…"

"Yeah, can you take them? Gram and I want to hit some garage sales this afternoon. She wants a recliner for her room."

I glanced back at Gram, who was searching quietly for something in her purse. She was getting so fucking old. So slow. I hated it.

"Yeah, but why can't CeeCee and Lily come over later?"

"Your sister is being a pain in the ass and I can't trust her to do what she says she's gonna do. So, no staying home alone at the moment."

"Christ."

"Pretty much."

"Whoop her ass."

"She's seventeen. Too old to spank, too young to punch in the throat," Mom said ruefully as CeeCee and Casper came walking out of the clubhouse, Lily trailing behind them.

Then my eyes registered the look on Casper's face and the tiny shorts Cecilia had on.

"What the fuck is she wearin'?" I hissed, my eyes shooting to Farrah's.

"Have fun!" she sang, laughing as she dodged my hand and ran around the hood of her car.

"You wait for me to come kiss ya, Ladybug!" Casper yelled before Farrah could climb into the car.

"I'm not waiting all day!" she yelled back as Casper stopped to hug the girls goodbye.

"You'll wait." He pointed at her, but kept his eyes on Lily as she hugged his waist.

How I'd ended up in that family, I had no idea. I was just thankful for it.

"I'm gonna head out," I called to Casper as he made his way over to

Farrah. "CeeCee and Lily! Let's go."

★ ★ ★

A FEW HOURS later, I was sitting on the couch enjoying a beer before the apartment was overrun. The girls were in Trix's bedroom doing makeup or face masks or some other mysterious girl shit, and for a few minutes, I had a little quiet time to myself.

I deserved it after the hour I'd spent following them around the grocery store. How a quick trip for groceries turned into twenty-minutes on the makeup aisle, I would never understand. None of them needed the shit, anyway.

"Hey, baby," Trix said quietly, waddling over to me and dropping into my lap.

"Nice toes."

"Thanks." She held up her feet and wiggled her green and yellow painted toes. "Lily thought the green and yellow would give me some good luck for my finals next week."

"You excited to be done?" I asked, rubbing my palm up and down her smooth legs. She'd changed and was wearing a pair of cut off sweatpants that she must have stolen from Leo, because they were tight as hell around her ass and loose at the waist. Easy access—not that I'd be getting any.

"Yeah." She sighed and dropped her feet, leaning her head against my chest. "Worried too, though. I need to find a job."

"No, you don't."

"Yeah, I do."

"I can take care of you." As soon as the words were out of my mouth, I knew they were the wrong thing to say, even if I'd meant them. I didn't want her to worry about finding a job—I had plenty of money I'd socked away for a rainy day—but Trix's body stiffened in offense.

"I can take care of myself," she snapped.

As she tried to push off my chest, I gripped her tighter.

"You don't have to—" My words were cut off by a knock at the front door.

I shifted her to the couch next to me and went to answer the door, checking the peephole and barely catching myself before cursing.

"You're early," I said flatly as Leo pushed past me into the apartment.

"Tommy, Mick and Rose are right behind me," he mumbled, carrying a paper grocery bag into the kitchen.

I didn't even get the door closed before I saw Grease and Callie's youngest, Rose, running down the breezeway.

"Is Lily here?" she asked excitedly.

"Yup. Doin' her nails, I think," I answered with a smile. I couldn't help it. Rose was born only six months after Lily, but she seemed so much younger—probably because she didn't have an older sister like Cecilia corrupting her.

Her little arms wrapped around my waist, squeezing tightly for only a second before she was tearing off through the entryway.

"Boys," I greeted as Tommy and Mick followed slowly behind their sister.

Tommy was only a couple months younger than CeeCee, which made Mick, eh, fourteen? Yeah, I think there was three years between them—not that you'd notice by looking at them. Tommy was leaner, built like Casper, but Mick was built like Grease, so even with the age difference, he was bigger than his older brother.

"Your brother comin'?" I asked as they met me at the door.

"Nah, Will's at the club."

"Figured," I replied with a nod. All the kids were here, but at twenty and with a prison record, Will was an adult. Leo was only two years younger, but he hadn't graduated high school yet. He was still stuck in that in-between stage where he acted like hot shit around the younger kids, but still wanted to have a movie night at his big sister's house.

Where Leo still watched the club members with a sense of awe, Will was trying his damnedest to fit in with them.

"Well, come on in," I said, taking a step out of the doorway so they could push past me.

"Hey, Trix," Mick called out shyly.

Oh, hell. With two words, I knew the kid had one hell of a crush on my girl.

I closed and locked the front door with a grimace. It was going to be a long fucking night.

Chapter 8

TRIX

"T HE NEW *TRANSFORMERS*," I called with a flourish as six teenagers and pre-teens fought for the best spots to sit in my tiny living room. "Has anyone seen it yet?"

"I saw it in the theater," Leo said nonchalantly as he sat down on the couch.

"Yeah, with Beth Miller," Thomas said, chuckling. "Bet you didn't see much of it."

My eyes widened as Cecilia, who was getting ready to drop down beside Leo, abruptly moved to the floor next to her sister.

"Shut the fuck up, Tommy," Leo hissed as Tommy dropped down in the spot Cecilia gave up. He glanced quickly over at CeeCee, whose jaw was tight as she acted like she wasn't listening to their conversation.

"Jesus," Cam mumbled, meeting my eyes.

"So, no one then," I said uncomfortably. Shit, I did not want to know anything about my baby brother and his conquests.

It was times like those, when I knew that Leo was doing shit with girls, or getting drunk, or making decisions about the club, that I wished my twin brother had lived. We'd been born early, and though I'd survived with no problems as I'd grown, Draco hadn't been strong enough. Even though I didn't remember him, obviously, sometimes I got this weird ache in my chest, like a part of me was missing. I thought that was probably the universe's way of reminding me that at one point,

I'd been half of a whole. And the other half? Well, he'd protected me, even in the womb, because when we were born, I was significantly larger than he was.

Draco would know how to talk to Leo. He'd know the right things to say and Leo would listen to him, because Draco was a brother and I was a sister and those two roles were very different.

"Bea?" Cam called softly, catching my attention. "You okay?"

I plastered a smile on my face and nodded, turning to put the disc into my Xbox. As soon as it was all set up, I stepped over the two little giggling girls and swept my hand down the back of Cecilia's head as I passed her before coming to an abrupt stop.

There wasn't anywhere for me to sit. The little assholes had taken up every available seat and every inch of the floor in my living room.

Cam chuckled at my disgruntled expression. "Come here, Bea."

He pulled me into his lap sideways and reached out to shove at Tommy's shoulder until the poor kid was practically sitting in Leo's lap.

"Hey!" Tommy grunted.

"Scoot over or sit on the floor," Cam replied gruffly, shutting him up.

"Be nice," I whispered, leaning into Cam as the movie previews lit up my TV.

"That was nice. If I wasn't bein' nice, I woulda kicked 'em all out hours ago," he whispered against my neck, making me chuckle. "You're good with them."

"They're easy. Give the boys soda and the girls nail polish. Boom. Everybody's happy."

"More than that, Sweetbea," he argued dropping his arm from the back of the couch to rest his hand on my belly. "You're gonna be a good mom."

My heart thudded in my chest.

"Why do you call me that?" I asked quietly, changing the subject.

"What? Sweetbea?"

"Yeah, or Bea."

Cam was silent for a long time, long enough for the movie to start and for Rose and Lily to pass out awkwardly, like little drunken sailors.

"My brother couldn't say your name right," he suddenly stated, not looking at me. "Called ya Bayatrix. Wouldn't shorten it, either. Guess it came from that—called ya Bay, then at some point it turned into Bea."

"Oh," I breathed, staring at his emotionless face. "I didn't remember that."

"Didn't think you would, baby," he said, giving me a small smile before kissing my forehead. "Watch the movie, yeah?"

"Kiss me first," I whispered.

His smile grew. "That's my line," he whispered back, right before his lips met mine in a soft kiss.

I WOKE UP a couple hours later as Cam laid me gently down on the couch. The TV was turned off and the apartment was silent as I watched Cam gently pick sleeping Cecilia up like a baby, carrying her into the spare room. Leo and Mick followed him silently, carrying Lily and Rose. Unsurprisingly, Tommy was asleep on the floor. He was almost always the first of the older kids to pass out.

I waited for Cam to come get me, and I kissed his neck softly as he carried me into our room, refusing to acknowledge his need to take care of me or my desire to let him.

★ ★ ★

"WAKEY, WAKEY, EGGS and bakey!" Leo yelled through my bedroom door the next morning, making me groan.

"Go away," I called back, glancing at my alarm clock. Seven a.m.

"We're hungry!" Leo called back, knocking a rhythm on my closed door.

"You don't stop knocking, you're gonna be eating through a fuckin' straw," Cam growled, rolling over to wrap an arm around my waist.

The knocking stopped abruptly and I relaxed back into the bed. I really didn't want to get up so early on a Saturday, but after a few minutes of listening to voices in my living room, I groggily sat up in bed.

"Where you goin'?" Cam asked quietly, his arm slipping down my waist to grasp my hips.

"Better get up before they tear up my house," I answered, turning to lean down and give him a kiss. "Good morning."

"Stay," he ordered, tightening his arm.

"Go back to sleep," I murmured back, kissing him again. "I'll make breakfast and wake you up when it's ready."

"Make 'em eat cereal," he argued.

I smiled at his grumpy expression and shook my head. Usually, I was the one who refused to get up, and it was a little funny being on the other side of the fence.

"I always make a big breakfast," I explained, peeling his fingers off my hip so I could climb out of bed. I stumbled a little as my feet touched the floor. God, I hated mornings. "Eggs, bacon, hash browns—the whole enchilada."

"Shit, Grams wanted to make us breakfast. I gotta call her."

I reached down and pulled his phone from his jeans and tossed it onto the bed as he pushed his face into the pillow, groaning.

★ ★ ★

"I LIKE MINE fried," Tommy said.

"Scrambled," Rose and Lily said at the same time.

"Over-easy," Leo mumbled, bent over his coffee cup. My baby

brother hated mornings as much as I did—I guess it was a family thing.

"She's not your fuckin' waitress," Cam snapped as he finally made his way into the kitchen. I'd already finished making the hash browns and sausage and was trying to figure out how to cook the eggs before everything else got cold. "Scramble 'em, Bea."

"Movie night was way better before you started comin'," Tommy mumbled, earning him a smack on the back of the head from Mick.

"Yeah, cause you got to walk all over her," Cam shot back.

"They're fine," I cut in, laughing. "Scrambled for the littles, fried for Tommy and Mick, Over-easy for Leo and none for Cecilia. I got it."

"Why aren't you eating?" Cam asked Cecilia as she came up beside me to help with the rest of the food.

"I am, I just don't like eggs," she replied, her eyes still a bit dazed from sleep.

"Since when?" Cam demanded.

"Since we got some farm eggs from one of Gram's friends and I cracked it open to find a chick inside," she mumbled back, wrinkling her nose.

"Ew!" Rose squealed as the rest of the kids groaned in disgust.

"No eggs!"

"None for me!"

"That's fuckin' disgusting."

"Wonder what it looked like."

"No eggs," Cam ordered, stepping over to take the spatula out of my hands. "We got enough food without 'em?"

"Yeah, if I make toast."

"I'll make it." He kissed me, then tapped me on the ass. "Go eat."

The girls sat with me at the table while the boys stood at the counter with their plates, inhaling their food like they were starving.

"Gram's birthday is next week!" Lily announced, around a mouth full of food. "We're having a party."

"Oh, yeah? What are you going to get her?" I asked, pushing my full plate of food away from me. Something tasted weird, but I couldn't put my finger on it. No one else seemed to be having an issue, though, so maybe it was just me.

"I made her a scarf," Lily answered proudly.

"It's summer," Cecilia scoffed, her tone surprising me.

"So! She'll love it! She said she wanted a scarf!"

"For Christmas, maybe."

"Shut up, *Cecilia*. Stop tryin' to show off in front of your boyfriend."

"I don't have a boyfriend," Cecilia hissed, her face turning beet red in embarrassment.

"I saw you kissin' Leo!"

"Jesus Christ, Leo," Mick said furiously.

My eyes widened as I heard Cam make a noise in the back of his throat, but before I could even turn to look at him, my brother was pulling my ponytail as he passed and practically running out the front door.

"Are you outta your fuckin' mind?" Cam yelled as the front door shut. "That boy's probably got the clap, he fucks around so much!"

"Hey!" I yelled, my chair scraping against the linoleum as I stood. "Knock it off."

"Hell, no."

"It's none of your business, Cam," Cecilia said forcefully.

"Fuck that."

"I don't need your approval!"

"You sure as hell do!"

Cecilia's fists clenched at her sides as she looked around the room at the stunned faces watching the scene unfold. "Get your stuff, Lil," she said quietly to her little sister, who was on the verge of tears.

"I'm sorry," Lily said guiltily, her gaze shooting back and forth from

Cam to Cecilia.

"Not your fault, baby girl," Cam said kindly. "You *should* say somethin' when your sister is makin' bad decisions."

The entire room went silent for a long moment.

"Oh, shut the fuck up, Cameron." Cecilia finally hissed, standing from the table and pulling Lily with her down the hall to the spare room.

The veins in Cam's neck pulsed as he glared in the direction Cecilia had gone, and I watched him get his shit together second by second as the Hawthorne kids sat in uncomfortable silence around us.

"We should probably get going, too," Mick said quietly, glancing from Cam to me. "Thanks for havin' us, Trix."

"No problem," I smiled at him, making him blush. He was such a little cutie. "We'll do this again soon."

Tommy, Mick and Rose left the table and went to the living room to roll up their sleeping bags and clean up their garbage from the night before. I loved that they did that. I never had to worry that my house would be a disaster after everyone left. Leo was a pain in the ass and rarely cleaned up after himself, but the rest of them always made sure they left everything as it had been when they'd arrived. Their parents must have been doing something right, no doubt about that.

"We're leaving," Cecilia said as she and Lily carried their backpacks out of the bedroom. "Thanks for having us over." She ignored Cam completely as she and Lily hugged me goodbye.

"This conversation isn't over," Cam warned as she opened the front door to leave.

"*Cam*," I warned.

"Fuck off." She flipped him off as she left, and I heard a murmured "Oh, shit" from the living room as I quickly stepped in front of Cam to keep him from following her.

"She needs her fuckin' ass beat," Cam growled as he came to a stop with my hand braced in the middle of his chest.

"She's a little old for that," I reminded him.

"Yeah, old enough to be fuckin' around with your whore brother."

"You know what? I get that you don't like it, but stop talking shit about my brother. You're twice as bad as he is," I snapped back, thumping my hand on his chest.

"He got up and ran like a pussy," Cam accused.

"Yeah, well you've got like a hundred pounds on him and you're almost ten years older, what did you expect him to do?"

"Defend Cecilia, for one. What kind of man leaves his woman to face shit without him?"

"Um, a boy? He's eighteen, Cam."

"Old enough."

"Not hardly."

"You remember me at eighteen?"

"That's not the same, at all," I reminded him softly. "You were a man at fifteen, maybe earlier. Completely different situations."

"Hey, guys?" Tommy called, "Uh, we're gonna go."

I spun from Cam and walked toward the living room to give everyone a hug goodbye. First Tommy, then Rose, but when I got to Mick, Cam's deep voice called out, "Mick," in warning.

"I'll see you later," Mick said, leaning forward at the waist to hug me awkwardly with barely any of our bodies touching.

They left quickly, and as soon as the front door was locked behind them, Cameron spoke.

"No more overnights with boys and girls," he ordered, his voice absolute. "You wanna have them over, I don't give a shit. But the boys aren't stayin' if the girls are."

"Since when do you get to boss me around?" I asked in a surprised voice, crossing my arms over my chest.

"You want them fuckin' in your bathroom?"

"My *bathroom*?"

"Only place in the apartment to get some privacy."

"Hell, no."

"Then no more overnights."

He turned and stomped toward the bedroom. "Come on—I'm going the fuck back to bed."

I snorted and followed him. Poor Cam. He looked like his head was ready to explode.

★ ★ ★

"It's been over twenty-four hours since I've been inside you," Cam murmured a few hours later, after we'd both slept. "Time to remedy that."

His open mouth ran down my throat and I arched against him, spreading my legs so he could fit his thighs between them. When we'd climbed into bed he'd insisted we sleep naked and I hadn't argued, even as he'd fallen asleep only minutes later while I'd lay there frustrated, feeling all of his skin against me with no relief in sight.

So now, there was nothing between us as he thrust his hips against mine, the underside of his cock rubbing back and forth against my clit.

"We need to talk," I mumbled, my eyes still half closed from sleep.

"Not right now, we don't."

"Later, then." It was probably better that I waited until he was lazy and satisfied anyway, he'd probably argue with me less.

His lips ran down the center of my chest as his hips continued to rock in a lazy rhythm. I wrapped my hands around the back of his head as he took one of my nipples into his mouth, sucking gently before moving to the other and giving it the same attention.

"Look how pretty and red they get for me," he mumbled, swiping his tongue over a nipple.

His lips slid down my stomach and I cried out as his mouth reached my clit, giving it a wet kiss. His tongue slid down, pressing inside me for just a moment before swiping back up slowly. By the time he reached my clit again, I was panting, and my entire body jolted as he made contact.

My knees pulled up as he pressed his mouth harder against me, my legs trembling. Then he pulled away.

"Up," he ordered harshly, grabbing my hand to pull me onto my knees.

He laid down on his back and slid beneath me, jerking my hips down to his mouth as a sound of surprised arousal flew from my mouth. Holy shit. I ran my hands down his smooth chest as his fingers dug into my hips, my nails digging into his skin as he suddenly sucked hard on my clit.

"Fuck," I yelled, my entire body jolting.

My hair fell in a long curtain as my body curled forward, and within seconds, Cam's hand was fisted in the strands, pulling me forward.

I braced my hands beside his hips as his knees came up and widened, his feet flexing against the sheets.

Then I took him into my mouth and felt him groan against me.

Sliding down as far as I could, I sucked hard as I pulled away again and I felt his mouth grow slack as the muscles in his thighs quivered.

"That's it," he moaned. "*Fuck*."

I arched my hips mindlessly against his face as I took him in again, and both of his hands slid to my ass, gripping me hard as he started sucking.

My hair stuck to my face with sweat as I sucked him deeper, not even pausing when he retaliated by working his lips and tongue harder against me. I wanted more, more, *more*.

I didn't even feel like myself. All thoughts had completely flown away, and the only thing I could concentrate on was his hips jerking at my movements and his mouth devouring me.

Then his hand slid back and his mouth moved to my clit as his fingers slid inside me, curling forward.

I exploded, crying out and gagging as I accidentally pushed my mouth too far down his cock.

His hand ripped at my hair, pulling me off him so he could push me forward. He sat up behind me and wrapped one arm around my waist, his hand coming to rest between my breasts.

"Condom," he gasped, reaching blindly for the box in my nightstand.

He frantically pulled one from the box and rolled it on, and then he was surging inside me as my back arched against his chest.

"Bea," he moaned as his hands slid over my slick skin. "Roll 'em, baby," he instructed as he guided my hips, making my ass slide against his stomach with every tilt of my pelvis.

I followed his movements while his hands slid up and cupped my breasts. His feet slid up the bed until his knees were raised against mine, his hips thrusting beneath me.

With just the right movement, my clit rubbed against his balls, and a shudder ran through me. Right there. I needed—oh, *fuck*.

I came again, my rhythm faltering as he thrust harder, his hands sliding back down to hold my hips as he came beneath me with a loud roar.

I continued to shudder as he spread soft kisses over my back and shoulders, his hips still thrusting gently.

"So good," he said softly. "Better every time."

Cam helped me off his lap and laid me gently on the bed as he left the room to get rid of the condom. When he came back, I was still sprawled out on my back, completely worn out.

"You're so sweaty," he said with a gentle smile as he climbed onto the bed on his hands and knees, coming to stop when he was braced above me. "So salty." He leaned down and ran his tongue along my belly and under the curve of my breast, making me shudder.

"I can't feel my legs, Cam. We're not going again," I told him seriously.

He burst out laughing and the bed shook as he dropped down beside me.

"Wasn't plannin' on it," he finally answered, rolling to his side and leaning his head on his hand. "Even though you're gorgeous when you're all sweaty and still shuddering."

He reached out to run a fingertip over my nipple and I shuddered again, making him grin.

"I'm getting a job," I announced as my sex high lowered to a reasonable level.

"What?" His face screwed up in confusion as he tried to follow my train of conversation.

"I don't want you to take care of me. I want a job. A good one—where I kick ass and make a shit ton of money and go on vacations."

"This is what you wanted to talk about?" he asked irritably, his hand pulling away from my skin.

"Yeah—we need to get a few things straight," I answered sharply.

"Fuck that." Cam rolled away from me and set his feet on the floor, scratching the back of his head for a moment before shaking it and standing up. "Do what you want."

My mouth dropped open in surprise as he left the room. Seconds later, I leapt from the bed when I heard the shower turn on.

"You're being an ass!" I yelled over the running water as I stepped inside the bathroom. "I was trying to talk to you."

"Fine. Talk," Cam replied from behind my blue shower curtain.

I opened my mouth, then closed it, then opened it again. I wasn't sure what to say. I'd started the conversation the way I'd wanted to, but his lack of response had me a bit stumped. He was clearly pissed, but he wasn't arguing with me and I needed that argument to state my case.

"I want to work."

"Yeah, ya said that. So work."

"I don't want you to make a deal about it, or be pissed off about it." I sat on the closed toilet lid, still completely naked as I tried to argue with him.

"Not doin' either one of those things, Bellatrix."

"You're being all pissy."

"I'm not. I'm showerin.' You're the one tryin' to pick a fight."

"I got a job offer in Portland," I announced. I hadn't even completed the sentence before the shower curtain was flung open and water sprayed out of the tub.

"Not fuckin' happenin'," he said flatly as I sputtered.

"I make my own decisions!" I snapped back, squeaking like a damn mouse as he leaned forward and dragged me into the shower with him.

"You wanna live hours away from me, Bea?" he asked roughly, jerking the shower curtain closed again so we seemed wrapped in our own little cocoon. "That what you want? Seein' me when I can get some time, or you can get some time, once or twice a month?"

"No," I grit back between my teeth.

"Then what the fuck are we arguin' about here? Fill me the fuck in—because I honest to God don't know what your fuckin' problem is."

"I make my own decisions," I repeated stubbornly.

"Yeah, got that."

"I plan my own life."

"Got that, too."

"Good."

Cam shook his head and turned away from me, dipping his head forward so he could get his hair wet.

"Sounds to me like you need me to tell you not to go," Cam said softly as I stood behind him with my arms wrapped around my chest. "You got this job offer—probably the only one you've got—but you don't wanna take it."

He grabbed my shampoo and poured a little on his head, scrubbing it into his scalp as I watched the muscles in his back and shoulders move and bunch.

"You need me to tell you I don't want you to go?" He paused for a moment, as if waiting for me to answer, then rinsed his hair. He turned to me when he was done and swiped a hand over his face to get the water out of his eyes. "I don't want you to take that job."

I bit my lip as my mind raced, and let him move me gently under the spray of water while I kept silent.

"You'll find somethin' down here, Sweetbea," he assured me as his fingers ran through my hair. "Just a matter of time."

"Are you sure?" I whispered back, the fear evident in my voice. I was terrified to leave him, but I was also terrified that if I didn't take the job in Portland, I'd never get another one. Then I'd be exactly who I didn't want to be.

"Hell, yes, I'm sure. You're smart and driven, and you'd look sexy as fuck in a business suit."

I couldn't stop the small laugh that tumbled from my mouth.

"There she is," he murmured, smiling as he leaned down to brush his lips against mine. "My Bea is fearless. She doesn't worry about the future because she's too busy kicking ass in the present."

"I'm freaked out," I admitted as I poured some shower gel in my hands and slicked them over his chest.

"Don't be," Cam replied, taking a deep breath as my fingers ran over his stomach. "You're gonna do it all and have it all, Bea. I promise."

Chapter 9

CAMERON

"Someone slashed my tires," Tommy told me over the phone. "I tried my dad and Will, but neither of them are answering and I didn't want to worry my mom."

It was Wednesday and I knew Grease and Will were meeting with some guys we were thinking of doing gun business with, but I couldn't tell Tommy that. I pinched the bridge of my nose.

"You sure they were slashed?" I asked stupidly, walking away from the noise of four air compressors going at the same time inside the garage.

"Yeah, I'm sure," he replied irritably. "My fuckin' car is sittin' on rims, man!"

"Shit. You at the school?" I asked as I motioned for one of the prospects to grab me the keys for the tow truck we rarely used.

"Yeah, me and Mick were supposed to get Rose from school, but we won't make it now."

"Call your mom and tell her—no. Fuck. I'll call CeeCee and have her pick up Rose when she gets Lily. You call your mom and tell her I needed your help today, so Cec will bring Rose home."

"Okay. You on your way, though?"

"Yeah, bud. I'll be there soon."

I sent a text to my little sister, who still wasn't talking to me because of the fight we'd had the weekend before, and thankfully got a text back saying she'd grab Rose.

Who the hell would slash the tires of two high school boys?

I clicked into my contacts list again as I started up the truck and nodded at the prospect when he asked if I wanted him to ride along.

"Hello?" Leo answered after a couple rings.

"Hey, man. You still at school?"

"I'm a little busy," Leo replied smugly as some chick giggled in the background, pissing me off. I thought he wanted my little sister? I didn't want him anywhere near Cecilia, but if he was playing her, I'd kill him and bury his ass in the woods.

"Pussy's gonna have to wait," I snapped as I pulled off the club's property, the old truck jerking as I switched gears. "Tommy and Mick are in the parking lot of your school with their tires slashed."

"What the fuck?"

"I'm on my way with the truck, but I want you to go wait with them. Not sure what's goin' on, but three of you is better than two."

"Yup, I'm goin' now."

The phone disconnected, so I stuffed it in the front pocket of my jeans.

"Fuckin' stupid to slash Tommy Hawthorne's tires. Who the fuck would have the balls to do that?" Price, our youngest prospect, asked from the passenger seat. The kid had graduated the year before, and he knew all about the Hawthorne boys. Even without the weight of their dad's power in the club, they were a force to be reckoned with.

Leo, Tommy and Mick owned the high school, like the fucking Three Musketeers… only with knives and crowbars instead of swords.

"I don't know," I answered Price a few minutes later as I pulled into the parking lot of the high school, seeing Tommy's Chevy Nova sitting in the middle of the lot.

I climbed out of the cab as I reached the boys and whistled between my teeth.

"Yeah, no shit," Mick mumbled, looking at the car sadly.

"You fuck someone's girlfriend?" I asked Tommy bluntly.

"Hell, no. I don't fuck high school girls."

"You fuck someone's wife, then?"

"Uh," his eyes widened comically before he swallowed hard. "Don't *think* so."

I rolled my eyes and stuck my hand out for his keys. What a fucking idiot.

By the time we got the Nova back to the club, the forecourt was filled with bikes. Grease, Will and Poet sat outside at a picnic table smoking, and all three came to their feet as they caught sight of us.

"What the hell happened?" Grease asked as I climbed out of the cab, Leo and the boys pulling in behind me.

"Someone slashed my fucking tires!" Tommy shouted, hopping out of Leo's car.

"You got any idea who it was?" Will asked as he climbed on the flatbed to get a closer look. "Shit, they weren't messin' around."

"No shit," I agreed.

Poet and Grease shared a look.

"Leo can you take my sons home?" Grease asked.

"Sure."

"What? Why?" Tommy asked as Mick crossed his arms over his chest. "I need to fix my car."

"You ain't fixin' nothin' tonight," Grease answered flatly. "Those tires are fucked and we don't have anything in the shop to replace them."

"This is bullshit!" Tommy's hands went to his hair and pulled it tight as he glanced wide-eyed at his car.

"Thomas," Grease warned, cutting off Tommy's ranting instantly.

"Let's go," Mick mumbled, pulling at his brother's arm. "We'll see you at home, Dad."

The boys climbed back into Leo's car and took off, leaving Grease, Poet, Will and I standing in a half-circle, staring at the mangled tires of the Nova.

"The fuck?" Grease mumbled.

"Who the fuck are these guys?" I asked in frustration. "And why the fuck would they slash a kid's tires?"

"Don't know that it's the same—" Will began to say.

"No coincidences," Poet cut him off, shaking his head as he started toward the front door of the club.

"We're runnin' in fuckin' circles here," Grease said, his voice laced with frustration. "None of this shit makes any sense."

I laced my fingers behind my neck and circled the car as I tried in vain to find some reason why, out of every vehicle of every member of the club, Tommy's would be targeted. It was flashy, yeah, because of the body style and the engine, but at first glance, it looked like a junker. The boys had covered it in primer, but they hadn't saved up enough money to paint it yet, so it was a flat grey. The back window was spider webbed and there was a black sticker in the lower right hand side that said "Ilusive"—some sort of snowboarding company the boys bought gear from.

While it was running, it was a beast. But sitting in the middle of a high school parking lot? It looked like a mangy old dog.

"How did the meet go?" I asked after a few minutes.

"Fine. Guy seemed interested."

"Nothing decided yet?"

"Draggin' his feet, I think."

"Huh." I glanced at the car again. "Ask my dad," I said finally.

"What?" Will asked, his head popping up from where he'd been staring at the ground.

"Ask Casper."

"Ask him what?" Grease was looking at me like I had two heads.

"For a pattern." I waved my arm toward the tow truck. "Tell him to think about it all. Everything that's happened in the past two months, even the shit that doesn't seem like it's connected. There's a pattern—there has to be."

"And you think he can find it? Then why hasn't he already?" Grease asked as I started backing away. "Where you goin'?"

"He's a genius," I replied seriously as I came to a stop. "Maybe he hasn't added everything in, or hell, I don't know. Maybe the shit today will clear it all up."

I turned and continued to walk over to my bike. "Goin' home."

★ ★ ★

"WHERE ARE YOU?" I snapped into the phone, standing in the middle of Trix's silent apartment.

"I stayed late with some people at the library," she whispered back.

"Jesus Christ, Bellatrix."

"What? What's the problem *now*?"

"Are you fucking with me right now?" I asked, lifting a hand to the back of my neck as I tried to get my racing heart under control. "You said you'd be home after class, I get here and you're gone."

"This is getting ridiculous," she replied, her words clipped. "I don't fucking answer to you, Cameron."

My hand tightened so hard on my phone that I heard the cover crack. There were so many things I wanted to say to that, but I knew they would get me nowhere. She needed to get the fuck back to the apartment—then I would deal with her bullshit. "Come home."

"I'll be back when I'm done."

Jesus.

It was so stupid. They'd fucked with Tommy's car, such an asinine thing to do. But that was the thing about people who didn't make any fucking sense—you never knew where they were going to aim next. We had no idea who they were or what their endgame was, and Trix was out doing whatever the fuck she wanted while I was literally sweating about her being the next target.

"*Now*, Bea. Don't make me come get your ass," I warned.

I heard her sharply inhaled breath and I knew right then that I was going to be even more pissed off by the time the night was over.

"Fuck off," she spit before the line went dead.

Looks like I was headed to the university.

TWENTY MINUTES LATER, I parked my bike next to her car outside the Knight Library. I pulled my phone out of my pocket and glanced around. The hair on the back of my neck was sticking straight up as I texted Trix.

Outside.

Less than five minutes later, a very pissed off Trix was stomping out the doors of the library.

"Get in the fucking car," I ordered as she came close, reaching behind me in a nervous gesture to make sure my piece was still tucked into my belt.

"I'm studying," she argued, situating her backpack strap higher on her shoulder. "I'll be home later." Her voice was even, but the look in her eyes was a giant 'fuck you.'

"Bellatrix, I swear to God," I grit out between my teeth, "if you don't get in the motherfucking car right now…"

She must have seen something in my expression, or maybe what little sense of self-preservation she had left finally kicked in, because suddenly she was unlocking her car and climbing inside.

My stomach was one giant knot as I followed her home, keeping one eye on my rear view. There was nothing.

By the time we'd finally pulled up and parked in front of her building, my hands were shaking.

"Get the fuck inside," I ordered. The sense of being watched no longer scraped at my skin like a thousand little razors, but my anger continued to rise until I wanted to smash something.

I followed her up the stairs to the second floor, and for the first time in a long time, I didn't even glance at her ass.

"What the fuck is wrong with you?" she yelled as she threw her bag across the room. "I'm not your kid. You don't get to fucking dictate to me."

I didn't answer her as I closed the front door and flipped the deadbolt.

I couldn't.

I knew if I opened my mouth when I was feeling so out of control, I'd hurt her. I'd say something that I couldn't take back.

I ignored her as I grabbed a beer out of the fridge and popped the top, and I didn't even glance at her as I made my way to the spare bedroom and closed the door behind me.

Carefully setting my beer on the bedside table, I sat down on the edge of the bed and pulled off my boots. My cut came off next, and then I pulled my piece out of my waistband and set it beside me on the bed.

I didn't move again except to lift the beer to my lips and set it gently back on the table over and over again until Trix quietly entered the room.

"This isn't going to work," she said, her voice shaky. "I'm an adult, Cam. I make my own choices. I want to be with you, but I'm not going to let you boss me around."

I lifted the beer to my lips and emptied it, wishing I'd thought to bring another.

"I'm sorry I didn't text you to let you know I'd be late. You're usually not home until after six, so I—"

"Came home after I towed Tommy's Nova to the shop." I cut her off. "Someone slashed all four tires."

"What? Why would someone do that? Did he sleep with someone's girlfriend?"

I chuckled humorously as she echoed my words from earlier.

"That's the question of the hour," I answered flatly. "Why the fuck would someone run Mack off the road? Why would someone slash Tommy's tires? Why the fuck are we getting nothin' when we put feelers out all over the state?"

"Wait, you think it's all connected? That doesn't even make sense."

"No, it doesn't, does it?" I looked up to find her changed into a pair of shorts and a tank top. "Doesn't make any sense to fuck with the Hawthorne boys. They might be young, but Mick is fuckin' big. Wouldn't make sense for someone to rough you up comin' out of the college library after dark, either. Wouldn't make sense for someone to rape you. Wouldn't make sense for someone to take you. Granddaughter of the Aces VP? It'd be a fuckin' death sentence, but there's no fuckin' logic with this shit."

"Cam," she said softly, walking further into the room.

"Don't come near me, Bellatrix," I warned, tilting my head to the side as I watched her. "Pissed as fuck with you right now."

"You wouldn't hurt me," she argued.

"More than one way to hurt a person."

"And you wouldn't do any of them. You love me."

"I do," I agreed, my voice still hard.

She stepped forward again.

"Can't be easy tonight," I said quietly as she reached me.

The moment her eyes went wide and she began to nod her agreement, I was all over her. I fisted her hair in my hands, ripping out the rubber band she'd used to pull it back. I pressed my mouth to hers, forcing my tongue between her lips as her body sagged toward mine—

but it wasn't enough.

I needed more. I needed to taste her skin, feel it gripped between my teeth and grow wet from my tongue.

I yanked her tank top over her head, watching her tits bounce with the movement for just a second before I was tearing her shorts and underwear down her legs.

"Slow down," she whispered, her hands coming up to run over my shaved head.

I shoved her backward hard enough for her to take a step back.

"Go," I barked.

There was no way I could slow down. No way for me to calm the way my hands shook and my heart raced. If she couldn't take what I was giving, she needed to leave. I didn't want to scare her, but there was no way for me to be gentle. She was right in saying that I'd never hurt her, but I was so close to the edge that if she wasn't *with me,* things would go bad fast.

"I'm not going anywhere," she announced stubbornly, her thumbs fisted inside her hands.

I stood from the bed, but even my size didn't seem to intimidate her.

"Fuckin' leave," I rasped, pulling off my shirt. "Got nothin' for you tonight."

Her chin lifted as she held my eyes defiantly, then without even glancing at my chest she reached up and traced the "B" there with one fingertip. "Mine," she whispered.

My head rocked back in confusion, and that was all it took for her to find her opening. She shoved at my belly, pushing me back onto the bed, and the moment my ass met the mattress, she was kissing me roughly, her nails biting into my shoulders.

"You gonna take me how I want it?" I asked her, sliding my hand between us to find her already growing wet. I thrust two fingers inside her without any preparation and her back bowed as she cried out. "Answer me."

"Yes," she said seriously, dropping her chin so she could meet my eyes.

My free hand went to my belt buckle and from the corner of my eye, I saw Trix pick up my pistol from the bed. "You gonna shoot me?" I asked, half serious.

"Not tonight," she replied, setting the gun next to my empty beer on the table. "Ask me tomorrow."

I thrust my fingers up hard inside her, relishing the sound she made as she rocked toward me. I finally got my belt undone and tore open my pants, lifting up a bit so I could push them to my thighs as I slid my fingers out of Trix.

"Knees," I ordered, gesturing to the floor in front of me. My chest was rising and falling heavily with each breath, and I wondered for a minute if she'd refuse me. It didn't matter if she did. I was getting inside her somehow, and if she wanted me in her cunt instead, I was happy to oblige.

She sucked me in as far as she could go on the first pass, and I swear I saw fucking stars. She wasn't kidding around. There was no tentativeness to her movements, no hesitation or shyness as her tongue rubbed hard beneath the head of my cock.

"Good girl," I moaned, making her eyes shoot to mine as she glared at me. She was weird about that shit. I usually watched what I said, but in that moment, I didn't give a fuck. She *was* a good girl. Such a good—fuck! She slid her teeth along the underside of my dick and instinct almost had me knocking her head from her shoulders.

I fisted a hand in her hair and pulled her off me as she panted, her lips rosy and swollen.

"On the bed." I let go of her hair as she climbed to her feet and laid down on her back in the center of the bed.

"I'm not a dog," she rasped as I stood, grabbed a condom out of my pocket and let my jeans and boxers fall to the floor.

"Hands and knees, Sweetbea," I replied.

My hands were still shaking as she positioned herself with her ass facing me. God, I wanted to taste her. I wanted to lick and suck every single inch of her skin. Push and pull at her until I knew for certain that she was okay, that the scenarios I'd had running through my mind that afternoon when I couldn't find her weren't real.

But I couldn't slow myself down, because the only thing I wanted more than the chance to map her body was to be inside her.

I dropped to my knees beside the bed and jerked her backward, giving myself just a moment to take her in before I lost my mind inside her. Her hips arched toward me as I sucked her clit into my mouth. She was wetter than I'd thought, and I groaned as I moved up, sliding my tongue through it as I pressed it inside her.

She clenched against me, and I couldn't wait any longer.

My trembling hands made condom application a fucking joke, but I got it done.

I stood up and gripped the cheeks of her ass, pulling them apart as I fed my dick into the tight hole that was fucking weeping for me.

Trix made a desperate sound as I moved slowly, then dropped her torso to the bed so she could tilt her hips even higher toward the ceiling. I began to sweat as I gently pushed inside. I wanted to fucking *move*, but I knew that I needed to get her ready for it. I loved the thought of taking her hard from the very first, but it just wasn't possible without hurting her.

Her tense body relaxed the way I'd shown her before, and as my balls finally brushed against her, she let out a feminine grunt.

"Hold on," I warned as I slid back out again.

I slammed back inside without warning, and her head flew back, flipping her hair all over the bed. It was so hot, I could have came right then.

I kept the same pace, sliding out slowly before slamming in over and over, and as she grew wetter, signaling her impending orgasm, I stopped, fully seated inside her.

"You want it?" I asked, sounding like some seventies porn star, but not giving a shit. She'd come into the room that night, flirting with the words that would have taken her away from me. Sure, she'd made some noise about how she couldn't stay if I was bossing her around, totally passive-aggressive, but I'd known what it was.

It was a fucking test. An ultimatum.

And fuck if I'd play into it.

"Please, baby," she gasped, rolling her hips against me.

"You gonna leave me?" I asked, digging my fingers into the cheeks of her ass as her hips continued to grind.

"No."

"No?"

"No, I won't leave you."

I pulled out and slid back in, watching a drop of sweat slide down her back.

I wasn't sure if it was hers or mine.

"I thought somethin' happened to you," I said, slowing my rhythm so I could watch my dick disappear inside her. "Came home and you weren't where you were supposed to be."

"I'm sorry," she moaned as she tried to move her hips against me.

She was almost crying in frustration, little sounds of pleasure falling from her lips every time I bottomed out inside her, but I wasn't giving her enough sensation to come. "I love you," she finally gasped, making my chest feel so tight that for a moment, I thought I was having a damn heart attack. "I love you."

Then my panic from earlier came flooding back with a vengeance, and the thought of something happening to her almost brought me to my knees.

Without thought, my hand raised up and landed on her ass with a loud crack.

I didn't put much force behind it. I'd never hit Trix hard, even on her ass, but the sound was loud.

Trix went completely still beneath me.

I paused for a moment, only for a moment, to see if she'd frozen in surprise.

But that wasn't surprise.

She was like a fucking statue. I wasn't even sure she was breathing, she was so still.

"Sweetbea?" I said, pulling out of her gently.

She didn't acknowledge me or move from the position I'd put her in. I kept a hand on her back as I stepped around the bed to see her face, and my stomach dropped as I took in her expression.

I could hear my heartbeat in my ears.

"Baby?"

Her eyes were squeezed tight and her jaw was clenched as if she was waiting for another blow.

"Hey, hey," I crooned, "Come here to me, Bea." I crouched by the side of the bed so I could put my face next to hers.

Her eyes opened and almost immediately filled with tears.

"I didn't like that," she whispered, the words shaming me in a way that I would never forget.

"I won't ever do it again," I promised, my voice strangled from the fucking knot in my throat. I slid my hand gently up her back so I could sweep her sweaty hair from her face.

She jerked toward me then, wrapping her arms around my shoulders as she pressed her face into my neck. Her fingers dug into my skin as she shuddered, and I swallowed hard as I picked her up and carried her into our room, shutting the spare room door tightly behind me.

All the anger and frustration I'd carried with me that night had vanished the moment I'd noticed something wrong. There wasn't any room for it alongside the panic that coursed through me as she trembled.

"Did I hurt you?" I asked as I climbed into the sheets, still holding her against my chest.

"No."

"What was that, Bea?"

"I don't know," she answered shakily.

CHAPTER 10

TRIX

I DIDN'T MOVE as Cam crawled out of bed early in the morning. I needed to get up soon, but as he left the bedroom without kissing me, I realized we both needed a little space.

Cam didn't understand what had happened to us the night before, but I couldn't ease his mind because I didn't understand it, either.

One minute I'd been close to orgasm, begging wordlessly for Cam to give me that last push into oblivion, and the next it had been like my entire body shut down. I was there, I could hear him talking to me and felt him pull away, but I couldn't move.

It was that sound. That godawful sound of flesh meeting flesh.

Our bodies slapped together on a regular basis, making noises that turned me on and strangely comforted me, but that fast, sharp sound? It had been disgusting. Horrifying. Nauseating. I'd barely felt it when his palm hit my ass, it got lost in the way the rest of my body had been practically singing, but I hadn't been able to escape that noise.

Hearing it, everything inside me, every single part of me, had instinctively curled into itself. Quiet. Still. *Small.*

I rolled to my back and pulled my quilt up to my chin as I stared at the ceiling. I hadn't had that reaction when Will and Cam had been fighting in the forecourt at the club. I'd hated it, but I'd stood there with my pop just fine.

I couldn't understand why I'd reacted that way with Cam. There was something I wasn't seeing, right in my periphery, but it was as if the moment I tried to look at it full-on, it vanished.

"Hey," Cam said tentatively as he came in, soaking wet from his shower.

"Morning," I mumbled back, watching him as he dried off a little and started getting dressed.

"Was gonna wake you after I started coffee."

"It's okay, I was up."

Our conversation was so stilted that it made a lump form in my throat. We'd never had a hard time talking before. Even when I'd avoided him, even when I'd had to see him at the club with other women, we'd still been able to bitch and bicker back and forth.

"You got—"

"I'm—"

We both stopped speaking and Cam sighed, walking over in bare feet to sit at the edge of the bed.

"Last test today, huh?" he asked, leaning over to brace his hand on the opposite side of me.

"Yep. Then I'm officially done."

An awkward silence fell and I looked back up at the ceiling.

"Sweetbea," he said softly, his voice pulling my eyes back to his face. "I'm sorry, baby."

My eyes filled with tears and I sat up in bed, reaching out to take his face between my palms.

"Don't be sorry."

"I scared you—"

His eyes had dark circles underneath and for once, he hadn't shaved before he showered. He looked like hell.

"We just won't do it again."

"Why didn't you warn me?" he asked raggedly, his bristly jaw moving against my hands.

"I didn't know. No one's ever—"

"Oh," he said, cutting me off before I could give any type of detail. "Was it because I was pissed? Because, swear to God Trix, I wouldn't fuckin'—"

"No." I scooted a little closer and pulled his face to mine, fitting my bottom lip between his as I gently kissed him. "I'm not afraid of you. You could break every single thing in this apartment and I'd stand in the middle watching you do it, knowing nothing would touch me."

"That wouldn't happen—"

"I know."

"—don't have the money to replace that much shit."

I laughed and he smiled back, his eyes still bleak.

"We good?" he asked, reaching up to cup the side of my neck.

"Yeah." I nodded, underscoring my answer. "I wish I didn't have to go to class today. Thursdays have been my day off for so long, I swear my body knows I'm supposed to be sleeping in."

"You can sleep in tomorrow and Sunday," he promised, his thumb tracing along my bare collarbone.

"Why not Saturday?"

"I gotta help my parents at the house."

"Oh, right. Gram's birthday dinner."

"Yep."

He leaned in and kissed me and I reveled in the novelty of his scruff rubbing against my chin and cheeks. I inhaled deeply as his tongue slid against mine, taking in the scent of his soap and the toothpaste he'd used before coming into the room. Cam pulled me into his lap sideways and I wrapped my arms around his neck as his arms banded around me.

"I gotta go now, or I'm not goin' and neither are you," he said gruffly, pulling away from my mouth. "What time will you be done today?"

"By eleven, maybe sooner," I answered as he stood up and laid me back in the bed, pulling the covers around my body. "I'll text you when I'm leaving school."

"Okay." He pushed some buttons on the alarm on the nightstand and leaned down to kiss me again. "You need some more sleep, so I set the alarm for an hour from now—I'll call and make sure it wakes you up."

"Thanks, baby." I gripped the back of his head to steal another kiss as he groaned.

"You're all naked and soft and sleepy and not acting like a bitch, and I hafta fuckin' leave."

"Quickie?"

"Nothin's ever quick with you." He stood up, pulling my hands away from his head. "Sleep."

"Okay."

"Good luck on your test."

"Thanks. I love you," I relaxed into the blankets and closed my eyes.

"Love you, too, Sweetbea."

I listened to him leaving the house as I drifted off to sleep, the knot in my stomach completely gone. We were okay.

★ ★ ★

"Hey, Bellatrix!" I heard called out behind me as I left the building after my last class. I'd made that test my bitch.

"What's up, Steve?" I asked as I slowed down so he could catch up with me.

"How'd you do?" he asked as he fell in beside me.

"Nailed it, you?"

"Same."

"Nice."

"So, a group of us are going to barbeque to celebrate the end of finals on Saturday, you wanna come?"

My brows raised in surprise. I'd never been invited to anything. I had a few friends that I hung out with once in a while, but they were all girls and mostly kept to themselves like I did. Basically, a bunch of introverts who got together to watch movies or whatever when we were feeling exceptionally bored.

"I can't," I finally answered with an apologetic smile. "I've got a family barbeque this weekend."

"Well, come afterward?"

"It's actually at my boyfriend's parents' house, and there'll be a ton of us. I doubt I'll be done in time to go anywhere else, sorry."

"Oh, okay," he said amiably. "So, you and the boyfriend—pretty serious?"

I stopped abruptly at the intrusive question and turned to look at him, a weird feeling growing in the pit of my stomach. I didn't know him well enough for him to ask me something like that. My instincts were telling me to get as far away from him as possible, but I couldn't just turn and run like a lunatic. We were surrounded by people, it wasn't like I was in any danger.

"I'm late," I blurted, a small part of me sure that I should tell him someone was waiting on me. "But have fun at your barbeque."

"Thanks, Bella," he said softly.

"That's not my name," I replied, taking a step back.

"It fits, though." He gave a little wave and turned away, walking toward the other end of the school. My stomach turned as he threw his arms high above himself in a nonchalant stretch.

Thank God, I never had to see that guy again.

I turned toward the parking lot where I'd parked my car that morning and pulled out my phone, letting Cam know that I was done with my test. We texted back and forth for a few minutes while he tried to convince me to come to the shop for a "nooner." I didn't say anything about Steve. By the time I sat down heavily in the driver's seat, I'd completely forgotten how uncomfortable he'd made me. I was too giddy about the way Cameron couldn't seem to get enough of me, even after my complete freak out the night before.

A few hours later, all that giddiness left me.

★ ★ ★

"Nan!" I yelled, pushing her front door open without knocking. My voice was panicked and thin, and I wasn't even sure how I'd driven to her house, my hands were shaking so badly.

"In here—what the heck is going on?" my nan asked as she rounded the corner into the entryway. "What's wrong?"

"I think I'm pregnant," I blurted, my hand flying up to my mouth as if I could catch the words before they reached her.

"Oh, Christ," another voice rasped as my auntie, Vera, walked out behind her.

"Vera," Nan hissed.

"Come sit down before you fall over," Vera snapped, spinning back toward the kitchen.

With my eyes miserably pointed toward the floor, I followed them numbly. They were whispering back and forth, but I couldn't hear what they were saying and didn't really care, anyway.

Vera was married to the Aces' president, Slider, and she'd been a constant in my life growing up. She'd practically raised my mom. She and Slider had known my gramps and nan since they were my age, and when Nan had gotten back together with my gramps, she and Vera had picked up their old friendship as if they hadn't been apart for thirty years. I should have known Vera would be there.

Where Vera was hard, Nan was soft. Vera spoke without thinking and Nan calculated every word. They were opposites in every way, yet they complimented each other.

"Come on, baby," Nan murmured, sitting me at a kitchen chair. "What's going on?"

"I thought I was due this week," I answered desperately, looking up to meet her eyes. "I thought I was due, so I stopped at the store to get some tampons. But then, as I was driving home, I realized I should've started last week, not this week."

"Hell, you know how many times I've been late?" Vera said.

"I'm not," I argued. "I have thirty days between periods. Always. Not twenty-eight, not thirty-one. Thirty."

"You haven't taken a test?" Nan asked kindly.

"No." That's when I started to cry.

Vera made a noise in her throat. "Why are you cryin,' Bellatrix? You're a grown woman with a good man. This is excitin' news."

I dropped my head into my hands and cried harder.

"Well," Nan said reasonably, "you need to take a test before you know for sure."

"I'll go get one," Vera offered, grabbing her ratty, fringed purse from the counter.

After she'd gone, I sat in silence, my mind spinning. I wasn't ready. I wanted to get set in my career. I wanted to be married. I wanted to be five years older before I had a baby. I didn't want a baby *now*, when Cam and I had just found one another again. I wanted to hop on the bike whenever we wanted and spend the day riding around. I wanted to go to club parties and concerts and vacations, just me and Cam.

Shit. I pulled out my phone and sent him a message, letting him know I was at my nan's so he wouldn't worry.

Nan rubbed my back as I tried to calm my breathing.

Then, before I was ready, Vera was back.

"Here," she said, shoving the pink and white box at me. "Go pee on it and we'll wait for you out here."

My heart thumped hard in my chest as I walked toward the bathroom. I could barely pee on the little stick, my hands were shaking so badly, but eventually I finished and sat the test on a little square of toilet paper as I washed my hands.

I hadn't even had time to dry them before the positive result formed. As I staggered backward, a loud, "Well?" came through the door and I caught myself.

I'm sure I looked shell-shocked as I opened the bathroom door, but Nan just gave me a small smile and pulled me into her arms.

"It'll all be okay, sweetheart."

"I'm getting an abortion," I said flatly, all my tears completely dried up. "I don't want this."

Nan's body stiffened, but she didn't say a word, just continued to hold me tight as my arms hung limply at my sides. It was as if my whole body had gone hollow, and I couldn't feel anything.

"It's not a 'this'," Vera snapped, yanking me out of Nan's arms. "It's a baby. Cam's baby."

"It's just a cluster of cells."

Nan made a noise of protest and looked away from me. When she spoke, her voice was the hardest I'd ever heard it. "Go sit down. We're going to talk."

I raised my chin and followed her to the kitchen, but feelings were already starting to flood in again. My small reprieve where I'd felt nothing was already ebbing away, and the room suddenly seemed colder.

"When I was younger than you are, I got pregnant with your Uncle Nix," Nan began, her voice strained but steady. "I didn't want him, either."

My head shot up in surprise at her words. I knew my gramps wasn't Uncle Nix's dad, just like my mom didn't belong to Nan, but I'd never heard the story of why that was. It had always just been truth, and I'd never had reason to question it.

"I'm only telling you this. . . Well, I just want you to have the facts, alright?"

"I'm gonna go," Vera said suddenly. "Can't take no more trips down memory lane."

She walked over and cupped my cheeks like she'd done when I was little, then kissed my forehead tenderly. "I love you, kiddo."

"Love you, too."

Nan was silent for a few moments after Vera left, then took a deep breath and began to speak.

"I was raped. It was brutal and demoralizing and completely shattered everything I'd thought I knew about the world and my place in it," she said flatly, her eyes steady on mine. "My rapist is the one who messed up my hand—well, he didn't cut off the fingers, that happened when I was a kid."

She raised her hand, gnarled and twisted with arthritis, the pinky and ring finger missing from the second knuckle.

"I'm so sorry," I whispered in horror.

"That was how Nix was conceived."

I felt my eyes grow wide as I inhaled sharply, but I couldn't stop my reaction. I'd never known. No one had ever said a word to me.

My eyes slammed shut as I grimaced, thinking about my handsome uncle, who looked nothing like my nan and towered over her by a foot. I'd always thought his dad must have been huge, and the implications of that were not lost on me as Nan sat across the table, wringing her hands.

"Bellatrix, I'm not telling you this so that you feel sorry for me, or feel some misplaced sense of guilt about your feelings. Okay, baby?"

I nodded, my throat so tight I didn't think I could get any words out.

"I'm telling you because I *know* how it feels to have a baby inside you that you don't want. I know how scared you are. But I want you to know," she reached out and gripped my hand hard, "you can do this. You can be a parent, even if you weren't prepared. Even if the thought scares you shitless. Even if this wasn't in your plans. Even if you think that having the baby might possibly break you into so many pieces that you'll never find them all again." Her voice had gone raspy, and I knew the last sentence didn't apply to me, but to her. "You will never understand the type of love you'll have for your child until you're a parent. It's all encompassing. It's the most important thing you'll ever do. It's your decision whether you're ready for that or not."

"I don't think I can," I whispered back, a heavy weight settling in my belly.

"I believe in a right to choose, always have, always will. I will never judge you and I will always love you," she said firmly. "But I want you to think this through, Trix. I want you to take a few days. Tell Cam. Discuss things with him. Because this is a decision that will never leave you, and you need to be absolutely sure it's what you want. After it's done, it's done."

"Do you think I'm horrible?" I asked as my eyes welled up.

"No," she said sympathetically, "I don't."

She came around the table and pulled me into her arms, letting me cry quietly into her chest.

I wasn't thinking about making a decision or the fact that I had to tell Cam. My mind was blank as tears rolled down my face.

★ ★ ★

HOURS LATER, I was curled up in the dark on the living room couch when Cam came through the front door.

"Bea?" he called out, flipping on the light switch. "Shit—what the hell are you doin' sittin' in the dark?"

"Too lazy to get up, I guess," I lied, pushing myself up until I was sitting. "You're home kinda late."

"Yeah, got bullshitting with Casper and lost track of time," he said, taking off his boots and cut. "Sorry, baby. How was your test?"

"It was fine."

"Just fine?" he asked with a smile. "Earlier you said you kicked ass."

I shrugged my shoulders and his smile dropped. "What's goin' on?"

"Come sit with me," I replied softly, meeting his eyes for the first time.

"Rather stand," he replied warily. He moved to stand in front of the couch, and I had to tilt my head way back in order to see his face. I wanted to stand up so I wasn't at such a disadvantage, but I was afraid if I did, he would pull me into his arms and I wouldn't be able to stop myself from sobbing.

"I'm pregnant," I announced steadily, trying not to flinch as he inhaled sharply, his eyes widening.

Chapter 11

CAMERON

I LOCKED MY knees to keep me upright and searched Trix's face, looking for any sign that showed me she wasn't serious.

She couldn't be serious.

I wrapped it up. Always. I was meticulous about that shit.

I knew that keeping her safe was all on me. She'd put that into my hands, had been clear from the very beginning. She didn't want kids yet, and it was my job to keep that from happening.

I swayed a little on my feet.

Then I couldn't help it—I felt a smile tugging at the corners of my mouth.

"You're pregnant?" I asked stupidly, my heart starting to pound.

"Yeah." The word was more of a sigh than an actual sound.

"Tha—that's—"

"I don't think I'm going to have it," she whispered.

It took a second for me to understand her words, and when I did, nausea hit me fast and hard.

"What do you mean, you're not going to have it?"

"I'm not that pregnant. We've only been together a little over a month, I can't be—"

"Not that pregnant?" I asked sharply. "You've either got my kid in there or you don't."

"It's just cells. It's just—"

"What?" my voice was louder than I'd planned, and it broke in the middle like a fourteen-year-old kid's.

"I'm not ready!" she yelled back, coming to her feet. "This is a fucking mistake!" She tucked her thumbs into her hands and dropped her head. "It's just a mistake."

A headache formed at the base of my skull, probably from the tightness in my shoulders as I stared at her.

"It's fuckin' magic."

"What?" she tilted her head up to look at me, and her face was so fucking wrecked.

"This is magic, baby." I said softly, stepping forward to lay my hand on her belly. "We were so careful. I was so careful—and he's still in there growin,' anyway. That's fuckin' magic."

Her head started shaking before she stepped backward, away from my hand. "No. It's—it's just biology. We weren't careful enough. We weren't—"

"What're you sayin'?"

"I want—I want—" her breath grew ragged as she tried to speak. "I don't want it."

I fell back a step, staring at her in confusion. I knew she was scared. Hell, fear was in every line of her body. But she *wouldn't* do that. She wouldn't get rid of our baby because she was scared.

I knew Trix. I'd known her since we were kids. She wouldn't do that. She wouldn't do that to *me*.

"You want an abortion?" I asked quietly. The word was so fucking heinous, my mouth felt dirty.

Trix made a noise in the back of her throat, one that sounded like a stifled sob. Then she nodded.

Everything inside me went cold. Everything. Every place inside of me that went soft for Trix, that warmed for her, completely vanished until there was nothing left.

"Your mother lost a son—your twin—because he was born too early, yet you're gonna take our baby out so it dies? You fuckin' heartless bitch."

I barely felt the fists that slammed into my chest.

"Fuck you!" she screamed, her entire body vibrating with anger.

"No," I hissed, taking a step back. "Wouldn't touch your ass with a ten-foot pole."

Her eyes went wide and filled with tears, but I had no sympathy for her. None.

I moved toward the door and slid my feet into my boots, not bothering to lace them before I grabbed my cut and stepped outside, slamming the door behind me. After I'd locked up, I went to the stairwell and sat down, dropping my head into my hands.

Holy fuck.

I couldn't believe that shit had just happened. What the fuck was wrong with her? What the fuck could make her even think about having an abortion? That fucking cunt.

My hands shook as I called Will.

"What's up?" he answered on the second ring.

"Hey, man." I pinched the bridge of my nose between my fingers. "Can you come hang with Trix tonight? I got some shit to do—don't want to leave her alone all night."

"Everything alright?" I almost lost it at the sound of those words. *That* was my little cousin. The one who stepped in when you needed it. The guy you called when you were having a shitty fucking day or the best day of your life, because he wanted to hear about it either way.

"Yeah." I cleared my throat and tried again. "Yeah. Just got some shit to do."

"No problem. Be there in twenty."

He hung up and I stuffed the phone back into my jeans.

I didn't know why I lied. I could have told him what was going on, but I hadn't. Maybe somewhere, deep down, I didn't want him to know that about Trix. I didn't want him to know that about our relationship—that I'd been so fucking all-in that it was pathetic and she'd... Well, she didn't want my kid. I guess that said it all.

I climbed to my feet and ran a hand down my face as I walked slowly to my bike.

I let the road do its thing, clearing my head and bringing everything into focus.

I'd always wanted a family. Kids. And from the beginning, I'd known that those kids would come from Trix.

When I was young, my mother, younger brother and three little sisters died in a house fire. One night, I was staying at a friend's house and the next morning I'd walked home to find a burned out shell of metal and ashes where my home had been. I hadn't understood it at first. I'd been confused, so I'd walked to Casper's apartment because his place had been the closest.

It hadn't been until later that everything sunk in.

My dad was alive. He hadn't been home during the fire. And after my mom was gone? Dude was a whole different person. Sneaky and furtive and fucking mean.

I'd eventually learn that he'd gone completely around the bend. Lost in his own little world where everyone owed him something and if they didn't give it, he just fucking took it.

He was the first man I ever killed. I'd shot him with Farrah's gun through the headrest of the passenger seat in her car.

He'd kidnapped her and little Cecilia. I hadn't had a choice.

There was no choice.

Didn't mean that I ever felt okay with it, though.

I pulled over to the side of the road and grabbed a pair of gloves, stretching out my hands before sliding them on. It was cold as fuck outside, and as I glanced around, I realized where I'd ended up.

The woods were familiar. I'd been up there a few times in the past couple of years, especially when I had shit on my mind—usually Trix. If I drove a few more miles up the road, I'd hit gravel. Couple miles past that and I'd find the property that I'd inherited from Tommy, my first dad.

The same clearing where I'd killed him.

And yeah, it was fuckin' weird that Grease and Callie named their son Tommy, too—probably weirder for everyone else, since I'd always called the guy Dad. But they'd named their son after someone else—I didn't remember who.

You didn't name your kid after a traitor. They don't deserve the honor.

I pulled my phone out of my pocket and checked for missed calls. Nothing. Trix hadn't even tried to contact me after I'd left the house hours ago.

I sniffed, pulling a handkerchief out of my saddlebags to wipe my runny nose. Fuck, it was cold. Swear to Christ, even my eyeballs felt frozen.

I fired up my bike and made a U-turn, taking my time driving back down the mountain. I was in no hurry to get home, but I needed to warm the fuck up before my balls became permanently imbedded in my stomach, where they'd crawled a couple hours before.

I didn't want to see Trix. I didn't want to look at her. I'd tried not to think about the situation as I'd ridden around, tried to just let my mind wander instead—but it was no use. Only thing I could think about was my kid in her belly.

It was my job to protect him. It was my job to protect them both—but this was a fight I couldn't even step into the ring for. I was damned if I did, and fucking killed if I didn't.

I got back to the apartment as the sun started coming up, and my body was so fucking tired I had a hard time climbing the stairs.

"Hey," Will mumbled from the couch as I let myself in. "All good?"

"Yeah, thanks, brother." I pulled my gloves off as I moved into the house, and my hands started to burn as they heated up. "You want coffee?"

"Nah, I gotta get outta here. Couch fuckin' sucks—gonna go catch some sleep in a bed."

"Why didn't you sleep in the spare room?" I asked, turning my head to look at him as I filled the coffee carafe with water.

"Wasn't offered," he answered with a shrug. "I'm out. See ya later at the shop."

"Thanks again."

"Anytime."

I walked over and locked the door behind him, checking it twice before I finished making the coffee. After the first cup, I knew it was no use. My eyes were heavy and my movements sluggish as I headed toward the spare room, barely glancing at the closed door Trix was sleeping behind.

I crashed on top of the blankets, barely kicking off my boots before I was asleep.

Sometime later, Trix crawled in beside me. I woke up enough to realize she shouldn't be there, her head on my chest and the rest of her body curled so tight that her knees pressed up against my side. I was livid with her.

I wanted to fucking shake her. I wanted to lock her in a room so that she couldn't go anywhere near a doctor. I wanted to push her off the bed.

But I didn't do any of those things. As her tears soaked the front of my shirt, I wrapped my arm around her, my hand resting on the side of her neck.

I let her stay.

I couldn't do anything else.

★ ★ ★

"Get off me," I ordered a couple hours later, pushing Trix aside as I climbed wearily from the bed.

I needed more sleep. I could feel it in every muscle. My eyes were scratchy and tired, but as soon as I'd woken up, I knew I wouldn't be able to fall back asleep.

Especially when Trix was curled up next to me, completely passed out.

"Cam?" she asked shakily, lifting her head from the bed.

Her eyes had dark circles under them and her entire face was swollen from crying.

I shut my eyes and shook my head.

"Cam, please," she whispered, coming up onto her knees.

"What do you want from me?" I asked harshly.

"I want you to support me. To love me." She stuttered through her words, and I wondered if she knew how completely fucked up her request was.

"Not gonna support you killin' my kid," I told her tonelessly.

"Can we at least talk?" she asked, her voice shaking.

"Sure. You agree how fucked up it is that you'd even think about having an abortion and we'll talk all fuckin' day."

"This isn't what we planned," she pleaded, reaching toward me.

I stepped back.

"That is *our* child, Bellatrix!" I roared, pointing at her belly.

How could she even consider this? How could she even—

"I know!" she screamed back, her voice breaking.

She crumbled into herself. Her head hit her knees as her arms pulled them tightly against her body.

I'd never heard the noise she was making before. It was so far beyond crying, it was physically painful to hear. She was wailing.

She was fucking wailing as she wrapped her entire body around where she carried our child.

I stood frozen while I watched her, unable to take that single step forward that would bring me to the bed.

Then she started barely rocking, back and forth, back and forth.

Like she was trying to soothe herself.

Like she was rocking our baby.

It broke me.

"Shh," I whispered through my tight throat. She jerked when I laid my hand on her back, but she didn't pull away when I climbed up behind her on the bed, scooting forward until my knees were spread on each side of her hips.

I curled myself around her, my elbows braced above her shoulders and my face buried against her neck.

Then I shuddered and began to rock with her.

Back and forth.

Back and forth.

We did that for a long time.

Chapter 12

TRIX

I DIDN'T GET out of bed all day.

At some point, Cam carried me into our room and tucked me between the blankets.

He left.

I stayed.

I didn't want to move.

I wished that he would have agreed with me.

That would have made things so much easier.

It would have made me feel justified.

It would have allowed me to ignore the voice in my head telling me I was making a mistake.

My arms felt heavy as I rolled over, pulling the quilt my great-grandmother had made years ago up to my eyes. I didn't want to see anything.

I didn't want to feel anything.

I didn't want to move.

I didn't want to think.

I didn't want to be so goddamn terrified.

I knew I wouldn't have an abortion.

I'd known it before I'd brought it up to Cam.

I'd known it before I'd made him look at me like I was a monster.

I'd known it before I'd ever left my nan's house.

But I couldn't *accept* it.

I felt it in every part of my body. I'd protect my child with every muscle. Every bone. Every fingernail and tooth.

But the terror that overwhelmed me didn't allow me to focus on the fact that I would be having a baby.

I literally couldn't even think about having a child without feeling like I was going to black out.

It was all encompassing.

I didn't understand it.

I heard the front door open and I burrowed deeper into the blankets. I didn't want to see anyone. I didn't want anyone to see me.

"Trix?" my brother's voice called through the apartment. "You home?"

Footsteps thudded down the hallway, and then suddenly he was there, standing in the doorway.

"You okay, sissy?" he asked quietly. "Why you in bed at four in the afternoon?"

"Just tired," I replied, keeping my face covered. "What are you doing here?"

"Cam asked me to stop by and stay for a while. Something's happening at the club, I think."

"Party?"

"Nah. Meeting."

"Oh."

"You sure you're okay?" He came toward the bed and sat at the edge, reaching out to put his hand on my back.

"Yeah, I'm sure," I replied raggedly. It took everything in me not to move away from his touch.

I didn't want anyone to touch me. I just wanted Cam. Only Cam.

"I'll make some dinner. What do you want?"

"I'm not really hungry, bubba," I whispered back, my stomach clenching at the lie. "Actually, maybe some grilled cheese?"

"Damn, that sounds good. You want some tomato soup, too?"

"Sure." My eyes filled with tears at Leo's easygoing words. He knew something was wrong, but he wouldn't push it. That just wasn't his way.

If I wanted to talk, he'd listen. If I didn't, he'd leave it alone.

Leo patted my back a couple times, then stood from the bed and left without another word.

I rolled to my back and stared at the ceiling while I listened to my little brother clanging around the kitchen. I'd picked grilled cheese because it was one of the only things he could make well, even though I knew my kitchen would be completely trashed by the time he was finished.

I needed to get out of bed. Just push back the covers and swing my legs over the side. It should have been easy.

It wasn't.

I did it anyway.

I went to the bathroom and cleaned off my face, but there was nothing I could do about my swollen eyes. Leo would notice them. I rarely cared.

"It's alive!" Leo called out as I walked into the kitchen.

"Ha."

"Your dinner," he sang, setting down a plate of grilled cheese sandwich cut in half with a coffee mug of tomato soup sitting in the middle.

"Fancy," I teased. "Thank you."

"No prob."

I watched him hustle around the kitchen, grabbing his own food, and noticed that sure enough, he'd left a huge ass mess.

"Is that tomato soup on my cupboards?" I asked as I blew on my sandwich.

"Uh, yeah." He glanced at me sheepishly. "I wasn't paying attention and it started boiling and popping."

I snorted.

"It was an accident!"

"You're cleaning that shit up."

"I cooked!"

"Yeah, and you also trashed my kitchen."

"You suck."

"You're still cleaning it up."

We went silent as we ate, and I tried not to let my mind wander. I was eating a meal that I didn't have to cook and sitting next to one of my favorite people in the world. That's what I tried to focus on.

It wasn't until later, when I'd climbed back into bed, that my heart started racing again.

What was I going to do?

I wanted to get my shit together so badly.

I wanted to somehow change my feelings.

I wanted to not be so afraid.

Why the hell was I so scared? I'd never been afraid of anything in my life. I'd always felt safe, even when I knew things were happening that were out of my control. Even when we'd had to go on lockdown at the club because it was too dangerous to be on the outside.

Nothing had prepared me for the debilitating fear that seemed to be growing.

I turned it over and over in my mind, trying desperately to find the root of whatever was going on with me, but I couldn't figure it out.

I'd always planned on being with Cam—of having kids with him.

I'd just wanted a job first. I'd wanted to contribute. I wanted to get my fucking feet under me before we had kids.

I wasn't stupid. I knew intellectually that I was being completely irrational—but that didn't help. I could say everything would be fine a thousand times, I could make it my fucking mantra, but that didn't change the fact that I was terrified.

A few hours after I'd gotten back into bed, I heard the front door open again and Cam's voice mixing with Leo's in the living room.

My entire body deflated into the bed. I hadn't been sure that he would come home at all.

I couldn't blame him for that.

I wanted to tell him everything that was running through my head, but I didn't understand it myself. I knew what he would do—he'd wrap his arms around me and tell me everything would be okay. He'd expect me to trust him.

But I couldn't. Not with this.

I couldn't trust anyone, even myself.

I heard Leo leave and waited anxiously for Cam to come to me. Would he sleep in the spare room again?

I'd tried to let him be when he'd gotten home early that morning, but after an hour of lying there listening to his snores through the walls, I hadn't been able to stop myself from crawling into bed with him. Even though he was angry, I needed to be near him.

I loved him more than anything. I loved him more than myself.

"You awake?" he asked gruffly as he finally came into the room, pulling off his hoodie as he moved.

"Yeah. Everything okay at the club?" My voice was hoarse.

"Found out some new shit—nothin' for you to worry about. You get outta bed today?"

"I had dinner with Leo."

"You get outta bed?"

"Yeah, we ate in the kitchen."

"That's good, at least," he mumbled.

He stripped down to his boxers then glanced over at my eyes peeking over the blankets.

"Let's go," he ordered.

"What?"

"Need a shower. Not climbin' into bed with ya like that. You need one, too."

"*Thanks.*"

He ignored me. "Need to strip the bed, too. You got extras?"

"Cam?" I asked softly.

"Come on, let's go."

I watched him carefully as I crawled out of bed, and followed behind as he grabbed my hand and towed me into the bathroom.

It was the oddest shower ever. Somehow he helped me clean up while keeping his distance. He never touched me softly or spoke low into my ear, he just made sure I was washing and then left me to it, even though we had barely any space to move around each other.

By the time we climbed back out, I was shivering, and it wasn't from the cold.

"I'm sorry," I said softly, reaching out to touch his back as he brushed his teeth. "I won't do it."

"I know," he said stonily around his toothbrush, meeting my eyes in the mirror. "You wouldn't do that to me."

"No," I said, relieved. "I wouldn't."

When I tried to step in against him, he moved sideways to the door.

I watched Cam walk into the bedroom, but I didn't follow him.

He'd moved away from me. God, that hurt.

Everything hurt. Why did everything hurt?

I brushed my teeth and went into the bedroom slowly, relieved that he'd found some sheets and had thrown them on the bed, along with an extra blanket I'd had in the closet. He was already lying down on his side, his back to me.

With my hair back in a braid and a long t-shirt on, I crawled between the sheets, shivering. It might be summer, but we were in Oregon. The nights were still pretty chilly. I moved in against his back, and his entire body tensed.

"No, Trix," he said quietly, the words like a knife to my chest.

"What?" I breathed, snatching my hands away from his back.

He didn't turn to me, but his next words were very clear.

"You asked for my permission for an abortion. You're not doin' it. I'm happy as fuck about that. Don't mean I forgot you askin.' You don't want our kid—you obviously don't want me."

"Baby—"

"Got that barbeque tomorrow," he reminded me. "I gotta get up early and help my ma. Need to get some sleep."

I scooted away from him quickly and lay there staring at his back, the dim light in the room from the streetlights outside casting shadows on his Aces tattoo.

He didn't want me.

I was lying next to him, the weight on my chest so heavy I felt like I could die from it, and he didn't care.

My fear became so massive in that moment that I couldn't even move.

I didn't sleep the entire night, and because he wouldn't allow me to touch him, I watched and listened to him breathe until the sun rose the next morning. I think that was the only thing that kept me from completely losing my mind.

★ ★ ★

"Leavin'," Cam said as I sat at the kitchen table with a cup of coffee. "You shouldn't be drinkin' that."

I looked down at my cup and back up to the censure in his eyes, then nodded.

Okay. No coffee. I slid the cup away from me.

"Can you drive yourself or—"

"Yeah, it's fine."

"I can have Leo or Will come get you."

I noticed he didn't volunteer, but I didn't let my expression change.

"Nope, it's fine. I can drive. I need to stop by the store and get some stuff for a pasta salad, anyway. Maybe some wine."

"You can't have wine," he snapped.

"It's not for me." I took a deep breath and stood up, picking up my coffee mug and dumping it in the sink.

"I'll see you in a few hours."

He walked away without kissing me goodbye and I firmed my jaw against the urge to cry. I looked like shit after my sleepless night—I couldn't add more crying to my completely pale and drawn face. I already knew I was going to have to pull out my rarely used makeup and attempt to fix the circles around my eyes.

If I knew I could skip out of the barbeque, I would do it in a heartbeat—but it was Gram's birthday. I couldn't miss it, not without catching major shit for it. It's not like I would have missed it, anyway—Gram was getting up in years, and we had no idea how much longer we had with her. My problems could wait until tomorrow.

As long as no one knew, as long as I didn't have to field questions and endure congratulatory hugs—I could get through the day.

I moved slowly toward the shower and started getting ready. It was going to take me a while to make myself presentable.

★ ★ ★

"There's my pretty girl."

"Hey, Gramps," I smiled as my mom's dad pulled me into a hug, turning my head to the side so I wouldn't get a face full of his beard. "Where's Nan?"

"Went up north to visit Nix," Gramps said, grinning as he

smoothed his hand down my hair. He'd always grinned at me like that, like I was a miracle that surprised him each time he saw me. "Didn't she tell you the other day when you were at the house?"

"Oh, maybe," I answered uncomfortably. "I probably wasn't paying attention."

Gramps chuckled and pulled the bottles of white wine out of my hands. "Fancyin' up the joint, eh?"

"It's from the grocery store," I said dryly, reaching into my car to pull out the pasta salad I'd brought.

Gramps chuckled and ushered me into Casper and Farrah's house. Mick and Tommy jumped up off the couch as we crossed through the living room and Gramps shoved the wine bottles into Tommy's hands.

"Not for you," Gramps warned.

"Damn."

"I can take that for you," Mick said quietly, reaching out to take the bowl of salad from my hands.

"Thanks, Mick." The poor kid blushed and hurried away.

"Poor kid." Gramps chuckled.

I ignored him, but shook my head, moving toward the back door where I could hear people talking and laughing.

When we got outside, the entire family was there. We were all part of the club, both as members and families of members, but this small group was even tighter than that. With so much intermarrying going on, it was kind of hard not to naturally navigate toward certain people.

I made my way around, giving hugs and saying hello.

"You look pretty," my mom said happily as she searched my face. "Leo said you weren't feeling good yesterday?"

"Just tired with finals and everything," I answered, giving her a small smile.

"Don't have to worry about that shit anymore," my pop said gruffly, pulling me into his side. "My Little Warrior is a college graduate." His voice rose on the last sentence and the backyard was filled with claps and cheers.

"Not quite," I said lightly, tightening my arm around my pop's waist. "I haven't got my grades back yet."

"You did good," he replied with a nod, as if there was no question.

"You feeling okay?" Callie asked as she walked toward us.

"Leo has a big freaking mouth," I grumbled, making my pop give me a warning nudge. "Yeah, I'm fine. I was just tired after staying up studying for finals."

I glanced behind Callie and noticed Grease checking out her ass. Gross.

"You're all done now, though, right?"

"Yep. All done."

"That's awesome, kiddo. I'm getting a beer, anyone else want one?"

I shook my head as both my parents said yes, making all three turn to look at me. "Could you grab me a water?" I asked quickly. "It's hot as balls out here."

Callie and my mom laughed as my pop made a sound of protest.

"What?" I looked up at him. "Balls isn't a bad word. Balls. Ballllls."

"I'll get my own beer," Pop grumbled, walking away.

"Give your pop a break, huh?" Mom said, reaching over to pull at my hair as she followed my dad to the coolers on the back porch.

"You think they'll get me a water?" I asked Callie.

"They sure as hell won't remember to grab my beer," she said jokingly as she followed them.

I stood by myself for a second, taking deep breaths as I watched the people in the yard. When my eyes met Vera's, I started toward her.

She was sitting at a picnic table with Gram and Slider, but the moment I reached her, she stood up to give me a hug.

"I'm not going to do it," I whispered shakily in her ear.

"I didn't think you would, baby girl."

"I did."

"I know."

She pulled away and gently cupped my cheeks, giving me a light kiss on the nose.

"I get one of those?" Slider asked, standing up beside us.

"Hey, Uncle," I said with a laugh, leaning over to hug him, too.

When he let me go, I turned to Gram. "Having a good birthday?" I asked, moving around so I could sit next to her. As I took my seat, my eyes accidentally caught Cam's across the yard, but I quickly looked away.

If I wanted to make it through the day, I couldn't think about how things were between us.

"Pretty good, now that you're here," she said, reaching over to pat my hand.

"I bet you say that to all the grandkids," I teased, leaning forward to brace my elbows on the table and my chin in my hands.

"Congratulations," she said softly, her lips tilting up just barely at the sides.

I jerked backward and glanced over at Cam again. He wasn't looking at me.

"What?" my voice came out slightly panicked.

"On your graduation," she clarified.

"Oh, right. Thanks!" My enthusiasm was so forced that she raised one eyebrow.

"Meat's done," Casper called out from the commercial sized barbeque he was grilling on.

"I better go help bring out the food," I said awkwardly, hopping up out of my seat.

All the kids came running as we piled food on the picnic table, and before long, we were spread out across the yard, eating and joking. I took a seat near my parents in the grass, grabbing the bottle of water my pop had been carrying around for me.

"You happy to be done?" he asked quietly, glancing at my mom to make sure she had everything she needed. He handed her his napkin when she started searching for one, her hands covered in barbeque sauce.

I smiled at their interaction. He always did stuff like that. She did, too. *Oh, you forgot to grab some corn on the cob? You can have mine. I didn't really want it, anyway. You forgot your napkin? Don't get up, I have one.*

"Yeah, I'm kind of worried I haven't found a job, though," I replied, stiffening as Cam came and dropped down beside me.

"Thought you got offered one in Portland?"

"She's not taking it," Cam butt in, making my hands clench on the flimsy paper plate I was holding.

"That right?" Pop asked me.

"I didn't really want to move so far north," I answered, not meeting his eyes.

Pop made a sound in his throat, but I wasn't sure if it was acceptance or irritation.

"I'll find something down here," I said with false cheer. "I just need to get my resume out."

"You ask Slider?"

"For what? The club?"

"Knows a lot of people in Eugene," he reminded me.

I nodded. Asking Slider was a good idea. He knew everyone, though I wasn't sure how. I also wasn't sure if I wanted to work with someone who had ties to the club—that was asking for a fucking audit every year.

We went quiet as we ate, and a little while later, we all surrounded the table where Gram was sitting to sing happy birthday.

It was a good day. I loved spending time with my family, I always had. I played horseshoes with Will, who was acting like a huge weight had been lifted off his shoulders since the last time I'd seen him, helped the little girls do their hair up princess style, helped Farrah clean up the mess in the backyard and brought beer after beer to Slider and my gramps.

It was so normal after the past few days, such a relief.

Cam kept his distance for the most part, barely talking to me. I knew my parents were watching us closely, wondering what the hell was going on, but they never said anything.

It wasn't until a couple hours later, when everyone was winding down and I was getting ready to leave, that Cam cornered me.

"Let's make an announcement," he said gruffly, coming up behind me as I picked up some empty soda cans off the edge of the porch.

"No," I replied sharply. I couldn't handle that today. I was barely hanging on, and I didn't know how I could even function if I had to discuss the baby with anyone. My hands had begun to shake when I spoke to Vera, so there was no way I'd be able to speak to my parents about it.

"Not askin' you, Trix," Cam snapped back.

"Fuck off," I said tonelessly, stepping away from him before stomping up the porch stairs.

"Trix, you don't stop walking away from me, I'm gonna paddle your ass!"

I spun to look at him in disbelief, and for just a second, his eyes looked pained. Then his entire face hardened.

"*Fuck off*, Cam!" I yelled back, carrying the empties into the house.

I heard him come in behind me, but I didn't turn around as I rinsed the cans and dumped them into the recycling container.

"What, you still lookin' for a way out?" he asked meanly, coming to a stop just feet from me. "Thinkin' if you don't tell anyone, you could still get that abortion you wanted?"

"I told you I wasn't going to do it," I hissed, turning to face him.

"Can't you just let me wrap my fucking head around it before we have to tell people?"

"Why?"

"Because I don't want to say anything yet."

"Yeah, you made that really fuckin' clear."

"Is this how it's going to be? You take shots at me, and what, I just have to sit back and take it? You've never once looked at this from my point of view!"

"Yeah, that's gonna happen," he replied nastily. "Let me try and understand why you'd want to get rid of my kid."

My jaw clenched and I wrapped my arms around my waist. He'd never see it. The man who had always known everything about me couldn't see past his own shit to notice that I was crumbling. There wasn't anything I could do. He wasn't going to forgive me.

"I'm gonna go home," I finally said, my eyes watering. "I'll see you there later… or not."

I turned and grabbed the bowl I'd brought with me and moved toward the front of the house, Cam's silence beating at me like a sledgehammer.

He went to the back door and stepped outside as I was grabbing the sweatshirt I'd worn this morning and walking toward the front.

When I got to the screen door, I stopped.

Everything stopped.

The sound of metal on metal met my ears and then a solid *thunk*. Then again. Then again.

I'd heard that before.

"Someone's here! Whose car is that?"

"I'm going to drop you out the window."

"You start running toward the clubhouse."

"You DO NOT stop."

I stumbled away from the door, trying to shake the confusion from my head.

"*I don't care what you see.*"

"*You absolutely do not stop until you get to Papa, Gramps or Vera.*"

"*Do you understand?*"

"*Do you understand?*"

"*Do you understand?*"

"*Run, baby. GO!*"

I spun on my heel and ran for the back door without understanding why I was doing it. I needed him.

Papa.

I needed Papa.

I hit the back door at a run.

I saw him as soon as I hit the porch.

Oh, God. There he was.

"Papa!" I screamed, diving for him.

Chapter 13

CAMERON

It all happened so fast that later, I would wonder if the sequence of events I remembered got somehow jumbled in my memory. I wished I could forget it.

Casper announced that he'd knocked Farrah up again, a smug smile on his face, and I couldn't keep our news in any longer. My eyes met Dragon's as I told them Trix was pregnant, too, then watched as he stomped toward me. My parents were a couple feet away, sitting in a rocking chair, and Brenna was chasing after her man to calm him down when the sliding glass door behind me slammed open.

I didn't even have time to turn.

Trix's shoulder hit me hard as she rushed past and I didn't have a chance to grab her before she was flying off the porch, hitting Dragon's chest as she screamed for him.

Her voice was so goddamn high-pitched that it was almost a screech, and thank God he braced himself, because she hit him hard, wrapping her body around his torso.

The backyard went completely silent aside from the radio playing softly in the kitchen window.

Then everything seemed to happen at once.

Slider pushed Lily onto Gram's lap as he and Poet rose from the table, while Dragon's eyes widened at whatever Trix was murmuring over and over again against his neck.

Will glanced at his brothers, who'd been jostling each other near the horseshoe pit, and Leo pushed past where Cecilia was standing near the base of the oak tree in the backyard, his face full of confusion.

And then—

Fuck.

Men came around the sides of the house. There were only three of them. Christ. Only three.

But it felt like so much more.

We weren't prepared.

We were fucking sitting ducks.

The first shot wasn't loud. Maybe that's why it took us a second to realize what was happening. Maybe not.

It didn't really matter.

They were indiscriminate.

I pulled my piece as Slider and Poet flipped the picnic table on its side, shielding Lily, Gram and Vera behind the wide, wood planks. Dragon shoved Trix at me as I fired at the man on my right, missing him as Trix's shaking body hit me. I threw her down behind me, against the wall of the house, as my ma dropped to the floor, crawling up beside her. Casper fired at the man on the right and took him down, but we couldn't get a clear sight on the fuckers on the left because of the angle of the house.

Mick went down first. Christ. He'd pushed Tommy behind him as they tried to find some cover, but they hadn't been goddamn fast enough. I wasn't sure if Tommy was hit, but he was beneath his younger brother, screaming and crying as Mick's huge, limp body refused to move.

Grease scooped Rose up and practically threw her to Cecilia behind the tree, and I could just barely make out my sister's feet as they tried to hide. That fucking tree wasn't big enough.

Will was shooting back, and I watched as his body jerked, but he didn't go down.

Poet and Slider were firing back from their perch in front of the table, but they barely got a shot off before Slider went down. The picnic table was shredded as one of the men swung his weapon in a long arc.

I ran toward the edge of the porch as Grease roared, and I caught sight of Callie falling to her knees in the yard.

One of the men went down, his weapon spraying indiscriminately through the carnage.

"Leo!" Trix screamed as my ma wrapped her arms and legs around Trix's body, forcing her back against the porch behind me.

Then the last man fell.

And all around me, all I could hear was screaming.

"You alright?" I asked Trix as I ran to her. She nodded vaguely, staring out into the yard.

"Okay, Ladybug?" Casper demanded. "Call nine-one-one."

We jumped off the side of the porch and paused.

I didn't know who to go to first.

Cecilia stumbled around the tree, her face so white it was nearly blue, carrying Rose, whose feet nearly reached the ground. Her hand was grasping the back of Rose's head to hide her face, but both looked unhurt. She stumbled forward and then stopped, as if she didn't know where to go.

"Lily," Casper murmured, running toward the mangled picnic table.

"Sheets, Ma!" I yelled at her as I raced toward Callie. She was on her back in the middle of the yard, Will trying to stem the blood pouring from her chest with his t-shirt.

I dropped my cut in the dirt and ripped my shirt off my head as I went, adding it to the blood soaked one under his hands. "You got this?" I asked frantically as I dropped down beside them.

"Yeah," he choked out, tears running down his face. "Micky."

I turned toward where Grease was bent over his sons and watched as the big man sobbed, picking Mick's limp body up off the ground and staggering to his feet.

Tommy stood shell-shocked behind him, his face completely blank.

Grease came toward us and fell to his knees, laying Mick beside his mother, who was unconscious, but thankfully, still alive.

Cecilia and Rose met my ma on the porch, and she pushed them toward Trix before dropping the phone and running down the stairs toward Casper, who was screaming for help.

I ran.

Fuck, I ran so fast I barely felt my feet hit the ground.

Lily.

As I circled around the back of the picnic table, I couldn't breathe.

Vera and Gram's bodies were in a heap, and beneath that heap was Lily. She was completely silent, and her eyes were wide and unblinking.

"Lily? Baby?" Casper asked frantically, pushing Vera and Gram's bodies off of her. They were gone. Completely ripped apart by bullets.

"Daddy? Where are you?" Lily asked in confusion, her arms waving around in front of her.

"Right here, baby. I'm right here."

Farrah made a mournful noise in the back of her throat as Casper gingerly picked Lily up out of the gore.

"I can't see you," Lily said dazedly.

"I'm holding you, Lilybug," Casper said gently, standing from the ground with my baby sister in his arms. "You're alright. Daddy's got you."

I glanced around me and noticed Poet sitting silently beside Slider's body, wrapping his t-shirt around his thigh, tying it in a tight knot.

"Shit," I hissed, running for him.

"I'm alright, boyo," he said achingly. "I'm alright. Go to my daughter."

I turned slowly, my stomach hollow, and caught sight of Brenna and Dragon bent over Leo.

As I got closer to them, I noticed they'd turned Leo on his side as he choked.

"You're okay, son," Dragon said gruffly, his hands steady on Leo's head as Brenna used her body to brace him. "Just breathe. You're alright."

Brenna was in her bra, and her shirt was wrapped around Leo's face as he jerked and tried to pull away.

"Calm down, baby," Brenna pleaded, her voice shaking. "You're okay, Leo. Help is coming, son."

Leo jerked hard and I caught a glimpse of his mangled face, the skin of his cheek almost completely severed from his jaw.

"I'll hold him," I said quickly, my hands shaking as I fell to my knees beside Brenna. "You go by his head."

We switched positions as I heard multiple sirens in the distance.

"Hear that, little brother?" I asked, leaning down near Leo's ruined face. "Cavalry is almost here."

Leo choked as he tried to reply, then without warning, passed out completely.

I leaned back on my heels and looked around the backyard. Jesus.

"Hulk!" Poet yelled, getting my attention. He was still sitting on the ground beside Slider.

I stood up and jogged toward him, noticing the way his face had paled in the last few minutes once the adrenaline began to wear off.

"Will's out on parole," Poet said sharply, glancing over to where Will and Grease were bent over Callie. "Get his piece, wipe it down, bring it to me."

I nodded once and ran to Will.

"Gun, brother," I told him quietly, reaching out.

His eyes didn't leave his mom as he handed it to me.

I ran back to Poet and dropped the gun in his lap. "Don't have nothin' to wipe it down with," I murmured.

Before I could say anything else, he was unwinding his shirt from the wound on his leg so he could use it to wipe Will's prints off the weapon.

"The fuck are you doin'?" I asked incredulously.

"I got this—you go 'round the house. Make sure we're all clear. Fuck. Bullets stopped flyin' and we started panickin.' Stupid."

I stood from my crouch and glanced toward the back porch to check on my girl. Cecilia, Rose and Trix sat huddled together in a little group, the older two watching the scene before them in horror as they shielded Rose with their bodies.

How the hell had this happened?

I jogged around the side of the yard and hit the left side of the house, finding the shooter Casper had taken out less than a foot from the corner of the porch. Casper had got him once in the neck and twice in the chest.

I moved silently around the front of the house and found a light blue pickup and two street bikes parked haphazardly behind the rest of the cars in the gravel driveway and cursed. Between the radio and everyone talking and laughing and yelling over each other, we hadn't even heard the two crotch rockets pull up. It was insane.

When I hit the far side of the house, I could see ambulances and multiple police cars flying up the driveway, and I knew I had just seconds to make sure the men were dead before we were fucking overrun. I stopped abruptly when the bodies came into view.

Because there weren't two.

There were three.

And the third was so fucking beat up, I had a hard time recognizing him.

"Hulk," he groaned, reaching out a hand that was still clutching a pistol. "Help."

I glanced at the men a few feet away. One of them was lying in a huge pool of blood in the packed dirt and the other was facedown, a bullet hole in the back of his head.

"Woody," I said, sighing as I dropped to my knees beside him. "Put it down, bud."

His fingers slowly loosened around the grip of the pistol.

"The fuck?" I asked, taking in his wounds.

It looked like he'd been sliced with a knife up and down his arms and his face was so swollen I had no idea how he was awake and talking. He also had matching gunshot wounds in each of his shoulders. I wasn't even sure how he was still moving his arms.

"Caught me last night," he mumbled, tears rolling down the sides of his face. "Didn't help 'em. Swear. Didn't help 'em."

"I know, bud," I soothed, glancing behind me as the vehicles started parking and doors started slamming. "You don't know anything, alright? Men picked you up, beat you up, dragged you here. That's all you know, right?"

"All I know," he said in agreement.

I'd just set my piece on the ground when two officers came around the side of the house.

"Hands where we can see them!" one of the cops yelled as I lifted my arms up by my head.

"I'm unarmed. Shooters are down," I yelled back.

I'd never in my life been so happy to see a fucking cop.

They swarmed into the yard like locusts, feeding off our misery. I got it. I understood that taking care of multiple gunshot victims was probably both incredibly hard and a rush like nothing else.

I was just glad they were good at what they did.

The cops were on us, asking questions and trying to work out some sort of timeline, but those of us who weren't hurt just watched anxiously as the paramedics did their thing. Farrah must have given a pretty clear account of what had happened when she'd called, because there were more than enough ambulances in the driveway. Within ten minutes, most of them had sped off toward hospitals, leaving a few of us sitting on the back porch, surrounded by blood and body bags.

"What happened here?" a plain-clothes cop asked me. He was new. He hadn't been there in the beginning as they'd patted us down.

"Having a barbeque," I told him gruffly. "Men came around the house, started shootin'."

"And you returned fire, correct?" he asked, bracing his hands on his hips.

"Tried to." I laughed humorlessly and gripped the back of my neck. "Don't think I hit nothin.' Too much happenin' at once."

I glanced at Trix, who was completely still, sitting in a rocking chair to my left.

"You have any idea why someone would target your family?" His voice was grating, and his insinuation clear.

"None at all," I told him flatly. "I need to get to the hospital."

"We're going to have more questions," he warned.

"Yeah, I figured."

It wasn't my first rodeo. I'd been held, booked and questioned so many times I could do that shit in my sleep.

"One last thing," the cop said before he turned to walk away. "Why would someone target Mark Eastwood?"

"No idea."

The cop walked away and I turned toward Tommy and the girls.

"Cam?" Cecilia asked quietly, her face swollen and blotchy from crying. "Why was he talking about Mark?"

I stared at her for a minute, wondering what was going through her head, but like always, I didn't have a fucking clue. When she was a baby, she was easy to read, but the older she got, the more mysterious my sister became.

"He was here," I said slowly.

Dad had ordered her to stay put, and for once, she'd done as she was told. She hadn't been around the side of the house, or even back into the yard. She'd stayed right there on the porch with Rose, Trix and now, Tommy. Waiting and watching.

"What?" she whispered, her eyes widening as they filled with tears. "No, he wasn't. He was—"

"You got somethin' to tell me?" I snapped, watching her closely.

"It wasn't him, Cam," she cried. "It wasn't him. He's on club property. They couldn't get to him there. It wasn't him."

"What the fuck are you talking about?" I hissed. We'd been looking for that boy for weeks.

"He was staying at the back of the property," she confessed softly. "He had a tent and everything."

I closed my eyes and dropped my head forward, squeezing the bridge of my nose with my fingertips. *Goddammit.* They'd taken him right off club grounds.

That fucking back entrance we'd ignored for years had been breached.

"He was here," I repeated, opening my eyes again. "Got no clue what the fuck you've been up to, but I don't have time for your shit right now."

Cecilia winced and wiped her palms over her eyes, a gesture that reminded me how young she still was.

I glanced to the side and went silent as a couple paramedics started picking up the body bags and putting them inside the back of an ambulance. One by one, they took them away.

"Let's go," I finally called out to the others. We no longer had reason to stay at the house. "We need to get to the hospital."

Chapter 14

TRIX

MY NECK SNAPPED back and forth as he shook me, but I didn't make a sound. He didn't like it when I was noisy, so I was very, very careful to stay quiet. He was saying something about toothpaste, but I couldn't understand him.

Where was my mama?

I tried really hard not to look at his angry eyes as he talked to me in the mean voice, and eventually my eyes wandered to the far side of the room, where my door was.

Mama. There she was.

I tried to stop the whimper. I kept my mouth sealed shut, but somehow the sound came out my nose. Oh, no. He didn't like it when I was noisy. I peed my pants like a little baby as my mama ran into the room.

"Ma'am, are you hurt anywhere?" the EMT asked, pulling me into the present as he crouched down in front of me. "Ma'am?"

"I'm fine," I replied hoarsely, unable to meet his eyes.

Chapter 15

Cameron

I GRABBED TRIX'S hand and pulled it to my chest as soon as we'd climbed into her car. She was okay. Thank fuck. If they'd hit only a few minutes earlier, she would've been in the yard, directly in their line of sight. I swallowed hard and kissed her fingertips, meeting her eyes for just a second before turning on the car.

Her fingers twitched, then straightened, rubbing softly over my cheek for just a moment. She was there, healthy and safe. I couldn't consider what-ifs. We had too many absolutes to deal with first.

Rose sat in Tommy's lap the entire way to the hospital, both of them completely silent. I didn't have the heart to make her buckle up. The poor kids were wrecked, and Cecilia wasn't doing much better.

I barely had the headspace to comfort them at all.

I think we were all still in a state of shock. None of us knew what we should be doing.

By the time we got to the hospital, it was already filled with club members.

As soon as we'd hit the waiting room, Grease, Casper and Dragon rushed over to meet us.

"You guys okay?" Grease asked gruffly, grabbing Tommy by the scruff of the neck and Rose by the back of her head, pulling them into his body. Tommy started to sob then, breaking his silence for the first time since Grease had pulled Mick off of him. "Thanks for taking care of them, Cam," he said softly.

I smiled a little and looked away. He hadn't called me Cam in years. There hadn't been much time when they were loading Callie into the ambulance, and I was glad he trusted me enough to leave them with me.

"Ma's with Lily," Casper said, wrapping his arms around CeeCee. "They're not sure what's wrong with her eyes yet."

I nodded and glanced over to Dragon, who was holding Trix's face against his neck. As I watched her, she began to tremble slightly, and his other arm came up to pull her more securely against him.

"Stitchin' Leo up now," Dragon murmured. "Plastic surgeon's workin' on him, but he's still gonna have a fuckin' gnarly scar. They said there might be some nerve damage. Coupla inches to the left—" He cleared his throat and shrugged one shoulder. "He'll be fine."

"That's good news," I replied. I glanced around the waiting room, taking in the brothers and old ladies filling up the space. "Where's Will?"

"Surgery," Casper answered. "Callie, too."

"What?"

"He was hit twice. Didn't even slow the crazy motherfucker down."

"Those steroids musta been good for somethin'," Dragon joked darkly.

"Jesus. Poet, too?" I noticed he was also absent.

"Nah, they dug his out. Admitted him, though. Should be okay. Amy and Nix are in with him."

"They're here already?" I asked in surprise.

"Must've fuckin' flew on that crotch rocket of his."

I nodded. Then I nodded again.

The pleasantries, if you could even call them that, were out of the way. I had no clue what to say.

"Why don't you go sit with Tommy—" Casper started to say to

CeeCee.

"What about Mark?" she asked, lifting her head. "Where's Mark?"

"Eastwood?" Casper asked in surprise, his voice carrying.

Both Grease and Dragon turned to look.

"Cam said he was there. Where is he?"

"What's it to you?"

"He's my friend. He—"

"Probably not a good time," I cut in, with a shake of my head.

"He's around here somewhere," Dragon said, watching CeeCee. "Patchin' him up. His mom's on her way."

"He's okay?" Cecilia asked, her mouth trembling as she reached up to cover it with both hands. "Oh, God," she whispered in relief.

"Your sister is in there fuckin' blind, your aunt and cousin are in surgery to take bullets outta 'em, and you're askin' about some fuckin' kid?" I snapped, finally at the end of my patience. What the fuck was her deal?

"Cam," Casper scolded.

"Ma's with Lily," Cecilia hissed.

"So that means you just don't give a shit? Your grandmother is dead, Cecilia. Slider and Vera and Micky are fucking dead."

"Cameron!" Casper said sharply, cutting me off.

"I'm done," I said in frustration, raising my hands as I took a step backward.

"We're all worried, kid," Dragon said, pulling my attention to him and Trix. "Ain't nothin' to do *but* worry. Cut your sister some slack."

★ ★ ★

A FEW HOURS later, Will was out of surgery, but Callie was still back in the bowels of the hospital, where they tried to fix the gaping hole in her chest.

We were all on edge.

Lily still couldn't see and they had no idea why. They thought she must have hit her head somehow, even though she seemed fine from the outside. It was taking a long ass time for them to do brain scans and whatever other shit they had to do, so we just waited.

Rose had fallen asleep at some point and was spread out on a couch in the surgical waiting room where we'd ended up. Lily and Ma were in another part of the hospital, so Casper, Cecilia and I were splitting our time between the different floors, pacing and drinking coffee.

Lily got really agitated if there were too many of us in the room, so we'd decided to let Ma stay with her. Dad went in a couple of times an hour, just to give her a kiss and remind her he was there, but she was so fucking out of it that I wasn't sure how much she'd remember.

I was going nuts. Seriously losing my shit.

I wasn't real patient on a good day, but that night, I was like a bomb waiting to detonate. So much fucking waiting. Waiting on Callie. Waiting on Lily. Waiting to find out if Leo was going to be able to move the left side of his face. Waiting for Poet to wake up so we could have a meeting and figure out what the fuck we were going to do.

Trix wasn't talking to me. She wasn't talking to anyone.

I knew that she and I had a lot of shit to deal with, but fuck if any of that mattered anymore. I just wanted her with me. I wanted to smell her and feel her skin and hear her voice. I needed her—but she wasn't moving more than a foot away from her pop. Hell, he'd gone to the bathroom and she'd waited outside the door for him. Every time I tried to sit with her or talk to her, she gave me the bare minimum of her attention, instead watching Dragon move around the room like she was afraid to let him out of her sight.

She didn't need me. She was making that perfectly clear.

I'd just sat down on the floor in a corner of the waiting room when a doctor came out of the back hallway, pulling off his surgical cap.

"Family of Callie Hawthorne?" he asked.

Shit, I'd forgotten that she'd married Grease. I had no idea why they hadn't had a wedding, but they'd obviously made it legal if her last name was Hawthorne.

Grease strode to the doctor and they spoke quietly for a few moments before the doctor turned and walked away.

"She's good," Grease announced hoarsely, meeting Tommy's eyes across the room. "Puttin' her in the recovery room now. We can see her in a coupla hours."

Casper's ass hit the floor next to me at Grease's words. He fell so hard it was as if his legs could no longer hold him upright.

"Thank fuck," he said on a shudder, drawing his knees up and bracing his elbows on them, his head bowed low.

I reached over and set my hand on his back as he sniffed hard, keeping his head low.

"She'll be alright, Dad," I said softly.

"My sister," he whispered. That was all he said, but there really wasn't anything else to say. He'd been hit hard that day, no doubt about it.

We'd lost four people. Four people, and all of them were related to Casper by marriage or blood. Father-in-law, mother-in-law, grandmother and nephew.

My entire family could have been wiped out. Again.

I squeezed my eyes tight and beat back the urge to weep. I didn't have time for that. I didn't have time to mourn.

Not yet.

We had people still fighting. We still had things that needed to be done, police reports to give, revenge to mete out. I couldn't let myself think of the people we'd lost.

"Better go give Farrah the news," Casper finally said, reaching over to pat my knee. "You're a good boy."

"I'm fuckin' twice your size," I scoffed, shaking my head.

His red eyes met mine and he gave me a small smile as he reached up and dragged his hand over my head. "You might be a fuckin' giant, but you'll always be my boy." He nodded twice and climbed to his feet as I tried to keep my shit together.

I may have had a shitty start in life, but I'd gotten really fucking lucky with Casper and Farrah.

My eyes went to Trix and I watched as Dragon looked at his phone and then said something quietly to her, making her nod her head. I climbed to my feet as they started walking down the hall.

"Hey," I said quietly, getting their attention.

"Gonna go down and see Leo," Dragon said gruffly. "Bren says he's awake."

I looked to Trix and met her nervous eyes. "You want me to go with you?" I asked her gently.

It was killing me to watch her from a distance. She looked so fucking fragile, so different from the girl I'd watched grow up. I wanted to pick her up and carry her out of that goddamn hospital. Take her away from all of it so I could find out what was going on in that head of hers.

"That's okay," she replied softly. "I'll be back in a little while, alright?"

I clenched my jaw against the need to argue.

Dragon snapped his head to the side, cracking his neck. Then he wrapped an arm around Trix's shoulder and gave me a pitying look.

It pissed me off.

"Yeah, alright," I mumbled, taking a step back so they could pass me.

I watched them walk down the hall until they reached the elevator doors.

"You were young when she and Brenna showed up," Grease said, coming up behind me.

"Yeah." I scratched a hand over my jaw, where my five o'clock shadow was bugging the shit out of me.

"She was quiet then," he said, nodding toward the elevator Trix and Dragon were stepping into. "Scary quiet."

I sighed, my stomach twisting.

"Seen a lot of shit. Been around a lotta kids with shitty backgrounds. But that little girl was a fuckin' mystery, man. Took to Dragon straight off, knew who he was, trusted him from the first. The rest of us? Hell, we may as well have been the monsters hiding under her bed."

"You got a point?" I snapped, instantly regretting it. He didn't deserve my shit. Not then.

"Yeah, I got a point." He shook his head. "You know what happened with my Callie?"

"A bit."

"Let's sit," he said, gesturing to a couple of chairs away from the rest of the group. We sat down and Grease leaned forward to rest his elbows on his knees, picking at the blood around his fingernails.

I looked at my hands. They weren't much better. Shit.

"Callie's parents were killed, fuckin' gunned down in their house." He looked at me to make sure I was following. "My woman was there, hidin' in a damn storage space. Heard everything." He swallowed hard. "She was like a fuckin' wild animal when I found her, sweaty, covered in piss."

He went silent for a long time, his eyes vacant on the floor in front of him.

"She seemed to get better, though. Had to move her north, set her up in a place, visited when I could. Took a while, but she started livin,' makin' friends with Farrah, goin' to school. Hell, she had Will up there while I was locked up. Kept shit straight and waited for me."

"Didn't know that," I murmured, rubbing at my hands.

"Yeah. Wasn't until somethin' happened that it all came up to fuck us." He looked at me. "She got attacked, had to kill my brother—blood, not club—and when I found her that time?" He shook his head. "She was gone, brother. Nothin' there. Found her beat to shit, holding one of Farrah's pistols in one hand and Will in the other. Couldn't reach her. She'd been okay, far as I knew, might've been okay forever, but that attack brought everything back for her. Spent weeks in the hospital, spent about a year after that gettin' her head on straight before she'd even see me."

"Musta been hard," I said softly.

"You tell me, brother. How you feelin' right now?"

His words knocked me back in my chair.

"Trix ain't Callie. Personalities couldn't be more different, but fuck me if she ain't got that same look in her eyes."

I lifted a hand to my face and dug my fingers into my eye sockets. All I could hear in my head was Trix screaming for her papa.

★ ★ ★

"Keepin' Lily here," Casper told me quietly around four in the morning, his eyes sunken and dark. "I'm gonna take CeeCee to a hotel for the night."

They couldn't go home. I didn't know how any of us would go back there. Fuck.

"Okay," I said with a nod, glancing over to see my little sister curled up in a chair. She looked about ten years old and my throat caught.

We'd moved out of the surgery waiting area once Callie had been put in her own room, and the new space was a lot smaller than where we'd been. Samson and his old lady had taken Tommy and Rose back to the clubhouse earlier to sleep in Grease's room. The kids had a hard time leaving with the long-haired man and his woman, but eventually they'd relented. All the adults from our family were staying at the hospital and they'd needed any sleep they could get.

"Everybody's outta the woods, need to get the kids to bed," he said tiredly. "You taking Trix home?"

"We know what the fuck's goin' on?" I asked. "Don't wanna take her home to more fuckin' fireworks."

"Poet's been on the phone for the last four hours. Pissin' off nurses and makin' a nuisance of himself. Got brothers from all over congregating in Eugene. Not sure what Poet's found out, but according to him, shit's mostly handled."

"'Mostly' don't exactly give me the warm fuzzies."

"Then stay at the clubhouse. You think I'd send ya home if I thought there was a problem?" he asked incredulously. "Get your fuckin' head on straight, Cameron."

"Yeah, I hear you," I mumbled, getting to my feet. "Sorry."

I made my way over to where Dragon and Trix were resting on a couch.

"Time to go, Sweetbea," I said gently, reaching under her back and thighs so I could pick her up.

I made eye contact with Dragon briefly to make sure he wasn't going to try and stop me, but all he did was give me a slight nod.

"Cam?" Trix asked sleepily as she wrapped her arms around my neck and pressed her face into my throat.

"Yeah, Bea." I swallowed hard as her body relaxed against mine for the first time that night. "I've got you, baby."

I took her straight to the clubhouse, nodding to the increased security at the gates as we pulled in. As they locked the rolling barbed wire fence behind us, I relaxed slightly. It felt really fucking good to be in a place where I knew nothing could touch her.

"You get that back gate checked out?" I asked Samson quietly as I carried Trix's still sleeping form past the bar where he was sitting in the main room of the clubhouse.

"Yup. Put a few boys out there. Found Woody's shit. Left it alone."

"Thanks, brother."

"Yup."

I kept moving through the room and into the back hallway.

When we reached my room, I didn't even bother with the lights. I walked straight to the bed and laid Trix down gently, climbing in beside her fully clothed.

I fell asleep still covered in dried blood, wearing nothing but my cut, jeans and boots.

Chapter 16

TRIX

I WOKE WITH a silent gasp and lay completely still as I took inventory of the room I was in.

Sunlight was pouring through the long, narrow window near the ceiling, and the sound of Cam's snores filled the room.

We were at the clubhouse. My body relaxed against the scratchy green army blanket we were lying on and I turned my head slowly to look at Cam. His mouth was open slightly, his face completely relaxed beneath a scruffy beard.

There was a smear of blood on his neck and a few more down the arm that was wrapped around my torso.

I swallowed hard at the nausea that threatened, looking toward the water-damaged ceiling.

Oh, God.

Everything from the day before came back to me in a flash, the scenes in my head bombarding me, one after another. I could barely breathe.

I'd gone screaming to my pop, babbling incoherently instead of telling him there were people at the house.

I'd never forgive myself for that.

What if I'd told him instantly that there were men in the front yard? What if I'd warned them?

Shame burned so hot in my belly that my body curled inward.

I gingerly grasped Cam's arm and moved it off me. I needed to get out of there. I needed to hide. I didn't want anyone to see me. I couldn't bear to look at anyone, knowing what I'd done.

I was scooting down the bed so I could crawl away when Cam's hand shot out, stopping my movements.

"Bea?" he asked roughly, his eyes still closed.

Then they opened widely, and he was frantically jerking me back up the bed.

"You okay?" he asked, ripping my shirt over my head before I could protest.

His hands ran over my torso, sliding up my belly and down each arm. Then his fingers were at my shorts, dragging them and my panties down my legs. My flip-flops had fallen to the edge of the bed at some point and he brushed them off with an impatient swipe.

"Oh, God," he mumbled, his fingers anxiously searching for any injuries. "Oh, God."

His voice was so agonized, my entire body locked up. I couldn't even respond to his words or reassure him as he rolled me to my side so he could check my back.

"Bellatrix," he groaned, burying his face between my breasts. His hands hurriedly tore at my bra straps, pulling my bra down my chest so he could feel the skin of my breasts against his face.

Tears ran down my face as I timidly raised my hands, wrapping them around the back of his head.

"You're okay," he breathed against my skin, one hand smoothing down my belly to right below my belly button. "Oh, God."

A broken sob tore out of my throat as he shuddered.

"You're okay," he repeated over and over, keeping his face against me as he tore off his cut and threw it off the bed.

He raised his head and his pupils were so huge they almost eclipsed the blue of his eyes.

With a moan, his lips met mine. He kissed me harshly, pushing his tongue into my mouth in desperation, his hands coming up to frame my face tenderly.

"I love you," he mumbled against my lips, "I love you."

His lips never left me as he dragged them down my cheek to the hollow place beneath my jaw. He moved to my shoulder, my collarbone, my breasts, my sternum, and the place beneath my bellybutton, before tracing his way back up again. His fingers pushed and pulled, squeezing my ribs between his hands before moving to grip my hips.

"Cam," I wheezed, trying to drag breath into my lungs as I pulled him upward so I could press my mouth against his again.

Then it was me pulling and pressing my hands against him frantically, tracing his ribs and belly and back with my fingers. I ripped at the button on his jeans, and he reached one hand down to help me shove them down his hips.

Then in one swift move, he was inside me.

Our first time without anything between us.

"Jesus," he sobbed. "Fuck, fuck, *fuck*."

My chest heaved as he slid back and forth, his arms coming up to wrap around the sides of my head.

Cam's left hand smoothed down my side to my thigh and he froze.

"Cam?" My voice wobbled.

His forehead hit my shoulder and I felt warm, wet liquid drip into the hollow of my collarbone.

Then he was up, pulling out of me and flipping my body facedown on the bed.

His entire body wrapped around me as he tilted my hips up and slid back inside.

"You're okay," he murmured against my shoulder, my hair catching in the scruff on his face. "I've got you, I've got you."

His thighs bracketed mine, his chest pressed to my back as one arm wrapped across my chest and the other settled on the bed, bracing him above me.

I reached back and gripped his head, holding his face against me as he thrust hard, over and over again. Tears leaked unchecked from my eyes as my body wound tighter and tighter, finally falling into a long, rolling orgasm as his body protected mine from the outside world.

"I love you," I whispered, making his entire body heave with a sob.

★ ★ ★

"Your brother's comin' home," Cam told me quietly as I sat on one of the couches in the main room of the clubhouse a few days later. "You wanna go see him?"

"No," I replied, not looking up from the book I was reading. My nan had brought it to me the day before when she'd caught me staring off into space.

We were all staying at the clubhouse for the time being. Some of the members had chosen to send their families out of town, so shit wasn't as crowded as it could have been, but it still sucked big time.

I hadn't been back to the hospital. I refused to leave the clubhouse, even to go outside. I didn't want to see anyone, and if most of the families hadn't been outside at the moment, I would have been barricaded inside Cam's room.

"He wants to see you," Cam said patiently, pulling the book from my hands.

"I'll go over tonight," I snapped, reaching for my book.

"You can't be there to welcome him home?" he argued, tossing the book across the room. "The fuck is wrong with you?"

"Nothing."

"Bullshit. You walk around like a fuckin' ghost all day. Only time I get a reaction outta ya is when I'm fuckin' nailin' ya."

My head snapped back at his coarse words.

"Fuck you."

He looked down at his bare wrist then back to me. "Nah, couple more hours before that happens again."

Tears burned the backs of my eyes.

He was right, but I'd never say that. I was having a hard time, such a hard fucking time. Every morning, I woke up desperate and sweating from nightmares that seemed never ending. They were a mix of memories I'd either blocked out or forgotten from when I was little, and scenes from the attack only a few days ago. They got so mixed up in my mind that at times, my stepdad's face was multiplied on each of the shooters. I couldn't cope.

I'd immediately reach for Cam, anxious for him to make me think of something else. He always complied, sometimes pulling me to him and sliding inside of me when he wasn't even fully awake yet. It happened over and over again, sometimes more than once in the middle of the night.

We'd begun sleeping with a fan in our room to air-dry our sweaty bodies, and by the time I crawled out of the bed each morning, I was sticky and smelly from the night before.

"I need to go out to my parents' place today," Cam finally said quietly. "They can't keep sleepin' at a hotel now that they're lettin' Lily head home."

"They're discharging her?" I asked in surprise.

"Yeah." He scratched at his face, then dropped his hands. "Can't find nothin' wrong with her. Can't keep her there."

"She can't see. That's what's wrong with her!"

"Physically, she's fine," he snapped back. "It's all in her fuckin' head."

He shot to his feet and twined his fingers together behind his neck as he began to pace.

"That can't be right," I murmured, shaking my head. "She can't fucking see."

"I gotta get goin'," Cam said abruptly. "Gonna try and clean up out there."

I wanted so badly to tell him I'd help him. I knew he wouldn't ask anyone else because he wouldn't want them to see his reactions to the destruction the attack had left behind. But I couldn't make myself go back to Casper and Farrah's.

I couldn't go there ever again.

"I'll be here when you get back," I said finally as his eyes searched my face.

I wasn't sure what he was looking for—what he was trying to find—but after a few seconds, he nodded and leaned down to kiss me. I was passive as his lips pulled at mine.

"Be back later," he said gruffly, then strode out of the room.

I glanced down at the book on the floor a few feet away, but I couldn't find the ambition to get off the couch and grab it. Instead, I stared at the side of the pool table and let my mind drift.

"Hi, I'm Bellatrix Colleen," I announced, coming to a stop in front of the old lady sitting in my backyard.

"Nice to meet you, Bellatrix Colleen," she said, reaching out to shake my hand, like I was a big person.

"You can call me Trix if you want." I shook her hand as hard as I could.

"Alright, then." She gave my hand a gentle squeeze before letting go. "My name is Rose, but you can call me Gram."

"Gram?"

"Yep."

I thought about that for a moment.

"Okay. I have a Gramps, but I don't have a Gram."

"You do now." Her face lit up in a bright smile, the corners of her eyes crinkling in the best way, and I felt an answering smile pull at my cheeks. I liked her already.

I shuddered and snapped out of my memory as someone sat down next to me.

"Hey, sweetheart," my nan said gently, reaching out to wrap her arm around my shoulders. "How you doing?"

"Fine."

"Don't bullshit me."

I tensed for a second and then relaxed against her, dropping my head against her shoulder.

"Shitty," I answered again.

"Yeah, you and me both," Nan replied.

"How's Gramps?"

"Pissy as hell and threatening to discharge himself from the hospital."

"How long are they going to keep him?"

"Just a few more days, I think," she said with a sigh, running her hand up and down my arm as she rested her head on top of mine. "They'll send him back here and then *I'll* have to fight to keep him off his leg."

"Sounds like Gramps."

"Could be worse," Nan said, her voice hitching. "He's still here, so I've got no room to complain."

"I think there's plenty of room," I argued, staring across the room at a broken bottle that had rolled under one of the tables. "How's Callie?"

"Why haven't you been to see for yourself?"

I shrugged my shoulders. I didn't want to explain myself. Not then.

"She's getting better. In a lot of pain, though."

I nodded.

"Nix has been working his way around the hospital, staying with Will mostly, since Callie's needed Grease. Can't imagine being Grease right now, one child gone, his wife and oldest in the hospital and his other children bein' passed around to family. He must feel pulled in a thousand different directions."

My eyes welled and I closed them tight, causing tears to roll down my face.

All of our families had been targeted, but the Hawthorne family had been hit hardest of all.

"I keep picking up the phone to call Vera," Nan said with a sad laugh. "At least they went together. Not sure she could have made it if he didn't."

"Bubby's coming home today," I told her, using the nickname I'd given my brother when he was born.

"Think he's already there," she replied.

"Oh."

"You gonna go see him?"

"Maybe later."

"Trix," she scolded gently. "He's been asking for you."

"I don't know if—"

"I know you've seen him," she cut me off, her voice growing more forceful. "But he hasn't seen you. He's been asking for you for days, getting frantic every time someone tells him that you're not there."

"What?" I shot up on the couch, turning to face her straight on. "Why didn't anyone tell me?"

"You've been locked up in here, not talking to anyone. Don't think your parents wanted to make things worse for you."

"Jesus, that's stupid," I snapped, sliding my flip-flops on. "You coming with me?"

"I'll be over in a little while," she said, climbing to her feet. "I want to clean up your Gramps' room a bit before he comes home."

I raced outside, shielding my eyes with my hands as sunlight hit them for the first time in way too long. There were brothers and their families hanging out at the picnic benches and kids running around in the grass, but I didn't acknowledge anyone as I jogged past them.

My eyesight went fuzzy for a second as I reached the long grass between my parents' house and the club, but I shook it off and kept moving. My legs itched as I jogged the distance to the house, but I didn't let that stop me, either. I'd walked through that long grass a thousand times, and I knew the itch would fade once I was out of it.

Tommy was sitting on the front porch when I reached it, and he came to his feet when he saw me. "Trix—"

I reached out and squeezed his arm, but didn't slow as I pushed my way into the house.

The living room was full of people, but I only had eyes for one person. Leo's back was to me, but I could tell by the set of his shoulders that he was wound up—practically vibrating with tension.

"Bubby?" I called, coming to a stop.

His head turned slowly toward me, and a strangled sound left my mouth as his face came into view.

My vision faltered, his swollen and stitched face replaced by my mom's for a split second, her cheek puffy and both eyes black.

"Sissy?" his voice slurred and his face changed back. I stumbled forward.

When I reached him, I fell to my knees, staring into his eyes.

How could I have left him alone so long when he needed me? I reached a new level of self-loathing as his nostrils flared and his eyes flashed back and forth over my face.

He reached out shakily and gripped my shoulder, raising his hand to my hair, his calloused palms catching in the strands.

"Out!" he garbled, raising his eyes from mine. "Ev'rbody OUT."

The house went silent.

"Leo," my mom called softly.

"Out!" he screamed, his hand tightening in my hair painfully.

My pop came in from the kitchen and took in the scene, then started ushering the brothers and their old ladies out of the house.

As soon as we were alone, Leo loosened his grip on my hair and ran his hand down the side of my head.

"Okay?" he asked, his eyes boring into mine.

"I'm okay," I rasped.

"Tried t'get to ya," he garbled. "Couldn't."

My lips trembled as I nodded.

"Okay?" he asked again.

"I'm okay, I promise."

He nodded slightly and his eyes closed, tears leaking out of the corners. He flinched as the tears hit the stitches along his face.

"Don't cry," I whispered, gripping his knees with my fingers.

"Couldn't get ya," he mumbled, taking a shuddering breath.

I climbed onto the couch next to him, sitting on my knees so I could put my arm softly around his shoulders. Without hesitation, he leaned into me, laying the right side of his body against my chest, his head resting on my collarbone.

"M'face," he choked out.

"It'll heal," I whispered into the top of his head, kissing it over and over. "I promise."

He cried silently, his body jerking slightly until he finally fell asleep against me. I leaned backward slowly, pulling my legs out from underneath me gingerly so I didn't jostle him. I was finally able to rest against the arm of the couch, my legs on either side of him, as he jerked and shuddered in his sleep.

Twenty minutes later, that was how our parents found us.

"Don't move him," I ground out, my arms tightening around his chest.

My pop inhaled sharply as my mom stepped forward.

"We won't," Pop said roughly.

He stepped over to the front door and slid the deadbolt home, then moved around the couch, meeting my mom in front of us. He sat at the far end of the couch, pulling my mom down onto his lap sideways facing us, before tenderly pulling my and Leo's legs onto their thighs.

I met my mom's watery eyes as she rested her head on my pop's shoulder and gave me a small smile.

"First fucker that knocks on the door is gettin' my foot in his ass," Pop growled softly, leaning his head on the back of the couch.

My mom's smile grew a little and I felt my lips twitch.

Then I closed my eyes, gripping my baby brother's t-shirt as my pop's hand came up to grasp my ankle gently, connecting us.

It was the first time I slept without nightmares.

Chapter 17

CAMERON

I'D SPENT THE day clearing out the backyard, using Casper's truck to haul broken chairs, the shot up grill and mangled picnic table to the dump. Even the horseshoes had fucking blood on them, and I got rid of everything. As soon as I'd finished doing that, I'd dragged out Casper's wheelbarrow and filled it eight times with bloodied dirt, digging into the ground over and over again until every speck was gone from sight. I'd left gaping holes all over the yard, but I couldn't find it in me to give a shit.

By the time I got back to the club, I had weeping blisters on my hands and my arms were pretty much numb. After I realized Trix wasn't in our room, I walked slowly over to Dragon's place.

I was tired straight to my bones. Even my teeth ached from clenching my jaw hard all day.

"Hulk," Dragon greeted from the porch steps as I reached them.

His hair was in a knotted mess at the back of his head, and his beard looked like he'd been scratching at it all day—the thing was massive.

"Trix here?" I asked, coming to a stop.

"Yeah," he reached over and tossed me a beer from the six-pack he'd stashed beside him. "Take a seat."

I looked at the small space between him and the porch railing and dropped my ass to the dirt. I wasn't sitting on his damn lap.

"How's she been?" he asked me quietly, jerking his head toward the door.

I pulled out my smokes and lit one, then used my lighter to pop the top of my beer. My lungs were screaming after all the smoking I'd done that day, but I took a deep drag before answering, anyway.

"Quiet," I told him.

"She looks like shit," he said bluntly, taking a long swallow of his beer, finishing it off and opening a new one.

"She's barely sleepin.' When she does, she's cryin' and jerkin' around."

"You wake her up?"

"No, she's not gettin' enough of it as it is," I mumbled around my cigarette.

"She tellin' you anything?"

I scoffed, pulling the smoke from my lips. "She's not sayin' shit."

"When she came runnin,' I 'bout had a heart attack," he said, looking over toward the clubhouse. "Fuckin' déjà vu."

"How so?"

"Back when I was gettin' custody of Trix, Bren's husband showed up. Man was fuckin' insane." Dragon shook his head. "Brenna dropped Trix through our bedroom window, told her to run to me so Bren could face the man by herself. Knew she had to protect our girl, did what she had to so Trix was safe."

I didn't say anything as he paused. I didn't think I'd ever heard the man string so many words together at once, and I sure as fuck wasn't going to interrupt him.

"Trix got to me and she was shakin,' she was so fuckin' terrified. Then she'd told me, 'Daddy'." He glanced at me. "That's what she'd called the fucker Brenna'd married. Fuck. That one word was enough to send me runnin'."

"I don't—"

"That's what she was saying when she jumped off your Ma's porch," he said gruffly, cutting me off. He lifted the beer to his lips and drank deeply until it was empty. "Daddy. Daddy. Daddy. Daddy." His voice was high pitched and soft.

My stomach turned at the look on his face.

"Not sure what knocked it loose, but she's rememberin'," he said softly, sniffing. "Shit we thought she'd forgotten."

"Fuck," I breathed, dropping my cigarette to the ground in front of me.

"Just thought you should know," Dragon mumbled, climbing to his feet. "You comin' in?"

"Yeah, in a minute," I replied, staying planted on my ass.

The door closed softly behind him and I rubbed both hands over my face.

Jesus.

I had no idea what I was supposed to do. Trix was wringing me dry at night, but during the day, she wouldn't even fucking look at me. It didn't matter what I did. I'd tried talking softly to her, pissing her off, cracking jokes, being mean. Nothing fucking worked.

The night grew darker and darker as the sun set, but I didn't move from my spot on the ground. I finally climbed to my feet as music started playing inside the house and the living room light switched on.

"Hey," Leo mumbled, nodding his head slightly as I walked in.

"How you feelin'?" I asked, looking past him toward the kitchen. I couldn't hear Trix's voice, but I could hear a couple people moving around in there.

"Where's Cecil'a?" Leo asked, ignoring my question.

"What?" I turned back to him in surprise.

"She hasn't been by." His face was so swollen that I could barely understand a word he'd said.

I opened my mouth to answer him, then closed it again. I had no idea why my sister hadn't been by to see him. I knew both Farrah and

Casper had stopped by at different times as they traded shifts at the hospital with Lily, and I guess I'd just assumed that Cecilia would have come with one of them.

"Haven't really seen her," I finally replied, watching him deflate a little.

"No big," he said, turning his face away from me.

Slender arms wrapped around my waist from behind, and I sighed, leaning back slightly into Trix as she laid her head on my back.

"Pop said you were here," she said against my cut.

"You ready to go home?"

"To the clubhouse?"

"Not safe for you on the outside yet."

She stiffened behind me, so I turned to look at her. For a few moments, things had felt almost normal between us, but the instant I got a look at her face, I knew that had been an illusion. She was still wearing the fucked up mask of complacency she'd been hiding behind for days.

"Maybe I should stay here," she said, glancing at Leo. "My brother is—"

"You belong with me," I interrupted, cutting her off.

"I'm just saying—"

"Trix," I warned, losing my patience.

Her eyes shuttered and she nodded jerkily, leaving the room. I stood by the couch and listened to her say her goodbyes in the kitchen, then watched her walk out and whisper something to Leo, making him nod.

I followed her out the door and we walked back to the clubhouse in silence.

I didn't know what the fuck to say to her.

She was hurting, I knew that. We were fucking mourning, all of us. But that was the thing—*we were all mourning*. Slider and Vera had helped raise me. I'd lived with Gram, she'd driven me to get my driver's license, and when I was a teenager, we used to stay up at least once a week playing cards and bullshitting. I loved her like a mother. I'd been there when Mick had taken his first steps and I'd been the one to take the training wheels off his bike when he was three years old. I was hurting, too.

She didn't get the monopoly on fucking grief. It didn't work that way. I understood that she was messed up from all that had happened, but I was, too, goddammit.

I'd just spent the day cleaning up after a fucking massacre, digging my family's blood out of the ground, and she didn't have one fucking ounce of comfort for me. Not a single word. Not a single touch.

Resentment burned in my gut.

"How you feelin'?" I ground out as we finally made our way into my room. We hadn't talked about the baby at all, and even though I knew she was glad for the reprieve, I couldn't keep my mouth shut any longer.

I thought about our kid constantly. It seemed surreal that he was safe inside her—the one person I hadn't had to worry about in the entire fucked up situation.

"I'm fine."

"Baby, too?" I asked, pushing her.

"I'd assume so. Everything feels the same." She began to undress, and I leaned against the wall as she stripped down to her underwear and slipped one of my shirts over her head.

"You need to see a doctor," I finally said after she'd crawled between the sheets.

"I'm fine, Cam."

"Didn't say you weren't. You still need to see a doctor."

She didn't answer me, just rolled over so she was no longer facing in my direction.

I clenched my hands, opening and closing them over and over again until I had my anger under control. I tried to tell myself that she just had to work out whatever it was she was dealing with, that she'd figure it out and start acting like the woman I'd committed to.

But when I got undressed and climbed into bed beside her, all of my understanding flew out the window as I tried to pull her in against me and she jerked away.

I rolled onto my back and breathed heavily through my nose as I pushed down everything I wished I could say to her.

★ ★ ★

When I woke up the next morning, Trix wasn't in bed with me.

I reached over to her side of the bed and found the sheets were cold. She hadn't reached for me in the night like she usually did, and I didn't remember her having any nightmares, either. I lifted my hands and looked at my palms. Shit. They were tore up and oozing from the shovel I'd used the day before. I should have worn a pair of gloves or something.

"Hey, Cam," Trix's nan, Amy, called out when I came out of my room a while later. As much as I wanted to lie in bed and sleep the entire day away, I had shit to do. Cars still needed to be fixed and I needed to go see my baby sister at some point.

"Hey, Amy. How's Poet doin'?" I asked as I grabbed a cup of coffee from the end of the bar. "And where is everyone?"

"He's being an ornery old goat, but getting better," she said with a tired smile. "Pretty much everyone headed home today—"

"What?" I snapped, glancing around the room. "You serious?"

"Patrick sent word. Not sure what's going on, but he told Dragon that it was okay for everyone to split, as long as they stayed vigilant."

"That's what they fuckin' said before," I mumbled angrily.

"You'll have to take it up with him."

"So, why are you still here?" I asked as she pulled her robe tighter around her body.

"Feel better in here with Patrick still laid up," Amy said with a sheepish smile. "I know everything is probably fine, but I'm not ready to go back to regular life yet."

"Yeah, I hear you. Trix and I aren't leavin' yet, either." I leaned against the bar top and sipped my coffee, grimacing when my palm brushed against the hot mug.

"What did you do to your hands?" she asked sharply, moving toward me. "Holy hell, Cameron. You idiot!"

I looked at her in surprise as she pulled my hand out in front of me.

"Come on, I'll clean these up."

"They're fine," I replied, shaking my head. "You seen Trix today?"

Her mouth firmed for a minute before she looked up from my hand.

"She went over to Brenna and Dragon's."

"'Course she did," I grumbled, shaking my head.

She ignored my words, but went silent for a moment before saying, "Come on, kid. I'll get these hands patched up."

As soon as my hands were disinfected and wrapped, I made my way to the garage. I had a couple of cars I could work on while the place was mostly empty, so I cranked up some music and started. Just because we were in the middle of shit didn't mean the work stopped—we needed the legal income.

Running illegal shit may pay the bills, but it didn't give us clean money to report to the IRS, and fuck if I was going down for tax evasion.

A couple hours later, I heard slow footsteps come into the garage, stopping next to where I was crammed underneath a car.

"What's up—" I asked, rolling myself out. "Will?"

"Hey," Will said, his mouth pulling up in a half-grin.

"When'd they let you out?" I asked happily, getting to my feet. "How you doin'?"

"All right," he replied, closing his eyes as his voice cracked.

"Fuck, man. I'm so sorry about Micky."

"Yeah," he whispered huskily, nodding his head and looking over my shoulder. "Yeah."

"How's your mom?"

"She's hangin' in." Will's body began to sway and I took a nervous step toward him.

"Let's sit down," I said calmly, waiting for him to get himself together before I led our way into the clubhouse. I knew he wouldn't want me to help him, but it was fucking slow going as he shuffled toward a chair and sat.

"Shoulda spoke up sooner," Will stuttered as we settled in. "Shoulda said somethin' about those boys when I first started buyin' off them."

"You couldn't have known, brother," I replied calmly, watching him closely.

The day before Gram's party, we'd all been called in to the clubhouse for a meeting. Turned out that Will knew the people that had been fucking with us. He hadn't put the two together at first—it had taken him a while to figure it out.

The guys he'd been buying his steroids off of for the past six months had decided to branch out. That's what they told him. Apparently, they'd thought he had some sort of allegiance to them because they were supplying his 'roids. They'd asked him to help them—be their muscle. It just went to show how completely fucking naïve the boys were.

There was no way Will would ever turn his back on the club. Even if he'd wanted to leave the only family he'd ever known, the brothers would never let him.

When we'd realized that the little shit—the slashed tires, the bike accident and the shady informants—were the work of some college students, we'd been relieved.

Christ.

We'd been fucking ecstatic. We could deal with a group of snot-nosed punks with too much time on their hands and not enough money. They were a fucking joke. All the stupid shit they'd done had made sense—it wasn't the work of men like us trying to fuck with our heads, it was immature posturing by a bunch of boys.

We'd agreed to handle it after the weekend, no one wanting to mess up Gram's birthday.

I clenched my hands at my sides. We'd underestimated them, and had no idea how many of them were left to fuck with us.

"You couldn't have known," I repeated as Will's eyes filled with tears and he turned his head away.

"Fuckin' pain killers," he mumbled, slowly reaching up to swipe at his eyes.

"Got nothin' to hide with me," I said softly, averting my eyes. "You know that."

"Sorry about that shit in the forecourt," he said suddenly. "I was bein' a fuckin' idiot."

"You wanna kiss and make up?"

"Fuck you," he snapped, a small smile pulling at the side of his mouth.

"All forgotten," I said seriously, leaning back in my chair.

"Can't believe Micky's gone," he mumbled softly after a few moments, his face screwed up in a grimace. "I mean, I saw it. I was right there, but *fuck*. I see Tommy and I automatically look over his shoulder for Mick."

I didn't reply. What was there to say? His baby brother was dead, shot down at fourteen in a war we'd barely known we were fighting.

"My mom's still pretty out of it—they're keeping her doped up. What the fuck is she gonna do when she realizes he's gone? She's gonna fuckin' lose it, man."

"Grease'll take care of her."

"Who's takin' care of him?"

"She will."

"That doesn't even make sense," he murmured tiredly.

I thought about the space between Trix and I. We weren't taking care of each other. In my mind, I knew that's what was supposed to be happening—her leaning on me and me leaning back. That's what Casper and Farrah were doing. Holding each other up, even though with Lily in the hospital, it meant they only saw each other in passing. But Trix wasn't doing shit for me, and she wouldn't let me close enough to help her, either.

"You'll get it when you find the woman you wanna be with," I finally said.

"You and Trix okay?"

"Yeah, we're fine."

"Where is she?" he asked curiously, looking around the empty clubhouse.

"Over at Dragon's with Leo."

"He doin' okay?"

"Best he can, I guess."

"Yeah." Will sighed and then pushed himself slowly to his feet. "Should probably get over there to see him."

"You sure you can make it?" I asked, only half joking. The guy looked like he was going to fall over.

"Got my mom's car. I'll drive," he replied ruefully before turning to walk away.

I stayed seated as he left, then dropped my head into my hands once I knew I was alone.

I was so fucking tired. So overwhelmed.

I'd been pretty good at tamping all of the shit down tight, getting things done that needed to be done and pushing everything else away. But the longer it went, the harder it was to keep the burn in my chest at a manageable level.

I knew what was going to happen. I was going to snap.

They didn't call me Hulk for no reason. Poet gave me the nickname when I was just a prospect after a crazy fight I'd had. Another club had come to visit, men we'd been friendly with for longer than I'd been alive at the time. Everything had gone like normal at first. Parties and barbeques and shit, just spending time with guys who held the same beliefs as us.

But there was one fucker, I couldn't even remember his name anymore, who had it in for me. I was used to getting fucked with—that was the name of the game during the club's probation period—but that didn't mean I had to take shit from someone who wasn't a brother.

I'd kept my mouth shut every time he'd made a fucking mess just to fuck with me, or made comments about what a piece of shit I was. My dad and the other guys were clearly having a good time with the other club's members, and I wasn't going to tattle like a pussy. So, it had just built and built, my body growing tighter and tighter as I'd dealt with his shit, until the night he'd had the bitch who'd been sucking him off in the main room of the clubhouse spit his cum on the floor and had loudly ordered me to clean it up.

I beat the hell out of him.

And the two brothers that had tried to step in.

From then on, I was Hulk. Mild-mannered and quiet until I just couldn't keep that shit locked down any longer.

And I was getting to that point. The point of no return.

I wasn't going to cry like a baby. I wasn't going to piss and moan about shit—it wouldn't change anything.

But all that emotion had to go somewhere. It had to get out somehow. And I knew that soon, it was going to push to the surface. God help the fucker that set it free, because I sure as hell wouldn't be able to.

Chapter 18

TRIX

I FINISHED CLEANING up after lunch and sat down at my parents' kitchen table with a sigh. I wanted coffee. Badly.

I was trying not to drink any, but I'd already decided that morning that a little cup wouldn't hurt anything. I couldn't have another. The blessed caffeine almost wasn't worth the guilt I'd felt as I drank it.

Cameron would have been pissed if he'd caught me.

I rubbed my hands over my face and tried not to cry.

Everything was so messed up. We were all so preoccupied with taking care of the living that none of us had been given the chance to mourn yet. My mom was walking around like a zombie, her usually happy face drawn tight, Pop's eyes had dark circles under them and he was talking even less than usual, which pretty much meant he was completely silent, and Leo was sleeping most of the time and not because he needed the rest.

And I was, well, just trying to keep my shit together and avoiding Cam.

I knew he was hurting, and I knew it was fucked up—but I didn't want to be around him. It was as if he'd forgotten everything that had happened before our families were attacked. I couldn't. Every single night, I laid down in bed and ran over and over the fight we'd had that week. The way he'd looked at me in disgust. The way he'd spoken to me.

The way he'd ignored how I'd been falling apart at the seams.

If I'd been afraid then, it was nothing compared to how I felt after I began remembering bits and pieces of the years my mom and I had lived with her first husband. The fights. The crying. The things she'd thought I didn't hear, but I hadn't been able to escape from.

I knew my mom thought she'd shielded me from the abuse she'd suffered, but she was wrong. I'd noticed every time she had to move slowly and carefully, the way she'd go quiet when her husband, Tony, was in the house, the way she'd taught me to protect myself.

I remembered it all.

And with those memories came a fear that was so overpowering, it was almost debilitating.

She'd married him. She hadn't loved him. She'd been pregnant and scared and young, and she'd made what she thought was the best decision at the time.

Later, she'd known it was wrong and we'd escaped, but that didn't erase the bad choices she'd made.

Not for her, or for me.

I couldn't let that happen to me.

Someone knocked at the door and I startled. Leo was asleep on the couch and my mom and pop had gone to see Callie in the hospital, so I stood from my chair and made my way to the front of the house.

"Hey, Will," I said in surprise as I swung open the door.

"Hey, beautiful." He stepped inside and gave me a kiss on the top of my head before moving around me. "Leo here?"

"Yeah," I tilted my head toward the couch. "He's sleeping."

Will nodded and moved forward, circling the couch before kicking it hard.

Leo jerked awake. "What the hell?" he slurred.

"Wake up, fucker," Will ordered, smacking Leo's legs off the couch.

My baby brother's eyes went wide and then he scrambled into a sitting position. "Will!"

I turned away and left them alone as Will chuckled. They didn't need me hovering, even though I wanted to.

"Hey, Trix," Will called to my back as I entered the kitchen. "Might wanna go check on Cam."

"Okay, thanks," I called back.

I went out the back door and sat down on the concrete stairs leading into the yard. I wasn't going to go check on Cam. Hopefully, I wouldn't even see him for the rest of the day.

My hand went instinctively to my belly and I left it there as I looked out over the large field behind our house.

I was so glad Will had come to visit, though I didn't know if he should be moving around so much. A part of me wished he had stayed home, though. Leo's face had become familiar, a problem to be solved, but seeing Will had brought the terror of the attack right back to me.

The screams. The sounds of the guns and bullets hitting bodies and other things around the yard. The way Leo had looked at me, then began to run toward me before he was completely knocked off his feet. The way Gramps had jolted when the bullet hit his thigh, but he stayed upright, firing back like he was at the fucking OK Corral or something.

The way Cam had thrown me toward the wall to keep me safe, and Farrah had wrapped herself around me to keep me still.

I closed my eyes and let tears roll down my face. I missed my aunt and uncle. I missed Gram. I missed Mick and his awkward attempts at conversation.

I was scared that Lily would never be able to see again. I was afraid something would go wrong with Callie.

I was afraid that it wasn't over and something else would happen.

Someone else would die.

I was terrified to leave my parents' house, even for the club. It was the first place I'd felt comfortable since I'd found out I was pregnant.

Not even Cam could console me anymore.

I no longer trusted him to be my safe place when I fell.

It probably wasn't fair that I'd expected him to catch me when I was falling. He had his own concerns, his own worries to deal with. I knew that. But I couldn't help but resent him for pulling away when I'd needed him.

And I guess a small part of me felt like letting him deal with his grief alone was a sick form of justice. I'd needed him and he'd been either too blind or too stubborn to see it, and now when he needed me, I couldn't find it in me to help him.

I ached with loss, my mind and body weary—but I wouldn't lean on him. I wouldn't go to him and tell him that I was scared. I wouldn't cry to him in my grief.

I'd tried that before. I'd tried to burrow in close to him like he could shield me from my fears, but he'd literally turned his back to me.

He hadn't left me, but he hadn't seen me, either.

So I no longer had anything to give him.

It was becoming clearer and clearer to me that I could have the baby, or I could have Cameron. My nightmares were only growing worse, my fears multiplying. I wasn't strong enough to have both.

"What're you doin' out here?" my pop asked, opening the door slightly so he could follow me outside.

"Hey, when did you get home?" I asked, looking at him out of the corner of my eye.

"Just now. Will and Leo are both passed out on my couch," he grumbled, making me grin.

"It's like old times," I said softly, leaning into him as he sat down and wrapped an arm around my shoulder.

"You okay, Little Warrior?"

"Yeah, I'm okay."

"Don't seem okay."

"I'm getting there. Pop—" my words stuttered for a moment, then came out strong but soft. "Pop, do you think I could have my old room for a while?"

His body stiffened beside me and I swallowed hard.

"Why?" he asked bluntly.

"I don't want to keep my apartment. I was hoping I could stay here until I—before the—while I'm pregnant."

"You don't think Hulk's gonna have somethin' to say about that? The fuck is going on, Bellatrix?"

I pulled away from his arm and stood from the steps, walking into the yard a little before turning to face him.

"I'm sure he'll be pissed, but he'll get over it," I told him tonelessly.

"You're sure," he scoffed, shaking his head.

"Yeah, I'm sure."

"What fuckin' planet you livin' on?"

"We're not good, okay? We haven't been good in a while. This'll be a relief."

"You're havin' his baby, Trix. I'm a man. I've been there. Ain't no way he's lettin' you go if he can stop it."

"He can't stop it," I snapped in frustration.

We both went silent for a long moment, staring at each other.

"You want me to step in," he said softly, looking me over like he was trying to figure me out. "You're askin' me to live here so you don't have to fight him on it. You'll just leave it to me."

"No—" I tried to argue as my pop's jaw clenched in frustration.

"You're always welcome here, Bellatrix," he cut me off, getting to his feet. "Love havin' ya. But this ain't my fight unless you tell me he did somethin' to you and I need to take care of it. That the case?"

"No," I whispered, tucking my thumbs into my palms so I wouldn't fidget.

"You tell Cam you're movin' in here—then you can." He stepped forward and kissed the top of my head. "Your mother is havin' a tough time as it is, girl—no way I'm havin' your man showin' up and causin' drama, makin' things worse for her. Understand?"

"Yeah."

"Okay. Sounds like your mom's makin' dinner early." Pop nodded to the window behind us. "You stayin'?"

"Yeah, I'll stay."

I watched him pull open the screen and reach for the door handle before he paused.

"I'll always look out for you, Little Warrior," he said softly, not turning to look at me. "Always. But don't do somethin' you can't come back from. That boy loves you—no matter what you're thinkin' right now, or whatever the fuck is goin' on. He's loved you since he was a kid, and that ain't gonna change."

"It's not enough."

"Sometimes it is."

He left me outside without another word.

★ ★ ★

WE WERE SITTING down to dinner that evening after Will had left for home when Pop's phone started ringing.

"Yeah?" he answered gruffly, his mouth full of food. He paused for a minute, stuffing food into his mouth while he listened to whoever was on the other end of the phone. "Fuckin' idiot. Sit tight, I'm on my way."

He stuffed the phone back in his shirt pocket and took another huge bite before rising from the table and leaning over to kiss my mom. She smiled fondly at him when he was finished, and wiped a little bit of sauce from his beard.

"Your pop's checked himself out of the damn hospital," he said quietly to her, their noses just inches apart. "Gotta go help Amy."

Mom sighed. "Goddammit."

"I'll take care of it, baby," he assured her, leaning forward to softly kiss her lips again.

"I know you will."

"Wait for me in bed."

"Always do."

"Naked."

"We're sitting *right here*," I snapped, my face scrunched up in disgust. I'd been watching them, because my parents were sweet as hell. My pop didn't show his soft side to anyone but Mom, and she soaked it up like a sponge. But I was seriously close to vomiting after their conversation went from sweet to sexual.

"You're an adult. You're livin' here, you get used to it," Pop said seriously, tapping the table twice before walking around the edge to kiss the top of Leo's head, then the top of mine.

He left without another word and I felt my mom's stare on the side of my face as I tried to finish eating my dinner.

"Bellatrix," she said warningly. "Explain."

I lifted my head and met Leo's eyes, but he made no move to help me. He was wondering what the hell was going on, too.

"I'm going to live here for a bit," I mumbled, my fork scratching along my plate as I moved my food around. "I asked Pop earlier and he said it was okay."

"Just like that?"

I thought back to my pop's words, then nodded. "Just like that."

"Cam know?" Leo asked in disbelief.

"Not yet." I shook my head. "I'll tell him tonight."

"What's going on with you, Trix?" my mom asked in frustration. "You *love* Cam."

"I'm fine." I set my fork down forcefully on the table and it bounced onto my plate, making a loud clanging noise. "It's just not working out."

"Then you probably shouldn't have got pregnant," Leo said derisively, dropping his eyes back to his plate.

My chair screeched across the floor as I stood up quickly and I felt tears build in my eyes as I watched my brother's once handsome face scowl.

"You think I wanted this?" I hissed. "We were fucking careful."

"Pun intended," he mumbled meanly.

"Leo," Mom snapped.

"You know what? Fuck you, Leo."

"Trix!" Mom turned her glare to me.

"No. He doesn't get to be a dick because he's hurt."

"The fuck do you know?" Leo yelled, rising to his feet. "Cam hid you on the porch. You were fuckin' safe and sound. Watched from a distance while the rest of us got shot down like dogs."

I stumbled back a little, staring at my baby brother in confusion.

"Enough." Cam's voice rumbled through the kitchen and my palms grew sweaty. "You talk to her like that again, I'm gonna fuck up the pretty side of your face."

"Cameron," Mom warned.

Cam came up behind me, and his hand slid around to rest low on my belly. "You ready, Sweetbea?"

I glanced at Leo, then at my mom, who was still calmly sitting with a fork in her hand.

"Yeah. I'm ready," I said finally, pushing my chair in carefully.

"You gonna tell—" Leo began, only to be cut off by my mom.

"If you say one more goddamn word, Leo," she hissed, slamming her hand down on the table.

"Let's go, Bea," Cam murmured, leading me out the back door.

"I love you, Bubby," I called softly, looking back over my shoulder.

"Yeah," Leo mumbled back, making my entire chest tighten.

That wasn't my brother. My brother would never have said those things to me. He loved me. Unconditionally. He was always on my side, no matter whether I was wrong or right.

That angry man in there was not my baby brother.

I stumbled as we reached the tall grass between my parents' house and the clubhouse and glanced down at my bare feet. I hadn't even remembered to slide my shoes on.

Without a word, Cam lifted me up bridal style and kept moving.

"He's dealin' with a lot," Cam ground out softly as I wrapped my arms around his neck and looked away from him. "Give him some time."

I nodded. I didn't want to talk. I didn't want to discuss how badly Leo had hurt me, how disillusioned I'd become with everyone I'd ever cared about. It seemed like I couldn't do anything right. My mom had argued with me at dinner, Leo was perpetually pissed, and even my dad hadn't welcomed me back without conditions.

I stayed silent as we reached the clubhouse, even as Grease's drawn face popped out of the meeting room and his eyes focused on Cam.

"Hulk, church," he ordered.

Cam nodded, but carried me all the way into his bedroom before setting me down.

"Don't go out there barefoot," he ordered as he let me go. "That floor's fuckin' disgustin'."

He left the room, shutting the door softly behind him and I dropped down onto the bed.

I was exhausted, but I was too afraid to sleep. Sleep meant nightmares, and after my argument with Leo, I wasn't sure how much more I could take.

I took off my t-shirt, bra and shorts without getting up, and snagged one of Cam's t-shirts off the end of the bed, pulling it over my head. I'd just lay down for a little bit.

Before I knew it, I was fast asleep and stuck in a nightmare.

Chapter 19

CAMERON

"What's up?" I asked as I entered the small room I was rarely allowed into.

Casper, Grease, Samson and old Smokey were sitting in their chairs at the table, but no one else was in the room.

"Dragon and Poet are on their way," Casper said tiredly, running his hand down his face.

"How's Lily?" I asked him, leaning up against the wall. It was weird as fuck being in the room with all the empty chairs. My eyes automatically went to Slider's place at the head and I jerked them away.

"She's good. Home with Farrah and CeeCee."

"I need to get over there," I said in apology, meeting my dad's eyes. The man was holding on by a thread and I hadn't been around like I should've.

"Sounds like you're dealing with your own shit," he said cautiously.

"It's fine," I replied automatically.

"Callie?" I asked, moving my attention to Grease.

"Told her about Mick and Gram today," Grease rasped, leaning back in his chair. "Had to sedate her."

"Fuck," I hissed, looking down at my scuffed up boots.

"Her body's healin'," Grease continued. "All I can ask for."

"Let me know if you need anything," I mumbled back, meeting his eyes again.

"Will do."

"You're a fuckin' idiot," Dragon's voice drifted through the door. "Makin' your woman cry. You see that?"

I didn't hear Poet's reply, but within seconds, I was moving away from the door so they could pass me. Poet was on a pair of shiny new crutches and was wearing a set of light blue scrubs, his cut thrown over the top.

Dragon hovered like a nursemaid, looking like he wanted to kill someone, until Poet dropped down in his seat with a sigh.

"Close the door," Poet ordered me sharply.

I met Amy's watery eyes as I glanced out the doorway, and nodded to her before she moved away.

Once the door was closed, I leaned back against my spot on the wall. There was an empty seat at the table, but it sure as fuck wasn't for me.

The room was silent as Poet's pale face turned to each man, silently meeting their eyes. "I'm steppin' down," he said softly, running his hand down the long beard against his chest.

Smokey mumbled something under his breath.

"What the fuck?" Grease whispered.

"Gettin' too old for this. Made some bad decisions—"

"We all fucked up," Casper cut him off.

Poet raised his hand for silence, then spoke again. "Don't want it. Not without Charlie."

My throat grew tight at Slider's real name, the use of it an indication of how long their friendship had run. Poet and Slider had joined the club as young men, Slider because his dad was the president, Poet because he'd been running from shit in Ireland. Their friendship had lasted longer than most marriages. A lifetime.

"I'm steppin' down. Gonna spend some time with my grandbabies, take Amy on a fuckin' vacation. Sit on my ass and watch fuckin'

Matlock in the middle of the day." Poet looked around. "Think I've earned it," he said roughly.

My softhearted dad looked like he was going to cry, but he beat it back, sitting up taller in his chair.

"Now the formalities," Poet said roughly, pulling off his cut. He looked at Dragon expectantly, then nodded as Dragon's switchblade slid across the table. Poet ran his fingers reverently over the vice president patch on his cut before flipping open the knife and slicing through the threads, neatly severing the patch from his cut.

"All in favor for Dragon as President of Aces and Eights Motorcycle Club, say aye," Poet said strongly.

A unanimous 'aye' went up around the table.

"All in favor for Grease as Vice President of Aces and Eights Motorcycle Club, say aye," Poet continued.

Again, a unanimous affirmative vote.

"All in favor for Hulk…" I zoned out a bit as I heard my name, my eyes growing wide.

'Aye's filled the room, and I turned my head to silently look at Casper, who gave me a proud nod. Then my eyes met Dragon's. I was taking his vacant spot.

He looked away.

"All in favor of Will—Christ, that boy needs another name," Poet grumbled, making low chuckles fill the room as he continued on.

Will was also voted in.

Poet stood from the table and glared at Dragon as his son-in-law moved to help him.

I stood straight as the men around me rose from their chairs and Poet moved against the wall, sweating as he stood straight and tall.

Then everyone moved.

Dragon swallowed hard as he braced his hands on the table in what was once Slider's place. Then he tapped it twice and sat down.

Grease followed suit in the seat Poet had just vacated.

Will's seat stayed empty. I wondered if he knew what was happening at the club and chose to miss it, or if his dad hadn't mentioned it.

"Well," Poet said roughly to me, gesturing with his arm when I was the last man standing.

I moved around the table slowly and pulled out my new chair, not meeting anyone's eyes as I dropped down.

Subdued clapping and cheering filled the room, and I was thankful for it. It sure as shit wasn't the best circumstances to become an officer, but it was mine. My night.

"Sit down before you fall down, old man," Dragon suddenly barked at Poet, who was looking really fucking gray.

Casper kicked Will's chair away from the table, and Poet hobbled his way over, taking a seat, but remaining separate from the table.

"News?" Grease asked, bracing his elbows on the table. I watched him silently for a moment as he fidgeted and noticed how much he'd aged in the past week. His hair and beard had little streaks of gray that I'd never noticed before.

"Congrats, Hulk," Samson said quietly, reaching over to grip my shoulder, and I nodded my thanks. He'd been completely silent at every other meeting I'd attended in that room, more of an observer than anything. I wondered if he ever gave input, or just stayed to keep on top of shit going down with the club.

"Two boys from Western Oregon University, one from University of Oregon," Poet announced to the room. "Those are the dead ones."

Grease turned his head and spit on the floor.

"Contact in the police department says the roommate of the U of O kid was involved. Haven't been able to find him. Not sure if he went home for the summer, or what."

"Name?" Casper barked.

"That's it?" Dragon asked in confusion. "Only four of 'em?"

"Looks like it," Poet answered, shaking his head. "They were doin' little shit. Kid shit. That fuckin' attack was—it didn't make any fuckin' sense."

"Little cunts," Smokey rasped, his breath labored.

"Name?" Casper asked again.

"Steve Smith," Poet replied. "Waitin' to hear where he's from. Maybe he's run home to Mummy and Daddy."

"He's mine," Grease announced, his voice resolute.

"Steven fuckin' Smith? Jesus, like finding a needle in a haystack," Casper commented in disgust. "Talk about the most average name in the fuckin' United States."

His words nagged at me. Average. There was something right at the edge of my mind, but I couldn't grab hold of it.

A knock sounded at the door and all our heads snapped up in surprise. Casper pushed to his feet and opened the door.

"I'm sorry. Really sorry, but Patrick's not supposed to be—"

"Wife!" Poet bellowed, his face a mixture of embarrassment and fury.

"Don't ye use that tone with me, Patrick Gallagher!" Amy's voice was shaking, and oddly had a hint of a Scottish accent. "I'll twist yer balls straight off yer body."

I covered my mouth with one hand to hide my smile and dropped my eyes to the table. If I met anyone's eyes right then, I'd fucking lose it.

Dragon helped Poet get to his feet, and the old man stomped off the best he could while putting very little pressure on his wounded thigh. When the door closed behind him and we couldn't hear him bitching at his wife anymore, the entire room roared with laughter.

"Did you see her face?" Grease asked, a small smile on his face. "She probably *woulda* tore off his balls."

"Nah, she needs 'em," Casper argued, his voice hitching as he tried to fight off his guffaws.

"Aw, fuck. That's disgustin'," I groaned, making a new round of laughter roll through the room.

Dragon's eyes were crinkled at the corners as he glanced around the table, meeting each of our eyes one by one. "I'll do my best," he announced seriously, his face falling back into severe lines.

Every single man went silent as we nodded.

"We gotta talk arrangements," he said roughly, leaning back in his chair.

"Farrah's been takin' care of Slider, Vera and Gram," Casper announced. "Got 'em at a funeral home—" his voice broke and he cleared his throat. "Waitin' on details from you."

Dragon nodded. "You got the cash for that?" he asked bluntly.

"No," Casper answered. "With Lily…"

My stomach rolled. "I got it," I cut in. "Got some savings."

"Got a baby on the way," Casper argued.

"And income comin' in, we'll be fine—" I shot back.

"Club'll handle it." Dragon cut me off. "Least we can do. Clear?"

"Yep," Casper said, his whole body seeming to sag in relief.

"Grease?" Dragon called, drawing attention to the silent man beside him.

"Cremated Mick," he whispered roughly. "Not doin' nothin' 'til my woman's out of the hospital."

I closed my eyes against the look on his face. The man was barely hanging on—I wasn't sure how he'd gotten that far.

"Ain't sure she's gonna want a club—" Grease said apologetically.

"No worries, brother," Dragon replied softly, reaching out to grip Grease's shoulder. "You do what's best for your family. Ain't no one gonna question that."

"You got the cheddar for that?" Samson spoke up, surprising us all. "Me and Ash can help with Micky."

"I got it, man, thanks," Grease said with a nod, a look of understanding passing between them.

Another knock broke into the tense silence and Dragon cursed. "Grand Central fuckin' Station."

"What?" Grease yelled sharply at the door, his nerves obviously fried.

Samson's woman, Ash, poked her head in, making him sit up straighter. If I didn't know better, I'd think the man was afraid his woman was going to drag his ass out like Amy had done to Poet.

"Sorry," she said worriedly, glancing around the room. "But someone's screamin' like they're dyin'." Her eyes met mine. "Think it's Trix."

I shot up from the table, glancing at Dragon.

"Go!" he ordered, standing up quickly.

I ran.

When I got to my room, I threw open the door, Trix's screams getting loud as fuck once they weren't muffled by the solid wood. She was thrashing around, tangled up in the blanket and sheets as she wailed nonsense.

I felt Dragon at my back as I stepped into the room and reached for her.

"Bea," I yelled over her cries. "It's a dream, baby. It's a dream."

Trix hit me in the face as she flailed, and I scrambled to grab her arms as she fought me in her sleep. She was pulling so hard against me, I was afraid she was going to hurt herself.

"You're okay," I murmured over and over as I tried to contain her. "Baby, wake up." My voice cracked.

Finally, I crawled completely on top of her, dropping my body over hers as she beat at my back. I pressed my face against hers, seeing stars as her forehead hit my cheekbone.

"Shhh," I whispered into her ear as she finally slowed her struggles, then went completely still beneath me. "You're okay, Sweetbea. It's just a dream."

I lifted my head and glanced quickly at Dragon, who was standing in the doorway. His eyes were dark and haunted as he nodded at me, stepping back and pulling the door closed, leaving me and Trix alone.

"Cam?" she asked softly, tears running down her face, into her hair.

"Hey," I whispered gently back, my throat tight.

It was too much. I was cracking. After everything that had happened that day, I was finally at the end of my rope. I wanted to weep.

"I was looking for you," she whispered back, her eyes glossy.

"I was right here, baby."

"No, you weren't," she murmured back, closing her eyes and turning her face away.

★ ★ ★

THREE DAYS LATER, we said goodbye to Gram, Slider and Vera. They were going to be buried in a cemetery on the edge of town, leaving a space between Gram and Vera for Micky's ashes. Callie had decided she wanted Mick in beside his great-grandmother, but they were waiting to lay him to rest until she could be there. Until then, his remains would stay in his bedroom.

As I helped a hollow-eyed Trix into one of the limos the funeral home had provided, I glanced around to the sea of bikes waiting to leave from the funeral. Aces members from chapters all over the west coast had traveled to Eugene to pay their respects. So had members of other clubs we were allies with, coming from places all over the US, from Florida to Montana.

"I'll see you at the cemetery," I said quietly to Trix as I helped her buckle her seatbelt. The limo was already full of family, her mom and Farrah, my little sisters, Tommy and Rose.

Leo was riding in the procession, his scar on full display for the first time since the shooting.

I nodded at my ma and backed out of the limo, walking over to where my bike was parked. The people of Eugene were going to be out in full force as we rode through town, and the thought of the police outriders stopping traffic along the route made me chuckle a little under my breath.

The day before, I'd finally heard from the cop who'd questioned me. They were closing the case. Between the boys' prints all over their weapons and the fact that our guns were registered, it was a clear case of self-defense. He'd sounded pissed. I was pretty sure Poet had something to do with the fact that the dogs had been called off. He'd probably called in every favor he had with the department, one last hurrah before he stepped away.

"Ready?" Casper asked, wrapping a bandana over his flattened Mohawk. Mom must have cut his hair the night before.

"Yup." I started up my bike.

Thank Christ it was almost over. Trix looked like she was going to fall over at any second. She was barely eating and she hadn't slept in days, beyond a few naps at her parents' house. She barely spoke to me.

She barely spoke to anyone.

I hadn't been able to corner her, there was too much shit happening, too much to get ready and plan for. There hadn't been time to make her talk to me.

I cracked my neck and slid my helmet on.

After this fucked up day was over, I was going to sit on a couch and drink until I couldn't stand up again. Then tomorrow, I was going to figure out what the fuck was going on with my woman.

This shit had to stop, one way or another.

Chapter 20

TRIX

I GLANCED ACROSS the crowded clubhouse and took a deep breath. I'd been mingling for over two hours and my feet were beginning to hurt in the shoes I'd borrowed from my mom. I hadn't had anything to wear to a funeral—I hadn't even been to one since I was a kid. If it had just been Slider and Vera, I would have felt comfortable in a nice pair of jeans and a tank top, but for Gram, I'd known I had to do better than that. Unfortunately, the only summer dress I'd had was getting too tight in the chest and belly, so I'd felt like I was wrapped in sausage casing all day.

I was ready to change into one of Cam's t-shirts and get off my feet.

My family had taken a little time alone at my parents' house to unwind after we'd finished burying Vera, Slider and Gram, but eventually we'd had to make our way back to the clubhouse. The reception—if you could call it that—was just as important as the procession of hundreds of bikers had been. It was a celebration of life, and Slider wouldn't have wanted any other type of sendoff.

I'd also spent quite a bit of time with Cam that day. It was odd, his presence soothed me as much as it hurt. I was so jumbled up inside that I wanted him close, but the minute he got too close, all I wanted was for him to leave. I hadn't told him that I was moving in with my parents yet. I didn't want to deal with the fight that I knew it would cause, especially right before the funerals.

Everything hurt, from my eyelids to the tips of my toes. I felt so worn down, so overwhelmingly tired. When I tried to sleep, I had unbearable nightmares, but when I stayed awake, I was so weary I could cry. The lack of sleep made the flashbacks even clearer during the day, almost like hallucinations that I couldn't seem to stop. I wondered if anyone else was dealing with the aftereffects of the attack like I was. If they were, they weren't admitting it.

I swept my eyes around the room one more time, but I couldn't see Cam anywhere. I wasn't really surprised. There were so many people in the room that they brushed up against me constantly. My parents and Leo were over by the pool table, beers in hand. Leo wouldn't be old enough to drink legally for years still, but I think my mom was giving him a pass for the day.

He'd been shot in the face—drinking beer seemed so insignificant in comparison.

Gramps and Nan were sitting a few bar stools down from where I was standing, and I caught Nan's eye as I made my way toward them.

"I'm beat," I told her quietly, leaning in for a hug. "I think I'm going to go lay down for a while."

"Okay, baby," she murmured back, looking closely into my eyes. "Get some rest, huh?"

"I'll try."

I pushed my way into the back hallway, and finally had some room to move. While the clubhouse was open for visiting members and friends, the hallway to the bedrooms was off-limits. A prospect that had been a few years behind me in high school stood guard.

When I reached Cam's bedroom, I let out a sigh of relief. Finally, a little quiet.

I pushed open the door and closed it behind me without turning on the light, cocooning me in darkness.

"You comin' to bed?" a voice slurred, making me jump.

"Cam," I sighed after a moment.

"Who'd you think it was?" he asked, and I could hear the sheets rustling underneath him.

"Why are you in here?" I replied without answering his question.

"Needed a couple minutes by myself," he mumbled.

"Oh, I'll just—"

"Don't open that fucking door," he snapped, making me freeze in my tracks.

"What's your problem?" The hair on the back of my neck stood up, the darkness making his harsh words seem almost threatening.

"My problem?"

"Yeah," I inched farther into the room, crossing my arms around my torso.

"You seriously askin' me that?"

I stayed silent as my eyes adjusted to the darkness, finding him seated on the bed with his elbows braced on his knees.

"What's goin' on with you, Bea?"

"Nothing," I replied automatically, the word coming out tonelessly. My limbs felt like dead weight as I tried to keep my body upright.

"Bullshit," he hissed, raising his head to look at me. "You're not sleepin,' you're not eatin,' you're barely fuckin' talkin.' What the fuck is wrong with you?"

"I'm not doing this with you when you're drunk," I snapped back, slowly turning toward the door.

"We're doin' this *now*," Cam argued, surging off the bed so quickly I took a stutter step away from him. "What's wrong?"

"Nothing."

"What's wrong?" his voice grew louder.

"Nothing."

"What the fuck is wrong with you?" he screamed, leaning forward a little at the waist.

"Fuck you!" I screamed back, my face heating.

"Oh, fuck me? *Fuck me?*"

"Get the fuck away from me!"

"I'm not anywhere goddamn near you! You don't let me near you!" He threw his hands up in frustration.

"That's because I don't want you near me," I hissed back, my hands shaking. "I don't even want to *look* at you!"

Cam stumbled back a step, his face creased in confusion. I took the opportunity to dart toward the door and I'd barely gotten it open before Cam's large hand was over my shoulder and slamming it shut again.

"You're not fuckin' leavin'!" he shouted.

That was the catalyst. Four small words that sucked me back in time to a place I never wanted to visit again.

Memory after memory filled my head until I was stumbling away from the door, pressing my hands against my ears trying to make the voice stop.

"You're not going to leave me."

"You're not leaving."

"You won't go anywhere."

"You've got nowhere to go."

"What, did you think you would run from me?"

"Cam? Everything okay, bud?" Casper's voice called, then the door behind me swung open and the overhead light was flipped on.

I didn't turn toward the door. Instead, I pressed my hands harder against my ears as the memories continued to flood in, even as light filled the room and illuminated the bed I'd been sleeping in for weeks.

"Stupid bitch."

"Did you think I wouldn't notice?"

"Come to Daddy, Trix."

"Don't," Cam's voice slurred as he moved toward me. "Get out."

"You're drunk, son. Come on, come back to the party."

"No. We're talkin'."

"Doesn't look like Trix feels like talkin'." Casper's voice was calm, even as Cam seemed to grow more agitated.

I stared at the dark green wool blanket covering Cam's bed.

"Prospect called me—what's goin' on?" my pop's voice rumbled through the room.

"Get out!" Cam yelled.

I jolted as Cam reached behind him, wrapping his arm around my waist and pressing me into his back.

But still, I was frozen. Stuck between the past and the present.

"Why the fuck are there toys all over the living room, Brenna?"

"You stay home all fucking day, you couldn't clean the fuck up?"

"Where's Trix? Trix, Daddy's home!"

"I'll see my kid when I want to, bitch. Trix, come on down, sweetheart!"

"You okay, Little Warrior?" my pop called, making Cam's arm tighten around my waist.

"We're talkin.' Get out," Cam slurred again, his fingers rubbing gently on my belly.

"Trix? Answer me," my pop ordered.

"Come on, Cameron," Casper said gently. "Just makin' sure everything's okay, boy."

"Everythin' was fine till you came busting into my room," Cam snapped.

"Bellatrix Colleen?" Pop called.

There was movement at the door, and then Casper cursed. "Get the fuck outta here, Ladybug."

"What's going on?" Farrah asked accusingly. "Cam?"

"Just tryin' to talk to Trix," Cam said softly to his mom. "Just need to talk some shit out."

"Why's she standin' behind you, baby?" Farrah questioned, her voice coming closer.

"Just holdin' her, Ma," Cam sighed.

"You okay, Trix?" Farrah called.

I couldn't answer her. My entire body had begun to shake, and within seconds, my teeth were chattering. I felt like my chest was caving in as I began to tilt to the side.

"Trix?" Cam's voice was alarmed as he spun toward me. He lifted me up as I raised my hands to my throat.

I was suffocating. I couldn't breathe.

"Cody, get me a paper bag," Farrah snapped, striding toward us.

Cam sat on the edge of the bed, settling me in his lap as his hands ran all over me.

"Are you hurt?" he asked frantically, testing my arms and legs and belly. "Where are you hurt?"

"Cameron, stop it." Farrah's voice made Cam freeze. "Trix, honey, I think you're having a panic attack."

I wheezed and scratched at my throat.

"It's okay, I promise. Deep breaths, come on. Take a deep breath for me."

My eyes searched the room frantically until they landed on my pop. Almost instantly, I pulled a huge gulp of air into my lungs.

"That's it," Farrah said soothingly. "Now, let it out slowly."

I kept my eyes on my pop, who was less than four feet away, and took another deep breath. Then I met his eyes, my heart in a thousand pieces.

"Fuck this shit," Pop mumbled, moving forward quickly.

"Don't," Cam growled threateningly, his arms tightening around my body.

"The fuck do you think you are?" Pop said incredulously, coming to a halt. "I'll fuckin' end you."

"Jesus Christ," Farrah hissed, reaching up to pull my hands from my throat. "The testosterone in here is so thick I can taste it—and it tastes like shit."

"Got a bag, Ladybug," Casper announced as he ran back into the room.

"Good, give it to Dragon. Trix is breathin' again, think he's the one who's gonna need it."

"Bitch—" Pop started to say.

"Don't go there, brother," Casper warned.

The skin on my arms prickled as I curled my body tighter into a ball on Cam's lap. I wanted everyone to go away. My mind was spinning.

"Cam, I don't think Trix is up for a chat tonight," Farrah said softly, turning her back on Casper and my pop as if she couldn't even be concerned with them. "Why don't you wait until the morning? Clear heads and all that."

"She stays with me," Cam ground out, his head tilting down to rub his hair roughened cheek over the top of my head.

"Okay, baby. But I think she needs some sleep, bud. She looks like she's ready to fall over."

"I got her."

"I know you do. I know. But you need to lay her down so she can sleep." Farrah's eyes met mine as she rubbed her thumbs over the backs of my hands. "She's growin' a baby. Pregnant women need their sleep." She gave me a small smile.

"She don't sleep," Cam whispered, his voice strangled. "She just lays there, tossin' and turnin,' and when she falls asleep, she screams."

Farrah's eyes drifted shut, and she swallowed hard.

"Well, maybe if you lay with her she can get some rest, huh?" Farrah finally said, opening her tear-soaked eyes. "Keep the monsters at bay for a night."

"I'm tryin'." I couldn't see if Cam was crying, but it sounded like it. I knew whatever he'd been drinking had probably brought his emotions to the surface, but I couldn't help him. I couldn't even help myself.

I wanted to reach up and pull him against me, to kiss his face and tell him that we'd be okay—but I couldn't. It didn't feel like anything would ever be okay again.

"Keep trying, baby," Farrah said softly.

Cam nodded against my head, then scooted back on the bed. I glanced at my pop and Casper as we moved, but both were frozen.

I let Cam move me so my body was between him and the wall, then shut my eyes as he curled his body around me.

"There you go," Farrah said softly, pulling a blanket up over our shoulders. "Get some rest."

The room went quiet for a moment before shuffling footsteps moved toward the door, and the light shining through my eyelids went dark. Then the door closed softly.

"I love you," Cam whispered against my ear as my heart thundered in my chest. "I love you so much. You gotta let me help you, Sweetbea. *Please.*"

His breath hitched once, then twice, and within seconds, he began to snore. I opened my eyes and stared at the ceiling.

I'd trusted Cam for so long, it had become second nature to me. We were a team. Soul mates. I'd never imagined being with anyone but him, never envisioned a life that didn't include him as my man.

So, I couldn't understand why I had this block—this feeling of apprehension and fear at the thought of settling down with him and a baby. Was it immaturity? I didn't think so. It went so much deeper than that.

I didn't want to be my mother.

What if, after a few more months, we'd decided that we didn't work as a couple? Without the baby, it would have been hard to leave him, but I could've. I could've stepped away and made a different plan, found a different man. Maybe.

But now? He'd never let me leave.

"You're not going anywhere," the voice in my memory hissed.

It wouldn't matter how bad our life got. If I stayed, I'd be stuck.

I could never imagine Cam abusing me the way my stepdad abused my mom. Never in a million years. But my mom hadn't anticipated it, either.

She'd married a man that was so clean cut he was squeaky. He had money, dressed well and asked her to marry him, even though she was already pregnant with someone else's babies. He'd seemed perfect on paper.

A lot like Cam seemed perfect for me—except Cam wasn't clean cut. He was rough. He lived outside the law. Rules and regulations didn't mean anything to him, and while that didn't bother me one single bit normally… it made the threat so much more significant.

I couldn't be sure. I couldn't be sure, and I couldn't take the risk. When I'd gone to him about the baby, terrified out of my mind, he'd looked at me like he hated me.

God, I could still see the disgust on his face. Why hadn't he seen how badly I was falling apart? And now, he acted like none of that had even happened—like it was all erased because of the things we'd gone through since that day.

The attack was so much bigger than my meltdown about the baby—I knew that. I knew that our problems were insignificant when I compared them to losing four people in one day. My worries about having a baby before I began my career seemed silly when I remembered the day of the attack, watching as, one by one, my family fell.

But that didn't mean that I'd forgotten the way Cam had looked at me.

What would have happened if we hadn't had to deal with something so devastating? Would he still be treating me like dirt beneath his boots? Would he still be looking at me like I was a monster? How could I live with him, knowing that at any point, he could just completely shut himself away from me?

He'd looked at me like my mom's husband had looked at her—like she was nothing. Like I was *nothing*.

It was better if I got out before that could happen—before he could look at me like that again. I didn't think I'd be able to live if, down the road, I did something to make him angry and he pulled away like that again.

I inhaled deeply, taking in the scent of Cam's deodorant and the smell of grease that he seemed to always carry around. I loved him so much.

But hours later, as the sun started coming through the small window high on the wall, I gently pulled myself out of his arms and got dressed, packing a few items into a small bag and throwing it over my shoulder.

Then I left him.

I didn't stop moving until I'd made my way to my parents' house and opened the front door without knocking.

"You okay?" Pop asked me as he came down the short hallway in nothing but a pair of ratty jeans.

"I don't want to go back," I replied, dropping my bag to the floor. "Please. I want to stay here."

Pop searched my face for almost a full minute before he nodded. "Your ma's in bed. Go climb in with her and get some sleep. I'll take care of it."

My entire body sagged in both relief and sadness.

My relationship with Cam was over.

Chapter 21

CAMERON

When I woke up, my mouth tasted like something had crawled in there and died. I smacked my lips, trying to make my mouth water a little, and reached across the bed for Trix.

The spot beside me was empty.

Fuck.

I rolled into a sitting position and clutched my head. Goddamn. Whiskey always gave me the shittiest hangovers. Unfortunately, it didn't affect my memory, so I recalled in vivid detail the shit that went down the night before.

I was such a dumbass.

I'd wanted to wait until after all of the funeral shit to talk to Trix, but after I'd finished off a fifth of Jack and she'd come into the room, all my plans had gone to shit.

I climbed to my feet and swayed a little. I needed a shower and a cup of coffee—then I'd figure out what I was going to do about Trix.

★ ★ ★

"How you feeling?" Farrah called out jokingly from across the main room of the clubhouse as I poured myself a cup of coffee a while later. My head hurt like hell, so I just flipped her off instead of responding.

"You guys get some decent sleep last night?" she asked as she and Casper moved toward me.

The people visiting the club had mostly cleared out while I was still in bed, and things were quiet as we sat down on a couple of couches. I could hear people starting up their bikes outside, but there wasn't anyone I wanted to say goodbye to, so I didn't even attempt to see who was still hanging around.

"Yeah, I crashed. Trix was gone when I woke up, though—not sure if she slept."

"Shit," Farrah sighed. "I swear to God, history repeats itself."

"What do you mean?" I asked, taking a small sip of my scalding coffee. Damn, that shit was good. One of the women must have made it.

"Don't you remember when I had a panic attack in Cody's room? God, I thought he was going to kill Slider."

"Would have," Casper mumbled, wrapping his arm around my mom's shoulders. "But you were so out of it, I couldn't put ya down."

"That's right," I murmured, remembering that fucked up night when I was a kid. "I thought you were dead."

Casper made a disgusted noise in his throat, but Farrah just laughed.

"Sorry." I gave Casper an apologetic look.

"Has Trix had panic attacks before?" Farrah asked, settling farther into Casper's side.

"Not that I know of. She's been actin' fuckin' weird for weeks, though."

"Hmm." Farrah met my eyes. "What started it?"

I opened my mouth, then snapped it shut again. I didn't like the idea of airing our dirty laundry in front of my parents. They loved me—and if they had to choose, they'd always choose my side. But that was the problem. I didn't want them to think badly of Trix, even when I was pissed at her.

"When she found out she was pregnant," I finally said, leaving it at that.

"She wasn't happy about it?" Casper asked.

"No." I swallowed hard, then took another sip of my coffee to stall. "She wanted an abortion."

Farrah's eyes grew wide and Casper scoffed in disbelief.

"What the fuck?" Farrah screeched.

"I don't know," I mumbled. "She was seriously fucked up about it. Don't know what was goin' on in her head."

"Jesus," Casper murmured.

"Are you fucking kidding me?"

"Calm down, Ladybug," Casper snapped. "He doesn't need your shit."

Farrah scowled at Casper, but took a deep breath and relaxed back into his body.

"She already said she wouldn't do it," I told them, shaking my head. "I think she might've been figuring her shit out, but then those fuckers showed up at the house and she's ten times worse now."

"You think she'd have an abortion?" Farrah asked quietly.

"No." My hand tightened painfully on my coffee mug. "No, she wouldn't."

"You sure?" Casper pushed.

"Yeah, I'm fuckin' sure," I snapped back, just the thought of it riling me up.

Casper raised his hands in surrender and I sighed.

"She told me last night she doesn't want me near her," I ground out, looking at my mom for some reassurance. "I don't know what the fuck to do. I've tried everythin.' She won't talk to me."

"You keep tryin'." Casper said, surprising me. "She's worth it, you keep pushin'."

"That worked real well last night," I laughed, scratching at the short beard that was growing in on my cheeks.

"You were drunk," Farrah said flatly. "I thought Dragon was going to kill you."

"Shit." I groaned. I'd conveniently forgotten about that part.

"Wasn't his place to step in," Casper cut in. "But can't say I wouldn't do the same with CeeCee or Lil."

I nodded. "How's Lil doing?"

"Better," Casper said with a nod. "A little better. She's with Cec at home so we could come here and check on you."

"Hell, you didn't have to do that."

"Yes, we did," Farrah argued. "You're our boy and you've had a rough time of it."

"I'm fine."

"No, you're not," Farrah said resolutely. "But you'll figure it out, bud. Nothing lasts forever—even bad times."

I nodded, accepting her words. "Have they said when they think Lil will get her eyesight back?" I asked softly.

We hadn't really talked about the chance of Lily regaining her sight. It could happen, and I think all of us were waiting for it to get better—but there were no guarantees. We hoped for the best, but in the meantime, we'd have to just accept her blindness as fact.

Lily was blind, and there was nothing we could do about it. No surgery that could reverse the damage, no drug that could fix her.

"We're going to start taking her to a psychologist next week," Farrah answered. "Hopefully, that will help her."

"It might not," Casper murmured. He raised his eyes to mine. "Might be that this is her life from now on. Gotta be prepared for that."

"Fuck," I hissed.

"Coulda been a fuck of a lot worse, Cam." Casper shook his head. "We coulda lost her. Eyesight is nothin' compared to that."

Farrah sniffed, but that was the only indication that she was feeling emotional. My adopted mother was tough, but she felt things just as deeply as everyone else, maybe even deeper. She'd never show that emotion at the club, though.

"You guys heard anything from Grease?" I asked, changing the subject. It wasn't any easier to talk about Casper's sister, Callie, but at least we wouldn't be thinking about what would have happened if Vera and Gram hadn't protected Lily with their bodies.

"Yeah, Callie's up and around now," Casper said with a nod. "They're not letting her out yet, but they've got her out of bed and walking."

"Damn, isn't that really soon?"

"Nah, they make you get up pretty quick these days," Farrah replied. "The quicker you're on your feet, the better you heal, I think."

"I need to get back up there." I'd barely been up to see Callie. With everything going on with Trix and then the funerals, I hadn't made the time.

"She'd like that," Casper said with a nod. "We'd better get going, Ladybug. Don't want Lil home too long without us."

We climbed to our feet, and I finished off my coffee before hugging Farrah goodbye.

"Cecilia doin' okay?" I asked, as I walked my parents outside.

"Yeah, she's okay," Casper answered. "Can you believe that shit with Woody? I think she's been talking to him on the phone since he went back to Salem with his mom."

"I didn't even know that they'd been talking before," Farrah said in irritation. "That girl is giving me gray hair."

"You don't have any gray hair," Casper scoffed, coming to a stop next to his bike.

"You brought the bike?" I asked in surprise, glancing at Farrah.

"Yeah, not too much longer before I'll be too big to ride. Gotta get our time in now," she joked.

"Can't believe you're havin' another baby," I said softly, wrapping my arm around her narrow shoulders.

"Me, either," Casper said ruefully, making Farrah smack him with the back of her hand. "Havin' a baby the same month as our son—fuckin' *Jerry Springer* around here."

I bust out laughing, and fuck, it felt good.

"You're such a dick," Farrah snapped, laying a hand on her belly.

"Aw, Ladybug." Casper grabbed Farrah's hips and pulled her toward him. "You know I'm excited as hell."

He leaned down to kiss her and I turned my head away. They'd always been really affectionate, which was cool, but that didn't mean I wanted to see my dad sticking his tongue in my mom's mouth.

"We'll see you later," Casper called, pulling my attention back as he climbed on his bike and reached out to help Farrah on behind him. "Come to dinner."

As they backed out of their spot, Farrah blew me a kiss, so I waved back in response. When I was a kid, she used to do the same damn thing when she dropped me off at school, and she wouldn't let me leave without acknowledging the kiss somehow. One year, she'd made me fucking "catch it" every day or she'd climb out of the car and start singing at the top of her lungs.

She was such a pain in the ass. I smiled at the memory. I guess that was what happened when your adopted parents were only like thirteen years older than you were—they were still young enough to feel the need to embarrass the hell out of you for fun.

I glanced across the field to Dragon and Brenna's place and took a deep breath. I knew Trix was there. She wouldn't have left the property without someone coming to tell me.

I started walking, but took my time making my way over to the small house that seemed so out of place in the large field next to the garage. Maybe I'd take Trix out on the bike. We hadn't had a minute to ourselves in a long ass time, and I thought she might like riding up to our old swimming hole and spending the day. We had to get shit worked out. The distance between us was fucking killing me.

I wanted to touch her. Fuck, it felt like years since the last time I'd been inside her—and even that memory was tainted. She'd been so desperate when she woke up from a dream that I'd got both of us off in record time so she could fall back asleep again. I hadn't realized that it would be the last time she'd reach for me, instead staying awake for as long as she could, so the nightmares wouldn't come.

The sexual frustration was a killer, but even worse than that was her complete personality change since she'd found out she was pregnant. She wasn't herself in any sense of the word. The opinionated woman I loved had become a fucking shadow. Barely speaking. Barely existing.

I finally reached the front porch of the house, and knocked on the screen door before letting myself in. Leo was sitting on the couch. He'd practically taken up residence in that exact spot since the attack.

"Hey, Trix around?" I asked him.

"Yeah, man. Think she's in the kitchen."

"Thanks." I walked toward the back of the house and found Trix eating a bowl of cereal as she stood at the counter.

Jesus.

She looked like my Trix again. She'd showered and the long black hair that I loved was wet and slicked back from her face. Her eyes weren't shadowed, and the dark circles that had seemed like they would never leave had faded quite a bit.

"Hey, Sweetbea," I said, announcing my presence.

Her head snapped up at my voice, and her eyes grew round in shock.

"What are you doing here?" she asked, taking a step back along the counter.

"What?" I watched in confusion as she set her bowl down and moved even further away from me.

"I thought—"

"What're you doing?" I cut her off as she took another step away from me.

"Cam," her voice was soft as her expression shuttered.

"Cam," Dragon's voice boomed as he came up behind me. "Need to have a word."

I glanced behind me at Dragon's expressionless face, then spun toward Trix again. "The fuck did you do, Bellatrix?" I asked, watching her face fall. "You fuckin' kiddin' me right now?"

"Cam," Dragon snapped, laying his hand on my shoulder. I shrugged him off and took a step forward, watching Trix in disbelief.

"I'm going to move back in with my parents for a while," she said softly, tucking her thumbs into her palms as she fisted her hands.

"No." My voice was resolute. She was out of her fucking mind if she thought she was going to run home to her parents because we were having a hard time. This was such bullshit.

"Hulk," Dragon called, authority ringing in his voice. It wasn't the voice of her father, it was the voice of my president.

"You fuckin' bitch," I whispered, shaking my head as the full significance of her words became clear. "You want out? Makin' your daddy step in because you can't even fuckin' tell me that you're gonna leave?"

Trix's lips trembled, and I hated that a part of me wanted to soothe her. She was so fucking fragile. She looked like one well-placed blow could completely end her.

"Hulk," Dragon called again in warning.

I raised my hands in the air, and took one step back. Then I spoke again.

"You want out? Fine. I'm so fuckin' done with your bullshit. So fucking done." I ran my hands over my head in disbelief. God, I'd been so happy to see her looking better. So glad that she seemed to be coming out of whatever the fuck was eating at her. I was such a goddamn idiot. "I wanna see my kid when it's born."

Trix nodded and inhaled a shaky breath.

"Fuck you," I whispered. Then I turned and walked completely out of the house.

"Hulk!" Dragon called again when I was halfway down their front porch steps.

"What?" I snapped, turning to face him. "I'm fuckin' gone, all right? You need somethin' else?"

"Who you think you're talkin' to?" Dragon growled, following me down the stairs.

"Jesus Christ," I hissed, shaking my head.

"She'll figure her shit out, boy. She just needs some time." His voice was once again mellow, almost friendly.

I laughed. I couldn't help it. I laughed so hard that it made my stomach roll with nausea from the Jack that was still sloshing around in there.

"She can have all the time she wants," I finally said, meeting Dragon's eyes. "I'm done."

"Cameron—"

I raised my hand for him to stop. I didn't want to hear it.

"Done," I said again.

I turned and walked away, through the field of tall grass and beyond the gravel in the forecourt to my bike parked on the pavement in front of the garage. I needed to get the fuck out of there.

Chapter 22

TRIX

"I LOVE YOU," my mom said a few days after my pop had escorted Cam out of the house. "But what you did was so fucking wrong, I don't even know what to say to you."

My mouth dropped open in surprise and I glanced over at my nan, who was calmly sipping her tea. We were having a "girl's lunch" before my first appointment that afternoon with my obstetrician. Mom had gotten the name of Farrah's doctor and had called for me the day before, making an appointment before she'd even informed me.

It was probably good that she'd taken the initiative, because I was still putting off anything and everything to do with the baby. I hadn't had a nightmare since I'd moved back into my parents' house, and I was afraid they'd come back if I thought of anything beyond eating and sleeping.

"Ouch," I finally murmured in disbelief.

"Truth hurts," Nan mumbled, looking at me over her mug.

"Seriously? Because I didn't want to be with Cam, I'm the bad guy?"

"Don't act like an idiot—you've never been stupid," my mom snapped. "You *used* your pop. Asked him to do your dirty work, because you knew he would, because you knew he'd do anything for you. You know the trust and respect that those men have to have for each other? Huh? When shit goes down, they have to be able to count on each other, Trix, and you shit all over that. Embarrassed Cam and *ruined* his relationship with your pop."

"Whatever." I pushed myself to my feet.

"Sit back down," Nan ordered, her tone making me drop right back into my seat.

The table went quiet for a long moment before my mom finally spoke up. "I'm not sure what's going on with you, Trix. Honest to God, I have no idea what's going through your head. But if you try to tell me one more time that you don't want to be with Cam, I won't be held responsible for my actions." She looked at me expectantly, but I didn't say a word.

I missed Cam like crazy. God, that first day when he'd stormed out of the house, I'd felt like I was dying. I'd curled up on the couch with Leo, and even though his disapproval was clear, he'd still pulled me into his side as we watched shitty television. I ached for Cam, but the thought of going back was too scary to fully contemplate. I was *safe* with my parents.

"What's really going on, Trix?" Nan asked softly.

"I can't—" I stuttered to a stop and tried again. "What if—"

"What, Trix?" my mom asked in exasperation. "Spit it out."

"What if he hurts me?" I said in one breath. "What if I stay and have the baby and then I'm stuck. What if I never get a job, and I have no way to support us? I'd never be able to leave. I'd be a single mother with no job and I—"

"*That's* your worry?" Nan asked in confusion. "Has Cam ever hurt you?"

"No!" The word came out louder than I'd intended. "No, but he *could*. He could, and by then I'd have a baby and I wouldn't be able to leave. You should've seen him when I—" My voice began to grow thick and I swallowed hard against the lump in my throat.

"What complete bullshit," Nan mumbled, shaking her head.

"You don't know!" I snapped, jerking to my feet. "You have no idea what—"

"No, but I do," my mom cut in softly.

I turned and met my mom's gaze and my heart sank into my stomach at the sorrow there.

"Sit back down, baby," she said, leaning toward me.

As soon as my ass hit the chair, she sighed and ran her hands over her face.

"I want to apologize to you," Mom said, her voice wobbling as tears filled her eyes. "First, that I didn't get away before I did, and second, because I thought you'd forgotten it all, so I haven't talked to you about it."

"Don't cry, Mom," I pleaded, her tears bringing forth my own. "You did the best you could. You didn't know—"

"I did," she cut me off, squeezing her eyes tightly closed as she shook her head. "I had that gut feeling, you know? I had it from the first. But I was so fucking stubborn back then, Trix. So sure that I was doing the right thing."

"I think we were all like that when we were young," Nan told my mom kindly, reaching out to pat her hand.

Mom scoffed, and wiped at her face. "I knew something wasn't right, but it wasn't until after we were married that I saw Tony clearly. But Trix, I knew something wasn't right, baby. Okay? I knew it. Deep in my gut, I knew I was making the wrong decision, and I made it anyway."

"You said it yourself," I replied hoarsely. "You didn't see things clearly until after you were married."

Mom sighed. "This is coming out all wrong."

"Oh, I don't know. Sounds right to me," Nan put in dryly.

"I didn't love Tony. I was scared and pregnant and he offered me a way out. I knew it was weird that he was okay with marrying me, even knowing that I didn't love him and I was already pregnant with another man's children, but I let the *idea* of him speak louder than my common sense."

"I didn't remember him before," I said when my mom paused. "But I remember it now."

"I'm so sorry, Trix," Mom rasped. "I knew I should get away from him, but I thought if I could just wait a little longer for you to go to school it—you know what? It doesn't matter. My reasons were ridiculous, and I've hated myself for them for years."

"I can't take the chance of that," I whispered, looking down at the table in front of me.

"What if Cam died tomorrow? What if the club got raided?" Nan paused to knock on the wood kitchen table. "What if you fell out of love with Cam? What if you weren't actually pregnant? What if the goddamn sky was falling? You can't live your life on what-ifs, Trix."

"I can't live my life regretting my decisions, either," I snapped back.

Nan scoffed. "You think you won't regret this decision? You *love* him. You've loved Cam since you were five years old!" Her voice dropped and went hoarse. "I used to lie in bed at night when Nix was a kid, wishing like hell that Patrick was lying next to me. I wanted to tell him about the trouble Nix had gotten himself into—to listen to Patrick's voice telling me that we'd figure it out. Every time something great happened, from a successful season of Little League to the day Nix lost his first tooth, I'd mourn the fact that I couldn't tell Patrick."

I closed my eyes at the pain in her voice. I wanted that, too. I wanted to be able to roll over and tell Cam that it was his turn to wake up with the baby, or that our little one had done something fantastic that day. But what if he didn't care? What if, for some reason, he started to hate me? What then?

"I can't," I said as I opened my eyes. "I haven't had nightmares since I came home. I'm getting better."

Nan scoffed as my mom looked at me sadly.

"Just because your body was so worn down that you've slept without nightmares for a couple nights, doesn't mean they're gone," Nan said flatly, meeting my eyes. "I still have nightmares from something that happened when I was younger than you. Those don't just go away, Trix."

"I just want to feel like myself again," I yelled, jumping up from the table. "I feel normal when I'm here!"

"Oh, baloney," my mom argued, rising to her feet so we were face to face again. "You're not yourself! You can't be—not after all that's happened. Hell, Trix. I don't know that any of us will ever be the same. Add your hormones to that, and right now you're teetering on the ledge of a very high cliff."

"But what if—"

"No," Mom snapped, cutting me off. "No more 'what-ifs.' Do you love Cam?"

I closed my eyes and braced my hands on the table in front of me. I did. I loved him more than anything in the world. I was just so scared.

"Yes," I finally rasped.

"He's a good man, Bellatrix." Mom's voice was low and serious. "I know that you're afraid. I even understand it, baby. But you're throwing away something good—really good. And for what? Fear? I didn't raise you to be a coward."

I lifted my hands and buried my face in my palms as the first sob was torn from my throat, and once I'd started crying, I couldn't stop. I curled forward as I sucked in a desperate breath of air, and my body sagged as my mom's thin arms wrapped around my frame.

"I don't know what to do," I cried. "I messed up so bad, Mama."

"It'll be okay, baby. Shhh," she soothed.

"What if he doesn't forgive me? I'm so scared. What if everything's different now? What if he turns into a monster?"

"If any of that was going to happen, you wouldn't have already loved him for so long," Nan said, standing up to swipe a hand down the back of my hair. "But right now, you need to get it together, because we were supposed to leave for your doctor's appointment ten minutes ago."

"Shit!" Mom yelped, pulling away from me and hastily wiping her face with her hands.

★ ★ ★

"Shall we take a look?" the ultrasound tech asked, lubing up a huge dildo-looking thing.

My eyes widened and my mom giggled behind my head.

"This isn't funny," I growled, glancing over to where Nan was sitting in a chair.

"Oh, yeah it is," Nan mumbled.

After a few very uncomfortable minutes, suddenly the coolest sound poured into the room.

"Is that the heartbeat?" I asked in wonder. It sounded different than I'd thought it would.

"Hold on one second," the tech replied, a look of concentration on her face. She laughed a little under her breath, and then the recognizable sound of a heartbeat reached my ears. "There you go."

Then she moved the wand, making me extremely uncomfortable. "And there you go *again*."

It took me about thirty seconds for her words to penetrate.

"What?" I snapped, trying to look closer at the little screen near the foot of the bed.

"There's Baby A," she used the mouse on her computer to point at one little flashing blob. "And there's Baby B." She moved just a fraction and pointed out a second blob.

"Holy shit," I murmured, staring at the screen. "Two."

"Twins," my mom said, squeezing my shoulders as Nan stood up from her chair and crossed the room to get a better look.

"Two for the price of one," Nan murmured, leaning forward over my chest so she could look at the computer screen. "Well, you've never done shit halfway."

I laughed a little, my eyes glued to the screen. I couldn't believe there were two of them in there. Cam was going to shit.

My eyes clouded with tears.

He should have been there.

"I wish Cam was here," I whispered, making my mom squeeze my shoulders again.

The rest of the appointment passed in a blur, and before I knew it, I was in the back seat of my mom's SUV and pulling inside the clubhouse gates. We'd stopped by the pharmacy to get some prenatal vitamins and my prescription for medicine to help me sleep. I hadn't wanted to say anything to the doctor, but my mom had spoken up when he'd asked me if I had any other concerns. The doctor said the sleep medicine was pretty mild and wouldn't hurt the babies, but I was skeptical.

I wasn't putting anything in my body that I didn't have to. If I started having trouble again, I'd think about the medicine, but until then, I wasn't taking anything.

The doctor had also said that she'd get me a referral to a psychologist she'd worked in tandem with before. I wasn't sure if that was the route to go, but I was grateful that I had options.

Nan had mentioned maybe going with her to yoga—she said that helped her when the memories got really bad. I wasn't sure how that could possibly help, but I was willing to try. If nothing else, maybe it would wear me out enough to sleep.

We pulled up to the house and climbed out of the car just as Leo was coming down the steps. His face was already looking so much better than it had a week before.

"Hey, Bubby. Where you going?" I asked, moving toward him.

"Club." He lifted his chin toward the clubhouse. "Big party tonight."

"Really?" I asked skeptically, glancing sideways at the big gray building. "For what?"

"Think they're letting Callie out tomorrow, so the boys are celebrating."

"Oh." I wondered if Cam would be there, then shook my head. He would be, of course he would be. "Do you want to see the ultrasound picture first?" I asked, digging into my purse.

"Sure."

I passed the photos to Leo and watched as he shuffled through them, his face blank. I knew that he couldn't tell what the hell he was looking at and I forced myself not to chuckle as he finally reached the last picture and his eyes got huge.

"Holy shit!" he blurted, looking up at me and then back down at the photo that was labeled with little arrows pointing to both babies.

"I know, right?" I laughed, my voice a little hoarse. "There's two in there."

"Holy shit, sissy." He lifted his eyes again and looked at me seriously. "But everything's good, right?"

"Yep. Everything's fine."

"Congratulations." Leo's face pulled up in a crooked smile, and even though my heart hurt to see it, I smiled back. His face wasn't completely paralyzed on the left side, but there was definitely some nerve damage, and the doctors didn't think it would ever get better. His smile would always be slightly uneven.

"Thanks, Bubby," I said as he pulled me into a hug. "Don't say anything yet, okay? I need to tell Cam first."

"All right. I won't."

He squeezed me tight before pulling away and heading toward the clubhouse.

"You're going to get huge, fast," my mom called from the front porch where she was waiting for me. "We should probably go shopping soon."

I laughed happily and glanced down at the pictures in my hand. I was having two babies. Holy shit.

★ ★ ★

"YOU GOING OVER there?" my mom asked quietly as we sat in lawn chairs in her backyard. The clubhouse was loud with music and laughter and I couldn't help but glance that way every few minutes.

"I told him I wanted an abortion," I replied softly, keeping my eyes on the gray building as I rested a hand on my belly, rubbing my thumb back and forth across my thin t-shirt. "When I found out I was pregnant, I freaked out and I told Cam I wanted an abortion."

"Oh, Trix," my mom sighed.

"I don't think I meant it," I continued, leaning my head back against my chair. "I was just so freaked out. Cam and I had just gotten together and I was graduating, but I didn't have job yet—I was terrified."

"I'm sorry, honey."

"I just—I needed him to reassure me, but then when he did, it only made me angry. So I lashed out. I was so overwhelmed."

"Is that when you started having problems?" Mom asked softly.

"Yeah. I told him that I wouldn't do it, and he was so relieved." My voice hitched as I thought about that day. "But he was still so *angry* with me. It was like he couldn't see how badly it was tearing me apart."

"Baby girl, I'm going to tell you something that I wish a woman had told me when I was young." Mom reached out and grabbed my hand, lacing her fingers through mine. "When it comes to men—the right men—they are just as ferocious in the protection of their children as women. We always hear about mama bears, and the way a mother would fight for her kids—but we rarely hear the same for fathers. When it comes to you kids, there is nothing your father wouldn't do to protect you—and that's a blessing. I wouldn't love him the way I do if that wasn't the case."

"Yeah," I sighed.

"But there's a catch with that," she said softly, rubbing her fingers over mine. "What if the person threatening his child is its mother? What then?"

"I just needed—"

"I know what you needed, Bellatrix," Mom cut me off. "But you need to see it from his point of view. You were threatening to have an abortion. You're lucky he ever spoke to you again."

"That's ridiculous," I spat, my neck heating. "It's my decision—"

"Bellatrix Colleen, what would you have done if you went to Cam telling him you were pregnant, and he told you he wanted you to get an abortion?"

My mouth snapped shut as my stomach rolled.

What would I have done? I imagined telling Cam and him not wanting the baby. I thought of the moment I told him I wanted to get rid of it and imagined if he would have agreed with me.

Vomit shot up the back of my throat and I swallowed convulsively, trying to keep it down.

I would have hated him. I would have walked away and never looked back.

"Cam's lost everything before, Trix," my mom said quietly.

"What?" The word came out as a croak.

"He lost his entire family when you two were kids, every single person. Casper and Farrah did a good job with him, they love him like their own and he loves them, too—but these babies are the only blood tie that Cam has, the family that he's always wanted… and you threatened to take that from him."

Her words hit me like a sledgehammer.

"Oh, God," I whimpered, leaning forward to brace my elbows on my knees. "Oh, God. I was so scared, Mom. I knew that he'd never let me do it—that's why I said it. I knew that he'd talk me out of it." I turned my head to look at my mom's shadowed face. "What if he never forgives me?"

"He will," she replied softly.

"I've been so horrible to him." My eyes watered and tears fell down my face into the short grass. "I felt so guilty, for so many things. I hated the way he'd looked at me, so I focused on that. I focused on how hurt I was that he'd been angry with me."

"Your hormones are seriously messed up right now, Trix."

"That doesn't excuse it," I sobbed, pulling my hand from hers so I could cover my face. "God, I didn't want to be *stuck* with him. I wanted to be with him more than anything else, but I didn't want to be trapped there."

"You're not making a whole lot of sense, baby."

"I know!" I spat hysterically, surging to my feet as I pushed my hair away from my face. "Why am I so messed up? The nightmares just keep coming, and during the day, I'm afraid of my own fucking shadow! I'm so sick of it. I'm so sick of all of it."

"So fix it," my mom said, climbing to her feet.

"I don't know how!"

"You could start with Cameron. Once that's taken care of, we'll do yoga or get you an appointment with that shrink."

"But what if—"

"Don't start with the what-ifs again, Trix."

I nodded, looking toward the clubhouse again. She was right. I couldn't deal in what-ifs anymore. I had two babies that needed me to get my shit together.

★ ★ ★

I DIDN'T DRESS up to go to the party, but I did fix my hair and put on some makeup. It felt foreign on my face, thick and annoying, but I knew if I didn't try and cover up the evidence of my tears, people would ask questions. I hoped that they would mostly ignore me when I got there, but I wasn't counting on it.

I'd barely spoken to anyone since the attack, so they'd kept their distance, but if I walked into a party, they'd automatically assume I was there to visit.

I walked quickly through the tall grass, clutching my envelope of ultrasound photographs in my hand. I couldn't wait to show Cam our babies, even though my stomach was in one giant knot about the looming confrontation.

Would he ignore me? What if—no. No what-ifs. I needed to see him. He deserved that after the way I'd behaved. He deserved me going to him.

I waved at the brothers and their old ladies sitting at the picnic tables outside, and averted my eyes quickly from someone nailing a woman against the wall near the garage bays. I didn't need to see that shit, especially if it was one of the men I'd viewed as an indulgent uncle growing up.

I caught my pop's eyes as I entered the rowdy clubhouse, and his eyebrows rose in surprise. I shook my head at him, then glanced around the room, searching for Cam. I quickly found him, a pool stick in hand as he laughed with one of the younger guys. I think his name was Mack, though I'd never really talked to him.

I moved steadily through the room, giving small smiles to people who said hello. I didn't want to stop and take the chance of Cam seeing me and leaving.

When I finally got to the pool tables, I froze, waiting for Cam to notice me.

"Trix," he said roughly as he met my eyes. He looked away before I could reply, and leaned over the table to take his shot, as if I wasn't standing just two feet away.

"Can we talk?" My voice trembled and I wanted to curse.

"No," he replied emotionlessly as his pool stick hit the cue ball and knocked a striped ball into the pocket.

"Please," I said over the noise as he moved around the table, lining up his next shot. "I went to the—"

"Got nothin' to say to you," Cam interrupted, standing up straight. "Go home."

"No." People began to stare as I held my ground, and my face burned in mortification.

"You have that abortion yet?" Cam's statement whipped through the room, and my hand went straight to my belly in horror at his callous words.

Everyone knew now. Everyone knew why he hated me. I clenched my jaw against the pain saturating my chest. He *hated* me.

"Of course not," I ground out, tears blurring my eyes.

"Well, you still got time."

I inhaled sharply as my resolve started to waver. He was hurting me on purpose. Lashing out in the only way he could. He couldn't hit me like he would have anyone else—he'd never physically hurt me, but he could use his words—and he was. He was breaking me on purpose, and it was worse than any blow he could have delivered.

"I just want to talk," I pleaded, searching his face for anything that would tell me to keep trying. I just needed a small indication—anything that would prove that I wasn't making a fool out of myself for nothing.

"Think my prez might have somethin' to say about that," Cam said with a harsh laugh. "I'm stayin' away like you wanted. Now get the fuck away from me."

I nodded, closing my eyes for a second as I tried to settle my shaking hands. "Okay," I whispered. "Okay."

I uncurled my fist from the envelope I was gripping, and took my time smoothing out the wrinkles in the paper. Then I set the entire envelope on the edge of the pool table.

"I thought you might want to see these." My voice wobbled and I swallowed hard, still looking at the white envelope. "I went to the doctor today and they, uh, they did an ultrasound and sent home some pictures."

I looked up and met his eyes as he gave me a short nod.

"I'm so sorry, Cam," I whispered, my voice barely audible. "I love you."

He didn't respond.

There was nothing left to say, nothing that he wanted to hear from me.

The clubhouse was oddly silent as I turned away, but I didn't meet anyone's eyes as I walked steadily back toward the front door. Every single part of me wanted to drop to my knees in agony, but I didn't. I wouldn't make things harder for him, I wouldn't cause more drama than I already had.

I reached the cool night air with an overwhelming sense of relief. I'd made it outside without breaking. I'd tried to speak to Cameron, and my "what if" had come to pass, but I was still standing. I was still breathing, even if those breaths were desperate and agonizing.

"Little Warrior," my pop murmured from the darkness beside the door, giving me permission to lose it.

"Papa," I whimpered, my legs suddenly turning to rubber. The sob that tore out of my throat was so ragged that it physically hurt.

Just before I went down, my pop was there, scooping me into his arms and striding toward our house.

"You did good, baby girl," he whispered against my head as ragged cries poured out of my throat. "I know it hurts, Little Warrior, but you did real good."

Chapter 23

CAMERON

I GRABBED MY beer after Trix left the clubhouse and carried it past the pool table, snagging the envelope she'd left on my way to my room. I couldn't believe she'd had the balls to try and work shit out with me in the middle of a room full of people.

Did she think I'd just welcome her back with open arms? Jesus, I still wanted to throttle her.

I grabbed another beer on my way past the bar and carried it with me into my dark room, flipping on the light and slamming the door behind me. I was pleased as fuck that Callie was going home the next day, but hell if I'd wanted to have a party. I was wound so tight that the slightest thing could set me off, and having the clubhouse full of brothers and old ladies was a bad fucking idea.

I dropped to the bed and stared at the blank, white envelope between my fingers. I should have been there. I wondered if she'd heard the heartbeat. Maybe she'd recorded it on her phone? I wasn't going to ask her.

If it was up to me, I wouldn't see her again until my kid was born.

I took a deep breath and pulled the shiny little black and white photos out of the envelope, immediately feeling a surge of disappointment. I couldn't tell what any of the shit in the picture was. I wondered if Trix knew, then shook my head. It didn't matter.

I flipped through each picture slowly, not having a clue what I was looking at. I mean, it must have been my kid, but all I saw was a blob in the center of another blob. Nothing recognizable. I searched each picture individually, turning it this way and that, trying to find a frame of reference. Nothing.

Then I reached the last ultrasound photo and the ones I'd slid behind it fluttered to the ground as I lost all feeling in my hands.

Baby A *and* Baby B.

My heart raced.

No fucking way.

I scrambled to pick up the rest of the pictures, laying them out on the bed side by side to try and find some similarities—some extra clue about what I was looking at.

I got to my feet and swayed to the side, catching myself against the wall.

Farrah.

Farrah would know what she was looking at.

I swung open my bedroom door so hard that it slammed against the wall, but I barely noticed it as I raced toward the front room. She'd been at the bar when I left.

If she'd already gone home, I was going to freak the fuck out.

Nope, there she was. I moved toward her at a fast clip, and slammed the pictures down on the bar when I reached her.

"Look," I demanded when she glanced at me in confusion. "Look at those."

"Oh, Cam," she said softly, giving me a small smile. "Trix went to the doctor?"

"Just look," I snapped before taking a deep breath. "Please, Ma."

She nodded once, then looked down at the photographs in front of her and slid through them one by one.

"What am I looking for, baby?" she asked as Casper leaned forward to look over her shoulder.

"You'll know when you see it," I mumbled, leaning heavily against the bar.

My heart beat so hard I could hear it in my ears, and only a few seconds later, Farrah let out a small gasp.

"Holy shit," she mumbled as Casper began to laugh. "Holy shit."

"Ma," I growled, my hands beginning to fidget.

"Twins, huh?" Casper asked teasingly. "Damn, you don't mess around."

My legs felt like they were going to completely give out as my head started to swim.

"Jesus, sit down before you fall down," Casper ordered laughingly, pushing me onto a stool.

"I wore a condom," I whispered to myself. How the fuck had she got pregnant with twins?

"Oh, fucking gross, Cameron!" Farrah scowled as Casper snickered behind her. "I don't want to hear that shit."

"No, really," I said seriously, shaking my head in disbelief. "I wore a fucking condom. Every time."

"Shut up, Cam! And don't laugh," Farrah shrieked, turning to swat at Casper. "I'm not supposed to hear that stuff. What if CeeCee was talking about condoms?"

All laughter left Casper's face and his jaw tightened. "Not funny, Ladybug."

"You think?" she snapped back.

"Twins," I whispered, barely hearing my parents as I stared at the pictures on the bar. "Kids. I have *two* kids."

"Hell, yeah, you do," Casper crowed, moving around Farrah so he could wrap his arms around me in a tight hug. "Congratulations, boy."

"Jesus, I need a second job," I mumbled, my hands loose at my sides as Casper hugged me. "And a car. I need a car."

Farrah started to giggle as I lost my shit.

"You are going to be an awesome dad," Farrah sang, pushing Casper out of the way so she could wrap her arms around my waist. "Even better than Cody."

"Hey!" Casper complained, pulling Farrah back against him.

I gave them a small smile, then swiped the pictures off the bar top.

"So, what's this then?" I asked, pushing one of the unlabeled photos into Farrah's face.

"That's the head and torso, see right here? That's the spine..."

I stood quietly as she explained each picture, pointing out little things that I would have never noticed. She knew what she was talking about, and by the time we'd made it through the photos, I had a lump in my throat the size of Texas.

"I'm gonna go—" I started to say, ready to go back to my room and stare at my children in peace.

"Hey, Cam," Dragon's low voice came from behind me, and without turning around, I felt my entire body tighten. Fuck. If he was coming to give me shit about Trix, I wasn't sure I could hold back.

My emotions were so close to the surface, they were practically fucking bubbling.

"Hey," I murmured, turning cautiously around. "What's up?"

"Just wanted to tell you congratulations," Dragon said with a small nod.

"Oh." For a second, I just stood there staring at him with my mouth hanging open. "Oh, yeah. Thanks, man."

I waited for him to walk away, but he didn't. Instead, he reached up and swiped his long hair back from his face. "Twins, uh—they run in Bren's family. I mean, she's not sure about her mom's history, but we had—" his voice trailed off for a second as his eyes lost their focus. "Uh, yeah. Don't know if you remember, but we had twins." Dragon cleared his throat, and I felt bad for the guy because he looked both uncomfortable and really fucking sad.

"Yeah, Trix is a twin, right?" I asked, just to fill the silence. What the fuck was I supposed to say?

"You know, I think you're the first person to ever say 'is'." After the words fell out of his mouth, Dragon looked even more uncomfortable.

"What?"

"You said Trix *is* a twin. And you're right." Dragon swallowed, his Adam's apple bobbing hard in his neck. He shook his head. "I'm fuckin' this up. You said Trix *is* a twin, not Trix *was* a twin. Big fuckin' difference—not that most people notice it. She is a twin, she'll always be a twin—not having her twin with her doesn't mean she used to be a twin. Just means her twin ain't with her."

His words became more agitated the longer he spoke, and by the time he'd rambled to a stop, I was nodding back at him. "Right, man. I get it," I assured him.

"Anyway, congratulations," Dragon said with a nod before abruptly turning on his heel and walking away.

"The fuck was that?" I asked Casper in confusion.

"No fuckin' idea," Casper said softly, clapping me on the back. "But if I had to guess, I'd say D's missin' his boy right about now. His oldest boy."

My stomach clenched as I glanced at my ma. "You don't think—"

"Nope," Farrah said strongly. "No way. They're fine. They'll *be* fine—both of them."

★ ★ ★

I SPENT THE rest of the night in my room, staring at the little photos until my eyes were red and burning.

I couldn't believe that Trix had two of them in there. I wondered how she'd felt when she found out. Had she been happy? Was she excited? Or had the thought of not one, but two children, completely freaked her out?

Who went with her to the appointment? I hoped she hadn't gone by herself.

She'd seemed okay when she'd cornered me that night, but fuck if I could read her anymore. She'd turned into someone I didn't know. Someone I didn't want to know.

No, that wasn't true.

I wanted her badly—any way I could get her. If I thought that I could get her back and keep her, I would. But after the shit she'd pulled with Dragon, there was no way I was ever going there again.

He'd overstepped. The little scene they'd played out at their house was so fucked up, it still burned days later.

She'd actually used her pop to kick me to the curb. So fucked up.

The next morning, I crawled out of bed and stashed the pictures in my dresser. I wanted to carry them with me, but with my luck, I'd fucking lose them. I needed to go over to Trix's old apartment and get the rest of my shit.

I'd been putting it off, but the day before, I'd ripped the ass out of a pair of jeans. I was getting seriously low on pants. It wasn't like Trix was living there. She'd only been back once as far as I knew, just to get something to wear to the funerals. I'd just get my shit and get out—no one would even know I'd been there.

The apartment had been closed up since we'd started staying at the clubhouse, and when I walked in, the entire place smelled like shit. I pulled my t-shirt up over my nose as I glanced around, my eyes watering. It had to be the garbage. I gagged as I made my way into the kitchen and held my breath as I grabbed the entire can and rushed it toward the front door. It only took me a few minutes to take it to the dumpster, but swear to God, that smell was lingering on my fucking clothes when I was done.

I opened every window as I made my way back through the house, and once the air started moving, I froze.

I knew I needed to get out of there. It wasn't my place to be anymore, I shouldn't have even had a key.

I should pack my shit and leave.

My heart thumped hard as I looked around the living room. The blanket Trix used was thrown over the back of the couch, like she'd just been lying down and had tossed it back when she got to her feet. There was a pair of slip on sneakers pushed halfway under the recliner, and a half-full glass of water on the end table.

I shook my head and turned toward the hallway. Fucking life interrupted. That's what this shit was.

I stopped at the hall closet and opened up the washer and dryer, rocking back on my heels when I found a full load of stinky laundry inside the washer. I looked at the clothes, then up at the laundry soap on the shelf above them. Then back at the clothes.

Fuck it.

I poured a bunch of soap into the washer and turned that shit on hot, startling myself when the water sprayed into the drum. What the fuck was I doing?

I leaned down and checked the dryer, pulling out the pile of clothes and taking them into the bedroom, where I tossed them on the unmade bed.

The entire room smelled like Trix. I didn't look around as I picked my boxers and t-shirts out of the clean clothes. My hands were shaking.

I sat down on the edge of the bed and scrubbed my palms over my face. It shouldn't be so hard to pack up some clothes. *What the fuck was I doing?*

Trix was going to have to pack the apartment up soon. It was coming up on the end of the month, and I knew she was staying with her parents for the foreseeable future. Probably a good thing with two babies coming. She would have to be packed up and gone by the time the first rolled around or she'd be stuck paying for an extra month. Did she line up a storage space—shit. *Not my problem.*

My leg bounced up and down as I stared at the open doorway.

Two hours later, I found myself folding yet another load of laundry. The baskets had been full of dirty clothes and I hadn't been able to leave them.

I also hadn't been able to leave the dishes in the sink, the trash in any of the garbage cans, the floor unvacuumed, the kitchen unswept, or the counter messy.

"Hulk, you here, man?" Will called from the living room.

I stuffed the last load of dirty laundry into the washing machine and closed the lid before striding out to the living room.

"Don't ask," I warned as Will looked around the spotless apartment.

"You call and I show up—just like always," Will mumbled, raising his arms in the air. "No questions asked."

"Good." I walked to the front door as I slipped a clean t-shirt over my head, then my cut on top of that. "I need a ride."

Chapter 24

DRAGON

I UNLOCKED THE door to my girl's apartment as Tommy and Leo talked quietly behind me. I'd dragged them along to help me get shit done, mostly so they'd finally get their asses off my couch.

Leo's ass had made a fucking indention in the spot he'd sat in for the last two weeks, and I swear to Christ, Tommy's ass was making a matching one on the opposite end of my damn couch. They didn't do anything but sit in front of the television all day long. I knew they were dealing with shit in their own way, but enough was enough. They needed some fucking fresh air.

I took two steps into the apartment and stopped dead.

"What the fuck?" I mumbled, looking around the living room.

The place was bare, completely cleaned out except for stacks and stacks of plastic bins.

I stepped farther into the room and looked around. There wasn't a picture frame or a scrap of paper anywhere. Shit even looked like it had been dusted.

"Whoa. Did Trix get robbed?" Tommy asked.

"No, you fuckin' idiot," Leo replied. "She got…packed."

I walked forward into the kitchen—same thing. A few bins stacked on top of the kitchen table, but nothing else. I opened cupboards and the fridge. Nothing.

I made my way down the hallway, checking the closets and the bedrooms. They were all the same.

Plastic bins stacked neatly in each room. The beds stripped. The windows and floors clean.

"Hey, Pop," Leo called softly. "Think I know who did this."

I glanced over my shoulder to where Leo was looking down at a couple of bins near the dresser.

"Who?" I stepped over to where he was standing, and finally noticed the masking tape across the lids of the bins.

CLOTHES—NOT FOR STORAGE

"The fuck?" I mumbled softly to myself. I pulled the top bin down and looked at the next in the stack.

6 – NAN'S QUILT – TRIX WILL WANT

Shit. I pulled that one down, too.

SHOES TRIX NEVER WEARS – STORAGE

Then I moved to the next pile, and the next, and the next, reading the labels on each one.

WINTER COATS – WON'T FIT BY THEN – STORAGE

SHEETS AND EXTRA BLANKETS – STORAGE

BOOKS – TRIX WILL WANT

SHOES – NOT FOR STORAGE

DO NOT OPEN – PRIVATE – STORAGE

CLOTHES – NOT FOR STORAGE

CLOTHES – PAJAMAS – NOT FOR STORAGE

BATHROOM SHIT – TRIX WILL WANT

TOWELS – STORAGE

"Cameron." I finally said as I hit the last bin. "He packed up everythin'."

"And labeled it," Leo said quietly. "What do you think's in the 'private' box?"

"Don't even think about it, kid," I warned, looking around the room. "Hell, this makes shit easy."

"Why'd he do it?" Tommy asked in awe, his eyes wide.

"Because he loves her," Leo answered simply. "Didn't want her to have to do it herself."

It only took about an hour for me and the boys to load the bins and furniture into the box van I'd brought. They were all labeled in Cam's handwriting, all stacked neatly in their allotted rooms and ready to be taken away. He hadn't used a single cardboard box, and he must have spent a couple hundred dollars buying those fucking bins, because they weren't cheap.

Brenna had planned to go over and clean the place after we'd packed it all up, but I had Leo text her that she didn't need to. Cam had taken care of that, too. There wasn't anything left to do but give the key back to the apartment manager and drop Trix's shit at storage.

I dropped the boys at the clubhouse with orders to sweep the garage and keep their mouths shut about what we'd found. It wasn't their place to run their mouths about Cam and Trix's business, and I knew Cam wouldn't want that shit known.

When I pulled up in front of our place, Brenna came out to the front porch to meet me. God, she was just as beautiful as the first time I saw her. She'd filled out since she had the kids and her body grew softer with age, but she was still hot as fuck.

"Hey, what was that text about?" she called as she bounced down the stairs. Jesus. Her tits looked amazing when she moved like that.

"Place was packed up when we got there," I answered, pulling her in for a kiss. I gripped her hand and dragged her to the back of the van.

She was climbing inside before I'd even got the back door all the way open, and her jaw dropped as she took in the six bins stacked near the cab.

"What the hell?"

"Cam packed up all her shit," I told her incredulously. "Even cleaned the motherfuckin' apartment."

She turned her face toward me and my body instantly stiffened. "Don't fuckin' cry. This ain't nothin' to cry about," I ordered gruffly.

"Did you see the way he labeled these?" she asked, shaking her head. "'Movies and Trix's favorite blanket, Trix will want.' What did the other ones say?"

"Pretty much the same shit. Labeled 'em all pretty good—what should go to storage and what shouldn't."

"Trix is going to—"

"You think we should rip the labels off?" I cut in.

"Fuck, no!" She looked at me like I was out of my mind. "She should see this."

"Baby, she's just startin' to get over the fucker—"

"No, she isn't," Brenna argued softly. "She's just getting better at hiding it."

I let her words sink in for a minute. Was my girl really hiding it?

She'd been doing better—not great, but better. Her nightmares had come back, but she'd only had one that week. Scared the shit out of me when she'd started yelling, but her mom had calmed her down pretty quick.

Amy came and took her to yoga a couple times. Wasn't sure if that was helping, but it did wear her out.

"Hey, did you get my stuff?" Trix asked, coming around the back of the van.

I nodded silently and gestured toward the bins. Shit.

"Wow, you sprang for the good stuff, huh?" Trix started to climb up the back bumper and I lurched forward.

"The hell are you doin'?" I snapped, grabbing her under her arms and lifting her away.

"Uh, I was going to get my boxes." She looked at me like I had two heads.

"Stay back, I'll get 'em," I snapped. Like I was really going to let her pregnant ass carry shit into the house. Was she new here?

"Just set them down out here," she called as I moved toward the bins. "I'll go through them and see if there's anything we can put in the storage. I don't have much room…"

I growled at Brenna as she tried to lift one of the bins, but she ignored me. I don't even know why I tried to boss her anymore—she never listened to a goddamn word I said.

By the time I got all of the bins unloaded, Trix was staring glassy eyed at the labels.

"This is Cam's handwriting. He helped you?" she asked quietly, her voice trembling. "I didn't think—"

"It was done when we got there." I sighed and ripped the rubber band out of my hair, scratching my nails along my scalp for a second.

"But—" Trix looked at me then back at the bins. "*What?*"

I pulled my hair back out of my face and tied it up. Jesus. This is why I thought we should take off the damn labels. If I'd torn them off before she saw them, our daughter wouldn't look a fucking wounded animal.

"He packed up your shit—all of it," I finally said. "Bins were packed and labeled when we got there."

"Why would he do this?" Trix whispered to Brenna, tears spilling down her cheeks. "I don't understand."

"Don't know, baby," Bren murmured back, wrapping her arm around Trix's shoulders.

"This doesn't make any sense," Trix mumbled, shaking her head.

"Nice thing for him to do—just leave it at that," I grumbled, leaning forward to pick up three of the bins. "Let's get these inside."

I watched Trix closely that night, and the night after. I was waiting for her to lose her shit. I thought for sure that she was going to break down about the little fucker again, and I hated that there was nothing I could do to help her.

Bren had filled me in on what had gone down between my girl and Hulk. Couldn't say I didn't understand where he was coming from, but I still wanted to rip the guy's head off and shove it up his ass. My Little Warrior was hurting—no doubt about that.

But she never lost her shit. She talked about telling Hulk thank you for a couple days, but she never did. I think she knew he didn't want her gratitude.

After a while, even though I hated that my child was in pain, a part of me was glad that Trix was forced to stand on her own two feet for a bit. It made her stronger. As the days went by, I listened to her bitch about the heat and complain about how tight her clothes were getting, but she never fell back into the pit she'd been in before. She still dealt with nightmares, especially after Micky's small funeral—but she snapped out of them faster and faster with each one.

Trix was getting her shit together, visiting a shrink and talking to her mother and nan. She fucking worked for it, and slowly, we all began to see a difference in her. The girl I'd raised gradually made herself known again.

She smiled. A lot. She went to yoga with Amy and Brenna. She made her brother paint her toenails. She bought a small, plastic pool and made Brenna sit in it with her, sipping on what she called virgin margaritas. They were fucking smoothies—she put fruit and ice in a blender. Smoothies.

One day about two months after she'd come to live with us, my girl cornered me as soon as I'd taken my boots off after a long day at the garage.

"Hey, Pop?" she said quietly, making the hair on my neck stand up. I wasn't used to a quiet Trix, and it made me itchy.

"Yeah?" I asked gruffly. I really fucking hoped whatever she had to say wasn't bad news. Couldn't take any more of that for the next few years.

"I'm sorry I asked you to help me with Cam. I shouldn't have done that." She rested her hands calmly on her belly, but I saw her thumbs slide between her palms and the fabric of her shirt.

"Water under the bridge," I mumbled back, raising my eyes to meet hers.

"No, you deserve an apology." She swallowed hard, and in that second I wanted to tell her to stop talking, but I knew that whatever she was trying to say was important to her—even if it hurt. "You stepped in when I needed you to, even after you'd said you wouldn't. I know that wasn't easy for you."

"You can always count on me, baby—"

"I know, Pop," she cut me off with a small smile. "I know I can. And I know this seems kind of silly, since I'm living in your house." She laughed a little, and I felt my lips twitch. "But I'm going to stand on my own two feet. I want you to know that I'll never ask you to do something like that again." She started to cry and I was on my feet in an instant.

"None of that, Little Warrior," I murmured, wrapping my arms around her.

It was weird as fuck, hugging my kid when she had that huge ass belly.

"I just—I want to be able to take care of shit on my own, you know?" she said against my t-shirt. "I don't want to rely on you or anyone else to make the hard decisions for me."

"Then don't," I said simply, ignoring the swear word that grated on my nerves. I fucking hated it when she cursed. She was my baby girl. Ugly words shouldn't be coming outta her mouth.

"I love you," she said on a sigh, resting her weight against me.

"Love you, too, Little Warrior."

And that was that. She started doing exactly what she'd said. Making her own doctor's appointments and making lists of things she needed for the babies. She even started looking for jobs, though I wasn't sure how she thought she'd be able to work any time soon.

She still drove me insane leaving her shit all over the house, but...

She grew.

She laughed.

And finally, she glowed.

I was so fucking proud of her.

Through all of it, the radio silence between her and Cam never faltered. They kept their distance all the way through summer and into the fall.

Chapter 25

CAMERON

"WE GOT HIM," Poet yelled, limping his way into the clubhouse. "Fuckin' got him."

I glanced at Dragon, who was watching Poet carefully, then followed his lead when he got to his feet. "Church," he barked, striding through the room.

The small meeting room was silent until everyone had taken their seats.

"Got a call from my contact in the office at U of O—" Poet began.

"How the fuck did you get a contact there?" Will asked incredulously.

"Shut the fuck up," Dragon growled, making Will jerk back in his seat.

"Got a call," Poet said again, a sly smile pulling at the corner of his mouth. "Little Steve Smith decided to transfer—needed his transcripts. University of Montana."

Grease, Casper and Dragon all leaned back in their seats with knowing smiles on their faces. I wasn't clear on why the kid being in Montana was a good thing, but I sure as shit wasn't going to speak up and have Dragon rip my head off.

The man wasn't my biggest fan.

"Called our old friends up there and they're takin' care of it," Poet announced.

"He's mine," Grease snapped.

"Know that," Poet replied respectfully. "Horsemen are playin' the game, bringin' little Steve down to us to deal with."

"When?" I finally asked, glancing around the table.

I didn't want to make a big deal of it, but Trix had her doctor's appointment the next day, and an ultrasound to find out if we were having boys or girls. She'd texted me earlier that day to let me know and invite me to come along.

I didn't know whether I was going, but I liked having the option.

"Boys'll be here by the weekend," Poet answered, giving me a nod. Right. He knew about Trix's appointment, of course he did.

My neck burned in embarrassment.

I'd tried really hard over the past few months to show how unconcerned I was with Trix's shit—but I think everyone probably knew that I was starved for news of her. I spent most of my time less than a half-mile away from her, but I hadn't seen her face to face since Micky's funeral.

She hadn't even come to say thank you for packing up her apartment, and it burned to think of how I'd waited for her to show up once I'd known she was all moved out. I'd thought for sure she'd say something, but she never did. She kept her distance, just like I'd told her to.

The one time in our lives that Trix had followed an order from me, and it was the only one I'd wished she ignored.

★ ★ ★

I STILL WASN'T sure if I was going to the appointment with Trix the next morning when I took a shower and put on a pair of jeans that weren't covered in grease.

I wasn't sure as I read a text from her giving me the address to the doctor's office.

I wasn't sure as I climbed on my bike and rode it slowly out the gates.

I still hadn't decided when I parked my bike in the crowded parking lot.

Hell, I still hadn't made up my mind when I walked in the front doors.

Then I saw Trix.

She was sitting in a chair, laughing at something her ma said, with both hands braced on her round belly. Her hair was up in a ponytail and her face had filled out, so her cheeks were round like they'd been when she was little.

The dark circles under her eyes were gone.

I stood frozen, watching them until Trix glanced up and met my eyes.

It felt like the entire waiting room went quiet as her eyes widened and her mouth dropped open in shock.

Then she smiled, and I felt my legs go weak.

"Hey, you came!" she called, using the arms on her chair to push herself to her feet.

I didn't say a word as she walked toward me, her belly swaying slightly from side to side. I was too busy staring.

When she finally reached me, I cleared my throat. "That okay?" I finally asked.

"Wouldn't have invited you if it wasn't," she answered, grinning.

I couldn't get over the difference a few months had made. Excitement was written all over her face, she was practically vibrating with it as we stared at each other.

She looked healthy. Happy.

"Come sit with me and my mom," she ordered. "They told me not to pee before the appointment, and if I stand here much longer, it's going to start running down my legs."

A surprised laugh tore out of my throat as she led me back to where Brenna was sitting. I couldn't help but glance at her ass as she walked in front of me. I was trying not to be a douche, but I was pretty sure I heard angels singing as I looked down again. Her belly wasn't the only thing that had gotten bigger—her thighs and ass had grown, too. Fucking beautiful.

"Hey, Cam," Brenna called dryly, making my head snap up.

"Hey, Bren," I said back, my neck heating up. Shit, it felt like my ears were getting red, too.

"The receptionist said that they're on schedule, so it should only be a few more minutes," Trix said as she sat back down and patted the seat next to her. "Thank God. This is actually starting to be a little painful." She squirmed in her seat as I dropped down beside her.

Sitting so close to her had my heart racing, and I wasn't sure what to do with my hands. I'd never been more nervous in my entire goddamn life.

This was Trix. My Bea. But I didn't know how to act around her anymore. Before we'd gotten together, I would have wrapped an arm around her shoulders. I would have hugged her. Teased her about her belly. When we were together, I would have kissed her. Put my hands to her stomach and rubbed the taut skin.

Now, I could only sit there like an asshole, trying not to fist my hands where they rested in my lap.

"Bellatrix White?" A nurse called from an open doorway to our right.

It should have been Harrison. She should have *my* name.

"Showtime," Trix mumbled as she pushed herself to her feet.

I lifted my hands to help her, but let them drop again.

If I touched her, I was afraid I'd take it too far. I wouldn't be able to let go, and I'd end up tracing her body with my hands in a waiting room full of people.

The nurse walked us down a short hallway and set us up in a tiny room, and Brenna filled the silence with chatter as she helped Trix pull up her shirt and move her pants low on her hips.

I silently cursed as I felt myself get hard. Jesus. All she had to do was push those pants a little lower and I'd get a glimpse of the Promised Land.

"I'm so excited," Trix whispered, closing her eyes as her lips tilted up. Her eyes popped open after a second and she turned her head toward me. "Are you excited?"

"Nervous," I rasped out.

She giggled. I hadn't meant for it to be funny.

Then Brenna leaned down and whispered something in Trix's ear, making her nod.

"I'll see you guys in a bit," Brenna announced when she'd straightened back up.

"What?" I watched in horror as she left the room.

"She thought it would be better for us to do this just me and you," Trix said softly, pulling my attention from the empty doorway.

"Oh." I looked at the doorway again.

"I'm so sorry for—"

"Don't," I barked, making Trix's mouth snap shut. "After the shit I said at the clubhouse?" I shook my head. "You got nothin' to apologize for."

"You were angry."

"I was a fuckin' dick."

"That, too," she said, her eyes tearing up. "But I forgave that a long time ago."

I groaned, taking a step forward. "Bea—"

A knock sounded on the door, cutting me off. "Hey, guys, you ready to see your baby?" a woman asked as she slipped into the room.

"Babies," I corrected, making Trix smile.

I swallowed hard as the woman came inside and started talking about all the shit she needed to do, and before long she was squirting what looked like lube on Trix's belly and pressing a little wand against it.

A heartbeat filled the room.

"Look, Cam," Trix said, nodding toward a big screen high on the wall.

When I'd gotten the first ultrasound pictures, I'd had no idea what I was looking at. Our kids had looked like kidney beans.

But fuck me, that wasn't the case anymore.

I took an involuntary step forward as the tech moved her wand, giving us a clearer picture of our baby, its hand in its mouth and its legs pulling toward its chest and then kicking out again.

"Whoa," I whispered, barely registering when Trix reached out and gripped my hand.

"There's Baby A," the tech said. "I just need to take some measurements here. Do you guys want to know what you're having?"

I kept my mouth shut as I looked down at Trix. Tears were rolling down her face.

"Yes," she answered, meeting my eyes.

"Well, this baby is not at all modest," the tech said with a grin as little lines appeared on the screen while she measured the baby's head. "Definitely a boy. I'll try to get a picture in just a minute."

Trix squeezed my hand, and my eyes slammed shut while I tried to just fucking breathe.

A boy. Baby A was a boy.

I leaned down and kissed Trix's forehead without thinking about it.

When I looked back at the screen, something seemed off.

"What the fuck?" I murmured, my heart beginning to race.

"Oh, that's just Baby B getting jealous of all the attention on Baby

A," the tech laughed. "That's Baby B's leg, I think."

Trix began to laugh, and her entire belly shook with the movement, making my son freeze for a second before he went nuts.

"He likes it when you laugh," I said in surprise, grinning at Trix.

"He looks like you," she murmured back, staring at the screen.

"How can you tell?"

"I just can."

I wanted to laugh at her words. You couldn't see what the baby looked like on the screen, just an impression of his face, but I could tell she was serious. She meant it.

"Okay, I got everything I needed, now let's take some fun pictures," the tech said. "Hold on, Baby B, you'll get your turn in a minute."

She took still shots of our son's profile, and I was pretty sure he had Trix's nose, not mine. She also snapped a few more shots of his spine and arms and one of his junk, typing in, "I'm a boy" on that picture.

"Okay, now let's find Baby B," the tech said quietly to herself.

The sound of more than one heartbeat filled the room for a minute, but suddenly, a single heartbeat became clear.

"There's Baby B," the tech announced.

Trix's hand squeezed mine hard.

"You okay?" I asked quietly, leaning down to get a good look at her.

"Now, I'm nervous," she whispered back, sniffing.

"It's all good, Sweetbea—" The name slipped out on accident and we both froze.

"Want to know the sex of Baby B?" the tech asked cheerfully.

"Yeah," I replied gruffly, standing up straight again.

"Baby B is also a boy," the tech said with a smile. "No modesty in these two."

Trix giggled as I looked closer at the screen.

Two boys.

The rest of the appointment passed by way too quickly. I could have watched my kids swimming around on that screen all fucking day, but unfortunately, the tech had to take her machine and look at other people's babies.

"Ugh, this shit is so gross," Trix bitched as she tried to wipe the lube off her belly with a handful of paper towels the tech had handed her before she left. "And I can't see it."

I glanced at Trix's face, then down at her belly where she was just smearing the shit around.

"Do you—uh," I swallowed hard. Jesus. "Want some help?"

"Could you?" Trix shuddered as she pushed the paper towels in my direction. "Get it off. Please."

I shuffled forward and pulled a few paper towels from the stack, clenching my jaw as I wiped across her belly.

She had stretch marks, one large purplish one that ran directly beneath her belly button, and then a bunch of smaller, jagged ones off to the side.

I wanted to trace them with my tongue.

"Thank you," Trix murmured huskily as I kept wiping the shit off her skin.

By the time I got done, Trix was breathing heavily and my dick was so hard it was painful.

"Oh, feel!" Trix said in surprise, grabbing my hand and pressing it hard against the side of her stomach. "Wait for it…"

My breath caught as I felt something pushing against my palm, then my fingers, then my palm again.

I'd been missing it. They were moving around in there, and I'd been missing it.

My throat tightened as I leaned toward Trix's belly.

"Hi, son," I murmured less than an inch from her skin. "I love you, bud, but you gotta stop showing your dick to random women."

Trix burst out laughing and I grinned against her skin, letting my lips make contact. She smelled like the lube they'd smeared there, but under that was all Trix. Spicy and warm.

"Oh, right here," Trix murmured, taking my free hand and pressing it higher on her belly. Sure enough, there was movement in that spot, too.

We stayed there quietly, feeling our sons move, until someone came to clean the room and kicked us out.

It was physically painful to pull my hands away from Trix's skin.

We stopped at a bathroom on our way back down the hallway so Trix could finally pee, and I stood there uncomfortably as she groaned beyond the door. She was going to the bathroom—that sound shouldn't have turned me on like it did.

"Well?" Brenna asked excitedly as we walked back into the waiting room.

"You want to tell her?" Trix asked, her eyes shining.

"She's your ma," I murmured back, a grin tugging at my lips.

"Two boys!" Trix announced before I'd even finished speaking.

"You're gonna have your hands full!" Brenna moved forward and hugged Trix, then turned to me and hugged me, too.

I didn't know if I should try and hug her back. Instinctively, I recoiled, Dragon's face flashing in my mind.

"Jesus, I'm your kids' grandmother. You can hug me," Brenna snapped.

Trix started laughing and she sort of danced toward the front doors of the office.

"I'll get you next time," Brenna warned, turning toward her daughter.

I really hoped she didn't.

When we got to Brenna's car, what little ease Trix and I had felt during the appointment was long gone, and her eyes were wary.

"Thanks for coming, Cam," she said softly as Brenna climbed in the driver's seat.

"Thanks for inviting me."

"Of course."

We fell into silence and I couldn't think of a single thing to say. Should I just turn around and leave? Tell her how beautiful she looked? How much I'd missed her? Should I try and make plans to see her again? Even if she didn't want to be with me, I was already anxious to feel our sons kicking in her belly again.

Trix finally gave an uncomfortable smile, and opened her door.

I still didn't say a fucking word, because I was an idiot.

After they drove away, I stood by my bike for a long time, going through the second set of pictures the tech had printed for us so we'd each have our own copies. Then I pulled out my phone.

"Hey, Ma," I said when she answered without even a hello, immediately bitching about my dad.

"Hey, bud. How'd it go?"

"Great. Both babies look perfect."

"They look like sea monkeys. Who are you trying to fool here?" she joked.

"Nah, they were…hell, Ma."

"I know, right? So cool to see them swimming around in there."

"They were—"

"Tell me right now," Farrah cut me off. "I mean, I'll listen to you moon all day if you want, but I want to know what you're having first. I'm pregnant and impatient—you don't wanna make me wait."

"A boy," I said, grinning.

"And?" she snapped, not finding me funny.

"And another boy."

"Holy shit! Cody!" she yelled in my ear. "Cam and Trix are having boys!"

"Shit, Ma. My fuckin' ear!"

"Oh," Farrah started laughing. "Sorry."

She didn't sound sorry.

"This is awesome, dude. Charlie's going to have two little shits protecting her in school."

"Charlie?" I asked softly.

"Yeah, we decided. Charlotte Vera Butler. Got a nice ring to it, right?"

"Yeah, Ma. It does."

"Does Trix have any names picked out?"

"No, uh, I don't think so." Dammit, I should have asked.

"You should have asked!" Farrah scolded.

"I know, I know. Maybe I'll text her or somethin'," I mumbled.

"So, wait. . . You guys are talking again?" Farrah wheedled.

"I gotta go," I answered.

"Cam! Are you guys talking again?"

"Bye, Ma." I hung up the phone, laughing as she bitched.

Two sons. I had two sons.

★ ★ ★

A COUPLE DAYS later, I still hadn't texted Trix. I wasn't sure what to say to her.

I wanted her back. I wasn't sure that I could have any contact with her without pressuring her, and I knew how that would fucking go. If she actually did come back to me, she'd bail again.

"Boys're almost here," Poet announced, dropping his phone into his breast pocket.

We were in a warehouse the club owned a few miles out of town in the woods and we were waiting for Poet's buddies to drop off little Steve Smith. If the kid had any idea what he was in for, I had a feeling he'd stink to high heaven from shitting his pants by the time we got him. We'd gotten the call earlier that morning telling us that the guys were in Oregon, so Dragon, Grease, Casper, Poet, Will and I had ridden out to the property we rarely used. It didn't have any neighbors for miles around, and we'd had to spend an hour clearing the dirt road of branches and shit before we could even pull our bikes in.

"They're here," Will said, rolling back the large metal door as a powder blue van pulled into the large space.

"Poet," the driver said with a nod, walking forward to shake Poet's hand as another man climbed out of the passenger seat.

"Thanks for doin' this," Dragon said, moving forward to shake hands, too.

"No problem. New president, huh?"

"That's what they tell me."

"We were real sorry to hear about Slider," the guy said, turning to glance at the van. Shit, his face was all fucked up. "Might've had a little fun with the fucker on our way down."

"He still alive?" Dragon asked. The man nodded. "Then it's all good."

I shuffled forward a bit as the men moved to the back of the van and pulled out the kid. His wrists and ankles were wrapped in duct tape and he groaned as they dropped him on the concrete floor with no way to break his fall.

"All yours," the man from the passenger seat said.

Poet nodded and said something I couldn't hear to the men, and then without another word, they climbed back in their rig and backed out of the warehouse.

"Hulk, get the door," Dragon ordered, moving forward toward the prone body.

I turned and strode to the door, pulling it shut and flipping on the fluorescent lights overhead so we could see what we were doing.

When I turned back toward the men, everything inside me stilled.

I knew him.

His glasses were gone and his hair was messy, but I'd know him anywhere.

I was frozen. I watched blankly as Dragon and Casper pulled the kid up, seating him in a metal folding chair and taping him to it. He was silent while they did it, not uttering a word of remorse or fear.

Then he looked up and met my eyes, his mouth forming a sly smile.

I didn't even realize I was moving until Casper's hands hit my chest hard, stopping my forward momentum just feet from the piece of shit.

"The boyfriend," Steve said calmly. "Nice to see you again." He turned his head. "You too, Will."

My hands clenched into fists, and it took all that I had not to go through my dad to get to him.

"You know him?" Grease asked roughly, glaring at me in accusation.

"He had a class with my woman," I clarified through clenched teeth.

"Ah, more than that," Steve murmured, staring at me. "Bellatrix and I were study partners…friends, even."

A rough noise broke from my throat and Casper's hands fisted in my t-shirt, still using his body weight to keep me in place.

"Shut your mouth," I growled.

"She was pretty," he continued, stopping only when the butt of Dragon's pistol smashed across his cheek.

"Talk about my daughter again and I'll have you gaggin' on your balls," Dragon warned.

"You're her dad, huh?" Steve murmured, then spit blood out of his mouth onto the floor. "Shoulda taught her not to tell her plans to just anyone." He smiled then, and his teeth were red with blood. "Makes it too easy to find her… and the rest of you."

That was the last word he said.

Gunshots filled the room as Grease and Will lit him up, his body jerking over and over in the chair as they filled him with bullets.

When they finally stopped shooting, we all just stood there in silence.

"He was gettin' off on that shit," Grease mumbled, looking at the floor as he stuffed his pistol back in his jeans. "Didn't want to listen anymore." Then he turned and walked out of the warehouse, Will following behind him.

"Trix doesn't need to know," I rasped as we heard their bikes fire up outside. "Not her fault—not somethin' she needs to worry about."

"Agreed," Poet murmured, watching me closely. "Got nothin' to do with her."

"Yup," Casper said.

"Course not," Dragon mumbled.

We turned toward the mangled body in the chair.

"Should we cut him up or just bury him like this?" Poet asked the room.

"Cut him up," Casper, Dragon and I said at the same time.

Chapter 26

TRIX

"Little Warrior, you got a visitor outside," my dad murmured, waking me up from a deep sleep.

I glanced at the clock and saw that it was ten-thirty at night, not super late unless someone had been crashing at nine the way I'd started to. I'd tried to stay up and watch TV with Leo, but that usually meant he was carrying me to bed an hour later because I'd fallen asleep on the couch, so I'd started taking my huge ass to bed early. I was getting too big for my little brother to carry me anymore.

"What?" I asked, pushing up on my elbows.

"You got a visitor." Pop walked back out of my room.

I groaned as I rolled to the edge of the bed and set my feet on the cold floor. I'd been wearing Cam's t-shirts to bed with some of Leo's boxers, but pretty soon, I was going to have to pick something else up at the store. The shirts were already stretching super tight around my belly, and by the time I woke up every morning, I'd pushed them to right up under my boobs in my sleep.

I stumbled toward the open front door and pushed open the screen as I adjusted the shirt, stopping dead when I saw Cam standing at the bottom of the stairs.

He'd let his beard grow in. I noticed it at my doctor's appointment, but it had gotten even thicker over the past few days. I loved it.

"Hey," Cam rasped, his face shadowed.

"Hey," I mumbled back stupidly, letting the screen door shut softly behind me.

We stood there silently for a few moments.

"That my shirt?" I could feel his eyes focused on my belly, but I couldn't see the expression on his face.

"Oh," I laughed uncomfortably, "Yeah, you packed it and nothing else fits, so…" My words trailed off as I realized what I'd said. I'd never thanked him for what he'd done, but I had a feeling if I did so then, he wouldn't be happy about it.

"Doesn't look like that one fits," he joked softly.

"It doesn't." I chuckled. "I usually end up pushing it above the belly to get comfortable."

Cam's hands fisted at his sides.

"Show me," he said.

My heart started thumping hard in my chest, the fact that I couldn't see his face making his order even harder to follow. Could he see mine? The moon was behind him, casting him in shadow, which meant it was shining directly at me.

My hands went to my top, and my fingers shook a little as I gripped the sides and pulled it up and over my swollen belly, tucking it under my breasts. I tried to ignore the fact that I wasn't wearing a bra, and that the movement made that fact perfectly clear.

"You're so beautiful," Cam whispered, moving up one stair. "Every time I see you, you get prettier."

"Fatter, too."

"Rounder. I like it."

I took a deep, shuddering breath and held it. He was so close now. I could reach out and touch him, but I was afraid to.

The close quarters and darkened room had created an intimacy during my doctor's appointment, but when we'd walked out into the sunshine, it had vanished again. It had been so long since we'd connected, I wasn't even sure that our jagged pieces would fit together anymore. I wasn't sure that he'd even *want* them to.

"Why are you here?" I asked hoarsely, dropping my hands to the bottom of my belly.

"I missed you," he answered.

"I've missed you every day," I said back, tears filling my eyes. "What makes tonight any different?"

Cam cleared his throat, then tentatively reached out to set one hand on my bare belly. "Some shit went down tonight," he murmured, glancing up at me. When I didn't ask any questions, his head tilted back down to look at where his skin met mine. "I was ridin' home, and I couldn't stop thinkin' about all that I've been missin'."

"You know you can come and see—"

"All I been missin' with *you*, Sweetbea," he interrupted gently. "All your smiles and your complainin' and trippin' over your shit, and tryin' to wake you up in the mornin' when you're actin' like a hibernatin' bear."

My laugh turned into a small sob, and I pressed my lips tightly together.

"I love you, Bea. Always have. Not sure where we went wrong, but I don't wanna be away from you no more."

"Are you sure this isn't because of the boys?" I asked softly. "Because you can come see them—feel them—whenever you want. I'd never stop you."

"The boys," Cam said in soft wonder. "Shoulda thanked you at the appointment for them, but I was so fuckin' floored, I was just tryin' to not pass out."

I giggled, making my belly jump.

"The boys are a bonus, baby. Don't you know that?" His hand left my belly and reached up to cup my cheek. "I loved you before the boys, and I'll love you after they're grown and makin' their own families. It's always been me and you, Trix."

I searched his face, cataloguing every freckle and eyelash that were as familiar to me as my own. The beard was new, but the jawline wasn't. The short hair on the top of his head was the same, his blue eyes were the same, the small scar near his mouth was the same. It *had* always been me and Cam—I'd loved him from some of my earliest memories.

"Me and you," I murmured finally, my eyes overflowing. "Okay."

"Yeah?" he asked, his voice so hopeful that I had to push back the sob caught in my throat.

"Yeah," I agreed.

The rest of my words were lost when he shot up the last two stairs and possessively pressed his mouth to mine. His kiss still held that same first shock and then became so powerful that I was completely lost to it.

"I love you so much," he whispered, pulling away before kissing me again. "Don't leave me again. Promise you won't."

"I won't," I whispered back, pressing my forehead to his.

"Even if bad shit happens, you stay with me."

"Okay."

"Don't care what it is—you stick it out."

"Okay."

"I mean it, Trix. Can't take that shit again."

"I promise."

We stood there kissing for a long time, our hands roaming leisurely, but never to arouse. We just needed to feel each other.

Cam finally pulled away when I began to shift on my feet.

"You tired, Sweetbea?" he asked, framing my face with his hands.

"Yeah," I groaned. I wanted to stay out there with him forever, but my back had begun to ache, I was shivering from the cool night air, and I knew my feet were swelling from standing for so long.

"Let's get you to bed," he said sweetly, bending down to grip me behind my knees and lift me into his arms.

"I'm a lot heavier now," I said in apology as I opened the screen for us.

"Still light as a feather."

"You're such a liar," I whispered as I shut the front door.

"Yeah, if I didn't know better, I'd think you had two kids in there or somethin'," he teased, his eyes twinkling.

We were silent as he moved down the hallway, past Leo and my parents' bedrooms, to my room at the end of the hall. The house was shaped weird because my pop had to add on when Leo was a baby. It wasn't meant for so many people, but my parents had made it work by adding on a bedroom for me that stuck out the side of the square house like a sore thumb. Literally. If you looked straight down at the house, it looked like a pixelated thumbs-up sign.

Cam set me on my feet in my bedroom, closing the door behind us without saying a word.

Then we crawled into my tiny bed and he tucked his front up tight against my back.

"I'm sorry for all the—"

"Told you not to apologize," he cut me off, kissing the side of my neck.

"I was messed up, Cam." I continued, knowing I had to get the words out. He might not have needed to hear them, but I needed to say them, anyway. "When I found out I was pregnant, it was like it knocked something loose. Well, maybe it was before then. Remember when you slapped my ass during—"

"I remember."

"I started having these memories. Flashes at first, and then after we found out I was pregnant, they got worse."

"Why didn't you say somethin'?" he asked softly, rubbing his hand up and down my belly.

"I don't know. I guess I was just trying to figure it out on my own, and I was so fucking terrified of having a baby that I completely lost my shit."

"Next time, you come to me."

"I did—"

"You tellin' me you wanted an abortion wasn't comin' to me with the shit that was draggin' you down. That was you pickin' a fight," he argued.

I took a deep breath, then confessed, "I didn't really want one."

"Figured that out a long time ago, Bea."

I sighed, relaxing my body farther into his chest.

"The shooting just made it worse," I said finally, letting it all out there. "It made the memories worse and the nightmares worse, and I felt like I was losing my mind."

"Still havin' 'em?"

"Not as much," I answered, reaching down to twine my fingers with his. "I've been going to this doctor, and that helps. Yoga with Nan helps, too."

"Gettin' all bendy and shit?"

"Of course *that's* the part you'd focus on."

"Just teasin' you, baby. They're helping?"

"Yeah. I'm getting better."

"That's fuckin' good news," he said, squeezing my hand. "'Course, I'd take ya batshit crazy—but I'm real glad you're feelin' better, baby. Real glad."

"I love you," I whispered, my eyelids drooping. "Don't leave, okay?"

"I'll be here when your grumpy ass wakes up," Cam promised. "Go to sleep."

★ ★ ★

THE NEXT MORNING, I woke up with a start, and immediately felt

Cam's hand rubbing over my belly and the boys moving like crazy.

"What time is it?" I rasped out, relaxing back into the bed.

"A little after eleven," Cam whispered back, his lips against my throat. "You slept through your parents and Leo leavin'."

"Where'd they go?" I asked, tilting my head to the side so he had more room to work.

"Who gives a fuck?" His teeth bit down on my skin and I shuddered. "I got you alone."

"Hold that thought," I said quickly, scooting away from the heat of his body.

"Where you goin'?"

"Your sons are on my bladder," I mumbled back as I got to my feet, pushing my pajama shirt down. "I'll be right back."

Cam groaned and I couldn't help but laugh at his grimace as I walked out of the room. Then I took a step backward and leaned my head back inside. "Thanks for staying."

"Told you I would."

I made my way to the bathroom with the goofiest smile on my face. I couldn't help it. I was so freaking happy.

When I got back to the bedroom a few minutes later, Cam was sitting up on the bed, putting on his boots.

"Wait!" I blurted. "I'm back. Take your clothes back off."

Cam laughed hard, his eyes crinkling at the corners as he motioned for me to come to him.

"Want you bad, Sweetbea, but I'm not fuckin' you here."

My stomach dropped. "What? Why?"

Cam grabbed my hips and pulled me forward until I was standing between his spread knees. "Well, besides the fact that your pop would see it on my face and cut my balls off—"

"No, he wouldn't."

"I'm also too old to be worryin' about your parents comin' home and catchin' us, and this bed is too fuckin' small."

"We need a place to live," I grumbled as he pushed my t-shirt back above my belly.

"I'll find one," he murmured, kissing my bellybutton. "But right now, I want ya to get dressed so I can take ya to the clubhouse and show ya off."

"They've seen me," I said back, reaching up to run my fingers over his bedhead.

"Haven't seen ya with me."

"I'm not taking a shower," I warned. "I'm guessing you wouldn't get in there with me, and I don't want to leave you yet."

"I'm not goin' any—"

"Nope."

"Fine, just get dressed."

Cam watched me closely as I stripped out of my pajamas, and groaned as I slid a pair of underwear up over my hips. "You're killin' me."

"You said you wanted me to get dressed," I replied innocently, jumping then laughing hysterically when he acted like he was going to lunge for me.

I pulled on a pair of leggings and a maternity shirt, and as soon as I'd pushed my feet into some sandals, Cam was up off the bed and dragging me toward the front door. I hadn't even brushed my hair, but I decided not to mention it as he mumbled about getting out of the house so he wouldn't fuck me under my parents' roof.

When we got to the clubhouse, there weren't many people there, which seemed to seriously bum Cam out.

"Wanna go to my parents'?" he asked as he glanced around the room. "Think Poet and Amy were headed over there today."

My body locked up and it took me a minute to answer him.

I hadn't been back to Casper and Farrah's house since the shooting, and a month before, I would have said that I'd never set foot on their property again. But Cam was looking at me with so much hope on his face, I couldn't tell him no.

Casper, Farrah and the girls had been living at home and dealing with all the bad memories on a daily basis since Lily had been released from the hospital. I could go for a few hours.

I was slowly learning that the things I'd thought would break me were smaller than I'd made them in my head. I had to just push through them.

"Sure, baby," I finally said with a small smile. "Wanna take my car?"

Cam's breath left him in a relieved whoosh and he grinned back at me. "Gonna have to—no way you're fittin' on the back of my bike."

★ ★ ★

THE DRIVE TO Cam's parents was hard. I felt completely on edge, even though Cam held my hand the entire way, rubbing my palm soothingly with his thumb.

"Want you to know, I'm not gonna be some controlling asshole," he said abruptly, pulling me out of my memories.

"What?" I asked in confusion.

"I like control," he started, making me snort. "I like it, because when I know where you're at—what you're doin'—I know you're safe. I know how to get to you if you're *not* safe."

"I'm not going to put me or the boys in danger," I retorted, turning to look at him.

"I know you won't," he said, lifting my hand to his mouth to kiss it. "But my mom didn't, either—you know? She was just... sleepin.' That's all it took, just sleepin' in the house with the kids, and it was all over. I got home to...nothin.' It was all gone."

"I'm not your mom, Cam."

"I know you're not, and I'm sure as fuck not my dad." He squeezed my hand and rested it on his thigh. "But not knowin' where you and the boys are when you're not with me? The thought of that makes me fuckin' crazy."

"I don't—"

"Baby, I'm not gonna boss you around, all right? Shit, that ain't true—" I laughed at his disgruntled expression. "If there's shit happenin' at the club, and I need you to be safe—I'll sure as shit boss you around. But otherwise? I just need to know that you're okay."

"Okay," I said, squeezing his hand.

"Okay? You're not gonna fight with me?"

"Cam, I grew up with my pop," I replied flatly. "I know what I'm getting into. I mean, I don't want to be my mom, just so we're clear. I want to work and have a life separate from the Aces, but I'm not going to bitch that you need to know I'm safe. The life we have isn't exactly easy, especially on you."

"Well, shit," Cam said softly, making me smile.

"We'll figure it out," I murmured, leaning back in my seat as we turned down Casper and Farrah's long gravel driveway.

"You and me, Sweetbea." Cam reached out and rested his hand on my belly. "And our boys."

"Finally," I sighed.

★ ★ ★

"WHAT IS THIS?" Gramps teased as Cam and I walked into Farrah and Casper's. "Finally got yer shit together, eh?"

"Yeah, yeah," I mumbled back, leaning in to give the old man a hug.

"Hey, sweetheart," Nan said, grabbing me as soon as I'd let go of

Gramps. "All good?" she whispered in my ear.

"All good," I whispered back.

"Hey, you want a beer, boy?" Casper asked, getting to his feet across the living room. "Trix, good to see ya."

"No thanks. I'm drivin'."

"You can't have one beer?" Farrah asked, walking into the room.

My entire body locked up as she came closer. I'd only seen Farrah a couple of times since Cam and I had our fallout, and she'd been cool toward me both times. Not hostile, really. More like she acted as if I wasn't worth her time.

I didn't blame her, but it had still hurt my feelings.

"Got precious cargo," Cam muttered, stepping forward to give Farrah a hug. "Where are the girls?"

"Up watching a movie in CeeCee's room," Farrah grimaced. "Lil's listening. She picked a musical." She gave us a tight smile, and I suddenly wanted to pull her into my arms.

"You're huge," she said suddenly, glancing down at my belly. "Holy shit, man. You're going to be massive by the time those boys come out."

Cam scowled, but I couldn't help the laughter that spilled out of my mouth.

"I know, right?" I gasped, looking down at Farrah's normal sized bump. "You obviously have only one."

"Thank God. I'll leave the twins to you two idiots." She smiled then, a huge, warm smile meant just for me. "Glad you're here, Trix."

"Me, too."

"Sit, sit," Casper ordered, falling back into his recliner. "Stay a while."

We all settled into our places, with Cam and I sitting on one couch, Gramps and Nan on the other, and Farrah on Casper's lap.

"What are you guys doing today?" Nan asked, settling into my Gramps' side. "Any plans?"

"Probably lookin' for a house," Cam answered, glancing down at me. "Need a place to bring the boys home to."

"An apartment would work," I interrupted, glancing quickly at Casper and Farrah. "It doesn't have to be a house."

"Boys need room to play, Sweetbea."

"They won't even be walking for like two more years!"

"Doesn't matter—need a place to settle—" Cam argued before Gramps cut him off.

"Well, I got an idea if you two are done bickerin'." Gramps said, waiting until we were both looking his way before he continued. "Came over today to talk to Farrah about Charlie and Vera's place. They didn't leave a will and it was in my name—but I figured they'd want Farrah to have it—take what she wants, at least."

"Okay," I said in confusion.

"Farrah and Casper wanna stay here, so that leaves a vacant house right near the clubhouse. Ain't like we could sell it."

"You serious?" Cam asked.

"Yep."

Cam turned to look at Farrah. "You sure, Ma?"

"Of course. Even after all that happened in this house—we love it here. We raised you and the girls here. Wanna raise the new baby here, too. If you want Slider and Vera's place, it's yours."

"Trix?" Cam asked, turning back to me. I didn't answer him verbally, but the indecision must have been clear on my face, because he was immediately pulling me up off the couch and dragging me toward the kitchen.

"What were you thinkin' for rent?" Cam asked, pausing to look back at Farrah.

"Place is paid off. You take care of the taxes and we'll call it even."

Then Cam was moving again.

"What're you thinkin'?" Cam asked the minute we were alone.

"I don't know." I tucked my thumbs into my fists, a nervous tick my psychologist had pointed out to me, and was startled as Cam gently raised my hands and loosened my fingers.

"Talk to me, Bea."

"I just—that's a big gift, Cam. That's huge. I mean, a *house*?"

"Yeah, that was my first thought, too," he replied, nodding his head. "But, baby. Think of how much we could save if we weren't payin' rent. You know?"

"Yeah."

"I wanna be able to set up accounts or somethin' for the boys—you know, in case they wanna go to college or a trade school or somethin'." He was looking over my shoulder like he was seeing into the future, and I felt my eyes start to water.

"Plus, you know you're gonna wanna go to work at some point, right? I mean, after the boys are a little older—or when they're little—whatever you want," he said hurriedly. "If we lived at Slider and Vera's old place, your mom would be *right there*. You know she'd babysit. And I'd work so close to home, I could be with the bo—"

I cut off his words with my lips as the first tears fell down my cheeks.

"Okay," I mumbled against his mouth. "Sounds perfect."

Cam lifted his fist and pulled it sharply down to his side in the dorkiest move I'd seen in ten years… and he was the one I'd seen do it back then.

"I thought you'd grown out of that shit," Farrah drawled from the entry to the kitchen.

"Hell, no," Cam replied, laughing as he wrapped an arm around my shoulders and kissed the side of my head. "I was savin' it for the right time."

Epilogue
CAMERON

"Time to wake up, Sweetbea," I called softly as I pulled the blankets down Trix's bare shoulder.

"No. Sleep time," Trix mumbled, scooting awkwardly down the bed and trying to stay under the covers as I moved them.

"Got a big day today."

"Don't care. Need sleep."

"You sure?" I leaned down and ran my lips over the poppies tattooed on her bicep, licking around the edges. "I can let you sleep for another hour, or you can have an orgasm."

"Sleep," she replied instantly, making me chuckle.

"Yeah, that's not gonna work for me."

"Does this really have to be a thing?" Trix gasped as she rolled onto her back. "I like orgasms as much as the next girl, but your sons kept me up all damn night."

"Yeah?" I asked, running my hand down her huge belly. Every day, she woke up bigger, and I kept thinking, there's no way she has any more room in there—and then the next day, she was even bigger than before.

"I love you," she said sleepily.

"Love you, too, Sweetbea. Kiss me."

"You're gonna have to come down here," she said ruefully, dropping her head back against the pillow. "I don't think I'll even be able to roll back over."

I grinned as our lips met.

"Let me help you," I murmured into her mouth, sliding my hand under her lower back to help her roll.

"I can't believe you got me to sleep naked," she said softly as I kissed my way down her back.

"Don't fit in your pajamas."

"I could have bought new—*oh*." Her last word ended on a sigh as I slid my fingers over her pussy from behind.

"Happy I woke you up?" I asked as her breath hitched.

"Yeah." She groaned. "Pretty soon, this isn't going to work anymore."

"Wrong." I stated flatly, pushing her upper thigh toward the bed. "Just gotta be creative."

I reached up to cover one of her tits with my hand as I canted my hips, sliding inside her easily.

Trix moaned into the pillow, then placed her hand over mine at her chest, lacing our fingers together. "Harder," she ordered, pulling her thigh up even higher.

God, I loved yoga.

"Slow," I argued. "We got time."

She pressed my hand harder against her tit and arched her back, shoving her hips back against me.

"So impatient," I said against the skin of her shoulder, making her growl.

I pulled my hand from her breast and ran my nails against the skin of her hip, making her jolt.

We'd figured out that Trix liked a little bit of pain, but she still couldn't handle the sound of my hand smacking her ass. Fine with me—I just got creative.

A pinch here, a little scratch or bite there, and my woman went off like a rocket.

"Cam," she moaned as I started to speed up, my fingers digging into the flesh of her thigh. She reached down and shoved my hand between her thighs. "You know I can't reach," she whined.

I laughed silently and found her clit, rubbing in circles as she tightened around me and came.

I followed her down the rabbit hole.

Goddamn, it got better and better every time.

"Sleep now?" Trix asked softly.

"Nope. Shower time."

I climbed off the bed and burst out laughing when I realized that she'd somehow gotten hold of the blankets as I moved and had pulled them up and over her head.

★ ★ ★

"YOU SURE YOU don't want to come?" Trix asked as she stuffed half a granola bar into her mouth.

"Hell, no."

"Oh, come on. We're getting presents," she complained as I ushered her out of our new house.

We'd moved into Slider and Vera's old place a few months before, and Trix was still trying to put her stamp on it. I didn't mind that she wanted to make the place ours, but swear to Christ, the FedEx delivery guy was stopping at the gates to the clubhouse so often, I think he was considering becoming a prospect.

"The *boys* are getting presents, I'm not gettin' shit," I said as I helped her into the car.

"Still—"

"Dicks don't belong at baby showers," I cut her off as I started her car and pulled down our driveway. "Only reason my boys are goin' is because they're stuck in there," I said, pointing at her belly.

"Fine." She pouted for a minute, then turned to me. "You think we're lazy for not walking to my mom's?"

"No, I think you're a thousand months pregnant and shouldn't be walkin' that far."

"Okay, so it's just *you* that's lazy."

"Funny."

Trix laughed merrily, reaching over to rest her hand on my thigh.

I loved when she did shit like that.

It took less than two minutes to drive to her parents' house, and when we got there, the driveway was already crowded as hell with cars.

"They didn't even leave room for me to drop you off," I growled, parking at the back and heading around the door to help her out.

"I think I can walk thirty feet," Trix said before she tripped in the gravel.

"Right," I snapped, wrapping my hand around her waist.

My ma came out to meet us, her belly leading the way.

"You're here!"

"You see how far back we had to park?" I barked, making her scowl at me.

"Ignore him," Trix mumbled, tilting her head back for a kiss.

"Wait inside till I come get ya," I ordered.

"Yeah, yeah. See ya later."

I stood there watching as Trix pulled away and linked arms with Farrah, walked into the house and let the door slam in my face.

Then I turned toward the clubhouse. Lazy, my ass. I was walking.

★ ★ ★

"MOOSE!" POET YELLED out happily a couple hours later, pointing at Will. "Name's Moose."

"Where the fuck did you get that?" Casper asked incredulously.

We were all well on our way to shitfaced. The minute I'd walked through the front door, Casper dragged out the moonshine one of Poet's contacts had sent down. The shit tasted like lighter fluid, it was so strong. Some asshole had probably made it in his damn bathtub.

"You're not callin' me Moose," Will grumbled, shaking his head. "No."

"Don't got a choice, boy." Grease said with a smile, tipping back in his chair. "Once it's said, it's yours."

"Fuck," Will hissed, taking another shot of moonshine.

"Gather round, children," Poet yelled, laughing. "Shit, me beards in me fuckin' booze."

The table erupted in laughter as Poet tried to wring the moonshine out of his beard and back into the shot glass in front of him.

"Fuck it," he mumbled, patting his beard against his chest. "Now fer the story of Will's name."

"There was once a president of these United States—"

"Jesus," Dragon bitched, running his hand over his face. "Seriously, man?"

"Shut yer gob," Poet shot back. "Now where was I?"

"The president," I reminded him, my lips twitching.

"Right! In 1912, President Theodore Roosevelt was givin' a speech in Milwaukee, Wisconsin—"

"This story have a point?" Will grumbled.

"—and a saloonkeeper shot him in the chest," Poet continued. "Good old Roosevelt kept right on with his speech. Told the crowd, 'Takes more than one bullet to kill a bull moose.'" Poet nodded, then pointed again at Will. "Moose."

We all sat in dumbfounded silence for a moment.

"I got shot twice," Will finally said, his voice devoid of emotion.

I laughed so hard I thought I was going to hack up that fucking moonshine.

Acknowledgements

Bloggers and Readers: This story really is for you. If it wasn't for your comments and messages, Cam and Trix's story wouldn't have ever been written. When I ended Casper and Farrah's epilogue so far in the future, I'd thought that I'd give a glimpse of everyone, healthy and happy, and that would be the end of the Aces. But you wouldn't let me get away with that – you wanted to see those babies I'd written turn into adults... and I'm really, really glad you did. Thank you.

Mom and Dad – I love you! Thanks for cheering me on, every time.

My girlies – thanks for being patient, yet again, while your mother got caught up in a story you knew nothing about. You guys are so incredible and my biggest supporters. There will come a day soon when you'll want me to go write instead of bugging you, but I'm really glad that for now at least, you still want to hang out with your dorky mom. I love you a ton.

Sister – thanks for listening to me yammer on about Cam and Trix and all of your help with the girlies. Love you.

Nikki – there would be no story if I didn't have you to talk to. You're my biggest sounding board and I couldn't do this without you. Ever. Thank you for making sure I don't look like an idiot every time I hit publish.

Wolfpack 1775: Thanks for the late night chats about... nothing. They're my favorite kind of chats. You keep me sane when I'm losing it – I hope I do the same for you.

Toni: Dude. You complete me. You had me at hello. You had me at,

"I'm going to wear this ratty assed sweatshirt in the middle of a Vegas casino in August while my husband stands beside me looking like he shopped at the GQ store… and I'm also going to smoke this cigarette and drink this cheap beer while I do it." You have no idea how awesome you are, and I kind of like that about you. Peas and Carrots.

Donna: Here we are again. Can you believe it? Thank you a million times.

Lola: Thanks for putting up with my, "It's too light, it's too dark, I don't like that font, could you move it to the right, no left, no right again." You were super patient even though I know I was a pain in the ass, and you rocked that cover design.

And to my cover models:

E – I know that you were nervous and I know that you thought I was crazy. I'm just glad I saw what you didn't. You're gorgeous, inside and out and I'm so unbelievably excited that you agreed to be my Trix. It couldn't have been anyone but you. Thank you for making the *Craving Trix* cover what it is.

J – thanks for being such a good sport every time I said to turn your head because I could see too much of your face. You're so pretty (Seriously. Pretty.) and professional, and you made E so comfortable at the shoot. I owe you big. I'm not sure I ever told you how thankful I am – so this is me telling you now. Thank you.

Sneak Peek

The Aces' Sons
CRAVING MOLLY

WILL

My mother was a pain in my ass. She irritated the hell out of me, but I loved her, so I could never tell her no. Even when she asked me to climb up on the makeshift stage at her birthday barbeque and jam with Leo and Trix like we were the fucking Partridge family.

Which was what I was doing at that moment.

It wasn't the first time she'd asked me to do it, and it probably wouldn't be the last—but I wasn't in the mood. Trix and Leo were insanely good. The brother and sister came by their talent naturally. I'd seen their mom, Brenna, wail on the drums more than once, and I'd heard that she could play a shitload of other instruments by ear. Her kids seemed to have followed in her footsteps. Both could play the drums, guitar and who knew what other instruments like they were born to do it, but I just barely got by on my bass, which made me feel like an even bigger asshole when I played with them.

We'd been playing at the barbeques on and off since we were kids, and for the past few years had begun our tried-and-true set with the same song. It was a tribute of sorts, and it didn't matter how many times we played it, all the women of the club stopped whatever they were doing and stood still, watching us. "I Will Follow You into the Dark" by Death Cab for Cutie wasn't really the older generation's style, but when Trix had sung it exactly a year after the shooting that killed my little brother, great-grandmother, the Aces president, Slider, and his wife, Vera, everyone had stopped and stared. A song about following your spouse when they died, even if heaven and hell wouldn't take them—well, that resonated with the rowdy bikers and their old ladies. It was also extremely fitting for our fallen president and his wife.

I glanced at my mom and met her eyes as Trix sang, and I couldn't help but nod when she mouthed 'thank you.' Yeah, I'd do anything for that woman and she knew it.

As soon as the first song was over, we fell into a familiar pattern of songs that rarely changed. Leo sang most of them and Trix led on a couple, too, but I kept my mouth clenched shut. I wasn't going to sing, I didn't care what kind of puppy dog eyes my mother gave me. I was fucking twenty-three years old, goddamnit. I'd been to prison. I wore an Aces' cut. I made my own damn decisions. Just for good measure, I didn't look her way again.

We knew the songs, knew that everyone liked them, and knew we could get our asses off the stage when we hit the end of our short list. So I was surprised as fuck when a few songs in, Leo completely stopped drumming and singing, well, yelling. We didn't have any mics or anything—so he had to sing pretty loud.

My hands went still as I glanced over my shoulder at him. He was staring emotionlessly off to the side of the clubhouse and when I followed his line of sight, I cursed under my breath.

Fucking Cecilia.

She'd just shown up in a barely decent top that I sure as fuck didn't want to see on my little cousin, and was chatting with a prospect. She knew that shit would piss Leo off. I had no clue what was going on with them, but they'd been dancing around each other, fighting and making up for the past few years.

Trix stopped when she realized we were no longer playing, and she turned abruptly to her brother.

It only took seconds for both of us to stop playing, but that must have been what Leo was looking for because as soon as we were silent, he started yell/singing again.

"La, La, Lalala," he sang, a nasty smile on his face as he started drumming.

Oh, shit. The familiar Offspring song made me groan and I immediately looked at Cam, who was standing near Trix's side of the stage with their sons playing in the grass at his feet.

He was livid at Leo's choice of music. It was a good song, but fuck, *Self Esteem* was about a chick that kept fucking around on her man and he just kept taking her back.

And Leo was staring right at Cecilia while he sang it.

Trix looked at her feet, then glanced my way, shrugging her shoulders as she started to play. She wasn't about to leave her brother hanging, even if he was making a complete jackass of himself. My fingers hit the notes on my bass without thought and I shrugged back as I joined in.

I watched the crowd as a few of the guys started laughing, but my dad, Uncle Casper, and Leo and Trix's dad, Dragon, were not amused.

They were even less amused when my little sister, Rose, led our cousin, Lily, onto the grass directly in front of the stage. The two had been practically inseparable since they were born just six months apart, so it wasn't surprising to see them together. What *was* surprising was the fact that they must not have felt the tension that filled the field we were standing in. As they came to a stop, Lily's head was nodding along with the beat, her thin, fourteen-year-old shoulders moving slightly while Rose stood still next to her.

Then my baby cousin surprised the fuck out of me when she started rocking. Hard.

I couldn't help but grin when Lily suddenly let go of Rose and threw up devil horns, her hair flying all over the place as she danced. She was really fucking moving, jumping and whipping her hair around, and most of the crowd around us stopped to stare. They weren't being rude—most had smiles on their faces, but they were definitely staring.

My little sister looked around with a scowl, then got this determined look on her face. I knew that fucking look, and I felt my shoulders get tight as I watched her.

My shoulders relaxed again as Rose began to move. She was tentative at first, barely nodding her head. Then she closed her eyes, shook out her arms, and started jumping and jerking alongside Lily, making sure that the crowd was watching *both* of them.

Christ, I loved that kid.

"*When she's saying that she wants only me, then I wonder why she sleeps with my friends,*" Leo screamed, his voice abruptly cutting off as he caught sight of the girls dancing in front of us.

Trix and I stopped, too, and it irritated the shit out of me. Couldn't we make it through one fucking song? I wanted to finish out the fucking set and get off that damn stage.

"Hey," Lily yelled, pulling my attention forward again.

She turned her face toward the stage, her unfocused eyes pointed in our direction. "I want more Offspring."

I smiled as Leo chuckled. "Nah," he called out quietly, knowing Lily would hear him. "Pretty girl deserves a pretty girl song."

Leo met Trix's eyes and I had no idea how she knew, but she immediately started playing. I laughed quietly, then joined in, looking back at Leo for a second.

His eyes were soft—that's the only way I knew how to explain it. They were tender, indulgent, and they were pointed right at Lily, who was smiling sweetly as her hips moved from side to side, her arms high above her head.

"*She's got a smile that it seems to me, reminds me of childhood memories. Where everything was fresh as a bright blue sky,*" Leo sang in his gravelly voice.

Lily's mom—my Aunt Farrah—whooped loudly, then made her way to our little makeshift stage, shaking her hips and singing along. My mom and Brenna followed her, shaking their asses, too, and I started laughing.

They were all dancing like crazy and signing along, and Lily was smiling so huge, her cheeks must have been aching.

"*Oh, oh sweet child o' mine,*" Leo sang, still watching Lily as she spun around and around in a circle.

We went through a lot more songs after that, and I couldn't even bitch about it. How could I bitch when Brenna's pop, Poet, and his wife, Amy, were dancing with his hands on her ass to the side of the stage? It was a little disgusting, but still sweet as hell. My mom had a dreamy smile on her face as she sat on my dad's lap—he was singing quietly in her ear, and Dragon and Brenna had disappeared not long after he'd pulled her from the dance floor and threw her over his shoulder.

It was fucking awesome to see everyone so happy. There was a time only a few years before that I hadn't imagined any of us laughing or having a good time again.

When we were finally done for the night and the boys were setting up the sound system, I had sweat pooling at the base of my spine and I was pretty sure I stank. Did I remember to put on deodorant that day? I wasn't completely sure—but I decided I'd just keep my arms down until I could grab a quick shower inside the clubhouse.

I was setting my bass back in its case when a bunch of loud voices came from the edge of the clubhouse to my left, not far from where Cecilia had been standing earlier. My heart thumped hard in my chest at the commotion, and my head snapped up to analyze the threat. I'd been caught unprepared in the past, but I never would again.

Then my jaw dropped as Samson and a prospect—I could never remember his name—came around the back, half dragging and half carrying a girl between them.

What the fuck?

My stomach sank as I recognized the yellow scrubs with purple fish the woman was wearing and I jumped down off the stage, my bass forgotten as I jogged toward them.

It couldn't be her. No way. She wouldn't come out to the clubhouse.

I took the woman in fully from head to toe. Fuck.

She was bloody. Her scrubs were dirty and ripped and her head was rolling on her shoulders as she tried really hard to keep her feet under her.

She only had one shoe on.

I told myself that lots of women probably wore those scrubs. Lots of women had that color hair and those same ugly as fuck tennis shoes. I'd almost convinced myself when her head rolled to the side and I caught a glimpse of her face. Her blue eyes met mine, and she let out a short sob.

No.

"Will," she whispered, her lips trembling.

"Aw, fuck, sweetheart," I groaned, lurching forward so I could lift her slight frame gingerly into my arms. "What the fuck happened?"